PROMISES AND PRIMROSES

This Large Print Book carries the
Seal of Approval of N.A.V.H.

PROPER ROMANCE

Promises and Primroses

MAYFIELD FAMILY SERIES

Josi S. Kilpack

THORNDIKE PRESS
A part of Gale, a Cengage Company

GALE
A Cengage Company

Farmington Hills, Mich • San Francisco • New York • Waterville, Maine
Meriden, Conn • Mason, Ohio • Chicago

GALE
A Cengage Company

LIBRARY OF CONGRESS CIP DATA ON FILE.
CATALOGUING IN PUBLICATION FOR THIS BOOK
IS AVAILABLE FROM THE LIBRARY OF CONGRESS

ISBN-13: 978-1-4328-6781-2 (hardcover alk. paper)

Published in 2019 by arrangement with Deseret Book Company/Shadow Mountain

Printed in Mexico
1 2 3 4 5 6 7 23 22 21 20 19

The English Primrose

Typically, the English primrose is a pale shade of yellow, though it can also be found in blue, pink, white, and purple. The primrose symbolizes youth, womanhood, patience, and gentleness. Primroses are a perennial flower, returning each year in a clustered arrangement that is easily divided and replanted. They are easy to grow and edible, tasting similar to lettuce. When given as a gift, primroses are used to tell someone you can't live without them.

Mayfield

FAMILY PEDIGREE

1822

HAROLD MAYFIELD
4th Viscount
Married: RACHEL

ELLIOTT
MAYFIELD
1762–
5th Viscount

THEODORE
MAYFIELD
1765–1794
Married:
CAROLYN

JANE
MAYFIELD
1766–1820
Married:
HORACE
STILLMAN

CATHERINE
MAYFIELD
1770–1800
Lived With:
MR. PENHALE

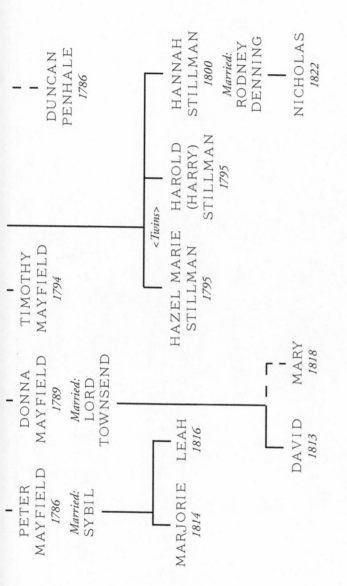

CHAPTER ONE:
ELLIOTT

March 15, 1822

Elliott Mayfield, the fifth Viscount Howardsford, looked across the desk at Peter, his eldest nephew and heir. *Destiny and opportunity are not that different,* he reminded himself in an effort to bolster his courage. As far as Peter knew, this was their usual quarterly review of the holdings that Peter would one day inherit. The meeting would be far more than that by the end, however.

"Thank you, Mr. Poole," Elliott said to his steward as he closed his book of accounts. "That will be all."

Mr. Poole inclined his head and left the study. Once they were alone, Elliott turned toward Peter. "Have you any questions for me?"

"I don't think so." Peter looked over the notes he'd been taking. "I'm eager to see how the new pasture rotation works in practice. You'll let me know if you need help

9

purchasing the additional stock?"

"I will, but we won't need help. Mr. Poole is eager to grow the flock, and I am bored enough with this gentlemanly life that I plan to attend the stockyards with him in work boots and a homespun shirt." He imagined himself in the disguise of a common man so that he might blend in at market. It sounded like fun.

Peter smiled, looking very much like his father, Teddy, Elliott's younger brother. Teddy had been dead thirty years now, and it was nice to catch a glimpse of him in his son.

"You should raise dogs," Peter offered. Not for the first time. The boy was obsessed. "They fill many a dull hour."

"I am sure they do," Elliott said. "However, seeing as how I had dog on my plate more than once during my time in India, I'm afraid it has ruined me for the species."

Peter shuddered. "That is horrific."

"Quite." Elliott leaned forward and put his forearms on the table. "There is another matter I would like to discuss with you, Peter, if you've time."

Peter took his pocket watch — a scratched and battered thing that had once belonged to Elliott's father — from his waistcoat. "I shall need to leave on the hour as I've an appointment to interview governess candidates in Norwich, but I am at your disposal until then."

"You don't mind if I move through the summation rather quickly, then, so that I might get through it before you need to leave?"

Peter spread his arms and sat back as though at his leisure, though that was rarely the case. Peter kept himself busy most hours of the day. To run from his thoughts, perhaps. Memories. Regrets. Elliott could relate. He had been a similar young man when he had arrived in India with his shirtsleeves rolled up, begging for someone to put a tool in his hand so he might lose himself in sweat and purpose.

"You have quite captured my attention with the introduction of your topic, Uncle. I am eager to hear the whole of it."

"Excellent." Elliott took a deep breath and laced his fingers together. "I've devised a plan I hope will save our family from the, er, dissolute course it has been on for a few generations now." Peter's face immediately went hard, but Elliott held the younger man's eyes. "Let us talk as men. You know as well as I that the Mayfield family is off course, though you are the exception."

Peter's jaw was still tight, but he nodded.

Elliott ignored the squirming in his own gut and continued. "Your father shall always have my respect for having done right by your mother and yourself, but that does not change the difficult lives you and your siblings have endured for their poor choices." Elliott paused, waiting until Peter acknowledged the truth with another nod.

They had never discussed the details of Peter's parents' relationship, but it loomed heavy above them both. Teddy had been the twenty-one-year-old second son of a viscount; Mara, a seventeen-year-old chambermaid. Their marriage had taken place only weeks before Peter's birth, making him legitimate, but his mother was as unsuited for the circumstance she had married into as Teddy had been for the role of a husband or a father. They had made one another miserable until Teddy's death eight years later, during which time, they'd had a daughter, Donna. Their third child, Timothy, was born three months after Teddy's burial in the family plot. Mara became a recluse for the decade that followed Teddy's death, refusing to leave her home and treating her various maladies with gin or laudanum, or both.

Elliott continued. "My sisters — your aunts, who I realize you never met in person

— made equally poor use of their privilege, and I fear that their children are following in their footsteps."

"I have attempted to live far above any censure, Uncle. If I have displeased —"

"I do not include you in my generalization, Peter. I could not be more proud of the life you have lived and the choices you have made. It is, in fact, your example that has led me to make a decision on behalf of *all* my nieces and nephews. I want to heal this family, mend the broken bonds, and help my relations find purpose in their lives by striving for more than what is in their grasp right now."

Peter's tension did not dissipate. He raked a hand through his dark hair, which was beginning to gray at the temples, and shifted anxiously. He glanced out the large window as if he would give anything to be on his way to Norwich rather than in this chair listening to Elliott's bungling attempts to explain what had seemed a very well-considered plan until just now.

There was nothing to do but move forward. "I have created a campaign that could save the others from their current courses by gifting them each a generous settlement upon an appropriate marriage. Your cousins are all of age, and with my sister Jane's pass-

13

ing last year, I have no more family to stand in my way." He attempted a smile, then realized he had made a jest that his siblings and their respective spouses — including Peter's parents — were dead. Perhaps not the best way to go about lightening the mood.

Peter looked less uncomfortable but more suspect. "A campaign?"

"A marriage campaign, you might say. I have seven nieces and nephews, all of whom I have cared for, but you are the only one who has married successfully and enjoyed the security and self-respect of a solid and loving union."

Peter looked at the desk and squared up the edges of the notebook with the table.

Perhaps it would have been better for Elliott to have relayed the entire plan in a letter where he could have found the perfect words to explain. In a letter, the recipient need never know how many drafts existed between first and final. For Elliott, those drafts often counted into double digits.

"I know you miss Sybil very much," Elliott said, his voice softening even as the awkwardness in the room increased. "Your daughters will benefit from the steadiness of their parents' characters for the rest of their lives. I would like my other nieces and

14

nephews to find similar happiness as you had with Sybil."

Peter leaned toward one side of his chair, rested one hand on the wooden armrest, and tapped his finger. "With all due respect, Uncle, my match with Sybil was not the result of a *campaign,* and I can't imagine we would have found happiness together had our relationship not started with love, commitment, and respect. I struggle to see how your . . . enticements will change anyone's course. A life of virtue and integrity cannot be forced or, in regard to this situation, bought. It must be an individual choice."

"I understand your concern," Elliott admitted with a nod. "But I fear that without my *enticements,* as you call them, the others will never change their current courses. I need them to *see* the benefits of an upstanding life, and I believe this is an opportunity to frame the future into something that it is both clear and attainable." He paused and took another breath. "This family is everything to me, Peter. I have sacrificed a great deal to provide for those over whom I have charge, but the hope that my efforts will heal the broken generations is faltering. There is no unity, no commitment to future generations — yourself

15

excluded — and a pattern of poor choices is beginning to be sewn into our family tapestry yet again. We have been given a noble trust of land, wealth, position, and opportunity. I cannot in good conscience do nothing to prevent it from being completely squandered."

Peter took a breath, then let it out. "I understand your motivation and admire your desire for them to rise above the pettiness of our parents, but appealing to greed does not seem to be a viable course for such a virtuous destination. The promise of wealth would not have changed Donna's course. She had wealth."

Donna. One of two nieces who had provided Elliott's strongest motivations. "If Donna had not needed to secure her future, and had she not been so desperate to rise above the same beginnings you have fought to rise above, she would not have married that man."

"Yet it is her action, not his, that has created her circumstance."

Elliott raised his eyebrows. "You condemn your sister?"

Peter shook his head and shifted in his chair again. "I know Donna was unhappy in her marriage and she was not treated fairly, but —"

"Never mind," Elliott broke in, sensing they were taking this tangential road too far and that Peter's piety, which Elliott suspected was compensation for his parents' dishonorable actions, had no place here. "This is not about Donna — it is about all of you. I want to present choices they have not had before so they might make wise decisions, not desperate ones, or, in the case of some, no decision at all. I do not believe the gifts I have arranged will appeal to greed so much as to responsibility. To say nothing of the fact that the offering gives me the opportunity to explain my position and, I hope, remind them of the place they can hold in history if they exercise the advantages.

"As our nation changes with the implementation of industry, I feel an undeniable anxiety regarding what the future will hold for all of us, and I feel it my duty to do all I can to restore respectability to our family name, both now and for the future."

Peter was thoughtful, and possibly humbled, by this explanation and nodded his head. "I would never argue with a man's convictions, Uncle. I shall set aside my initial judgment so you might explain this campaign more fully."

Oh, bless this boy and his steady nature.

17

Elliott spent the next ten minutes explaining how he had created an individualized gift for each niece or nephew that contained something that would assist in securing their future. He had spent the better part of a year drawing it together and finalizing it by way of his solicitors to make sure it was legal, ethical, and unbreakable should there be any disputes.

"I will not be orchestrating the matches," Elliott said, "only approving the decision to ensure that the person they choose is of the quality required for a suitable match. Upon the marriage, I will then transfer the holdings designated for that couple as outlined in the campaign. Of course, everything entailed through the title will go to you as already stipulated. These gifts have been arranged and financed wholly through my individual interests." Elliott had no family of his own and therefore had little more to do while in India than restore the family coffers and then grow his personal wealth. He'd returned to England a very wealthy man. The family holdings had been secured and then made profitable. Now he wanted to save their name and their futures.

Peter cleared his throat. "I fear my cousins will manipulate this situation, Uncle, and you will feel the fool."

"They could take advantage, yes," Elliott agreed. "I am hopeful, however, that they won't. In addition to the offers I have tailored to each of them, I am also no longer willing to pay their way in the world. You are the only one not living out of my pocket. The marital gifts will give them the ability to care for themselves and secure their future without my ongoing support, which I shall be withdrawing as determined by each circumstance."

Peter raised his eyebrows. "There is a deadline for them to make a match?"

"Or to change their lifestyles to fit the income and allowances already afforded them. I spent thirty years hoping that my financial support would put my siblings' feet back on a respectable path and set a new standard for their children. That plan failed. Therefore I have created a different one that I hope will result in self-respect, accomplishment, and success."

Peter was listening closely, a crease forming between his eyebrows. He had stopped tapping his finger, but he had not lost the tension in his body — the strong and solid body of a man young enough to work hard every day and old enough to see how it had blessed him. "And the gifts are all financial?"

Elliott considered how much detail he wanted to disclose to Peter and then chose to be vague. "The gifts are investments with growth potential."

If Peter were curious as to what exactly that meant, he did not betray it by even a quiver. Instead he smiled politely and leaned back in his chair as though having made a decision regarding the campaign. He had lost his defensive posture and, seemingly, his objection, but Elliott knew better. Peter had puzzled out how this related to him and determined that it did not — that was why he could be calm. Elliott had led him to that assumption on purpose. A man did not learn what Elliott had learned, built what he had built, and managed the number of people he had managed without learning a thing or two about how to approach people based upon their particular situations. He only hoped he was as good at that as he believed he was when he'd created each campaign. Peter's included, though he was not yet ready to broach that topic.

Elliott held Peter's eyes. "All I can do is trust the instincts and convictions that led me to this course. Ultimate outcomes will be determined by the choices of each individual, but I hope giving them additional options will help them better understand the power they have to shape their own futures."

"I do agree that every man should be the ultimate decider of their fate. It is surely such with my dogs. Those eager to learn and please are quick to hit the markers I set for them. Those who are willful and disobedient are the first ones sold off so as to preserve the quality of my pack."

Elliott could not appreciate the analogy as well as Peter certainly hoped he would, but he smiled anyway. "Thank you, Peter." Elliott stood from the desk and went to the credenza beneath the bank of west windows that overlooked the immense estate. He had inherited it thirty-six years ago when his father had died unexpectedly, but Elliott had spent less than three full years in this house — in this *country* — since then.

He pulled open the top drawer and removed a blue leather folder from a stack. He walked back to the desk, where Peter was watching with new wariness.

Elliott resumed his seat and slid the folder across the smooth surface of the desk.

Peter looked at the folder but made no effort to pick it up. He looked at his uncle. "What is this?"

"It is the details of your wedding gift." Elliott nodded toward the folder. "I have

21

created it especially for you."

Realization slowly dawned, and Peter's jaw tightened. His words were clipped when he spoke. "I am touched to have been included, Uncle, but I have no desire to marry again, as I believe you are aware. With an estate already under my care and your holdings that will one day pass to me, I do not need the security you have put forward for the others, nor do I need motivation toward living a respectable life."

"You are exactly right," Elliott said with a deep nod. "You do not need motivation or financial security, but, as I told you, each gift is tailored to the person. Aren't you the least bit curious as to what I devised as a gift for your future?"

Peter put his hands in his lap. "I am not."

Elliott sighed. "You are still a young man, Peter. You deserve a companion to see you through the remaining years of your life, and your daughters deserve a mother. I believe with my whole heart that Sybil would want that for you."

"Forgive me, uncle, but you did not know Sybil and have no basis for such an assumption."

Elliott inclined his head, acknowledging the truth of that observation. "And the fact that you do not have an heir?"

Peter stood abruptly. With his broad shoulders and athletic physique, he was quite the commanding presence when his ire was fueled, as it was now.

He grabbed for his jacket. "Timothy's son will be my heir just as I was heir for you."

"Timothy has no son."

"But he will. Especially now that he will have additional reason for doing so." Peter's certitude was admirable. "So, while I thank you for *this*" — he waved toward the untouched folder, barely concealing his bitterness — "I do not share the circumstances of my siblings or my cousins. I married well, I am raising my daughters in the privilege they deserve, and I am living an upstanding life. I have no desire for anything else. Now, if you would excuse me."

Elliott stood and hurried around the table to take hold of Peter's arm before the boy could escape. "I did not mean to offend you, Peter. I am sorry."

Peter's dark eyes were cold. "Apology accepted. I truly must be on my way, uncle."

Elliott dropped his nephew's arm, and Peter left, the door closing behind him with a snap. This was not how Elliott had hoped the first campaign proposal would go. He'd imagined Peter defensive at first, of course, but eventually seeing Elliott's motivations in their purest light and being gracious and touched, not offended. Perhaps Elliott did not have the people-management skills he so highly prized after all.

Elliott walked to the east window of his study and scrubbed a hand over his face. Peter was right about Elliott having never met Sybil. But he still believed Sybil would not want her husband and daughters to be alone. Elliott had hoped the wedding campaign would bring Peter out of mourning. It had been four years.

Then again, what could Elliott say against Peter's decision to remain a widower? Elliott had never loved anyone the way Peter had loved Sybil — though there had been a woman he *might* have loved that way.

Amelia Edwards had filled him with light, and he had expected that they would marry. Then his father had died and everything had changed. Elliott had stepped into the title, the debts, and the role as head of the family, and the young woman he'd wanted to be his wife had instead become a part of his past and his sacrifice. The life that had followed had not brought love again.

Elliott's ambition now was to see his nieces and nephews secure and his family name restored for the benefit of future generations. The satisfaction of those things

24

would make up for what he'd wanted for himself but could not have. At least that was what he had hoped. It might take a bit of time before he recovered from the unexpected conclusion of his first presentation. With a bit more attention, and perhaps tact, he vowed the next would go better.

Chapter Two:
Peter

The wind chafing Peter's cheeks helped keep old ghosts at bay as he galloped away from Howardhouse. He had no time for ghosts; life took place in the present and, *at present,* he was in need of a governess. That was his focus.

The sooner he filled the position, the sooner he could return to the routine of daily life. The only thought he spared toward Uncle Elliott's plan was hope that it would lead the others to live respectable lives, as he had always tried to do. Having a responsibility to rise to had set Peter on a path that required his best. He hoped Uncle Elliott's offer would become the same motivation for the other members of his family, but he feared it would not. There were certainly some of his cousins, and his own sister, who did not seem to have much ability to do anything different than what they had seen all their lives. But he could only manage himself.

And so, the governess situation . . .

After the birth of their first daughter, Sybil's cousin Lydia McCormick had joined the household as a nursemaid. After Sybil's death four years later, Lydia had agreed to stay on. Without her constancy, Peter did not know how he would have managed, to say nothing of his daughters, who needed attention he didn't know how to give. Since Sybil's death, he had focused on his estate and his pack, which was earning him both money and a reputation now that he had a few years' worth of experience under his belt.

But now Lydia had gone and fallen in love with the parish vicar, leaving Peter without anyone to look after the girls.

It was difficult to be happy for Lydia when her transition complicated his life so drastically. When he'd said as much, she'd reminded him that the girls would see her at church. As if he needed her sass at a time like that. He'd been tempted to not take the girls to church in protest but then realized he might be overreacting. Might. He *was* glad Lydia had found happiness with her vicar; she was nearly forty years old and had given up years ago on making a match. But he could not imagine his household without her, and he felt quite anxious about the prospect. He had procrastinated finding Lydia's replacement as though that would somehow change reality, and now he needed a new governess by Friday next — the day Lydia would become Mrs. Oswell and stepmother to the vicar's three children.

By the time Peter reached the village of Norwich, the horse's sides were heaving with exertion and Peter's mouth was dry. In another life, he would stop at the pub to wash the dust down with a pint while he talked up the locals for the sheer entertainment of it, but that was not the life he lived any longer. He needed to be home in time to say good night to the girls and get to bed early — tomorrow was his physical training day with the hounds. His life had become smaller since Sybil died. His desire to socialize and build relationships had worn away to almost nothing. What ambition and engagement he had left went to his dogs . . . and his daughters, of course.

Peter stopped in front of the public stable and handed the reins and a coin to the lad who scampered out to meet him. "I shall return within the hour," he said over his shoulder as he strode toward the employment office.

He ran a hand through his hair, gritty with

road dust, and remembered he was in need of a trim. Luckily, the footman was handy with the shears. Haircuts and hiring governesses and attending meetings were not the way Peter liked to occupy his time, and he felt anxious about the time spent away from home today.

Peter stomped his feet on the mat outside the employment office, wishing he could dispose more of the traveling dust, and then pushed through the wooden door, setting off a bell that jangled to announce him. Once inside, he attempted to brush dirt from his overcoat, hoping he did not look too rough. He had said in the advertisement that the governess position was within a gentleman's household, but he looked the part of a ruffian right now.

"Ah, Mr. Mayfield," the round man behind the desk said, coming to his feet. He was not much taller standing than he had been when he was sitting. "I've settled each candidate in a separate room, per your request."

Peter pulled out his watch, worried he was late but, in fact, he was nearly ten minutes early. "They have all arrived already?"

"Yes, sir," Mr. Hastings said proudly. "Punctuality is a virtue I prize above all things."

"As do I," Peter said as he shrugged out of his overcoat. The office smelled like gravy, which was strange.

Mr. Hastings waved down the hall. "I put one lady in each of the three rooms on the left. The last is a broom closet, I'm afraid, but I cleared it well enough to accommodate your purposes and ensure a private interview."

Peter nodded and hung up his coat, then slapped the man on the back as he made his way down the hall. With a bit of luck, he would be finished in under an hour.

Mrs. Grimshaw, the candidate in the first room, had recently left a teaching position at a girls' school. In her midforties, plump and gray-haired, she had been widowed, still childless, five years earlier. Her lined face and sad eyes reflected a life that had not turned out as she'd planned. She said she hoped for a new start, and since her sister lived in Westfield, she was particularly interested in positions in this part of the country.

Peter was sympathetic to her struggles yet worried she was applying for the position out of necessity and not because she would enjoy the work. He also wondered if she could keep up with Leah's energetic nature while not losing patience with Marjorie who, at eight years old, questioned every-thing. Mrs. Grimshaw seemed so very tired.

Peter thanked Mrs. Grimshaw at the conclusion of his interview and said he would send word of his decision through Mr. Hastings in a few days. He then moved to the second room. Mrs. Grimshaw *might* be the right woman for the job; he'd know better when he finished interviewing the other two. That he *had* to choose from these three was a fact — he had no time for ad-ditional interviews and did not keep suf-ficient staff to attend to the girls' needs without a governess.

Miss Lawrence had the firmness and energy Mrs. Grimshaw lacked. She was a small woman and had been a governess for the same family for eighteen years. She was nearly fifty years old, she told him proudly, and as well-educated as any man. She had a long face, flat brown hair, and a stern countenance. He worried she would not have the tenderness he saw in Mrs. Grim-shaw, but her references were exemplary, and Lydia had encouraged him to find someone who would educate the girls, not simply take care of them, which had been Lydia's focus. Peter concluded the interview and repeated that he would send word through Mr. Hastings. Between the two women, Peter thought Miss Lawrence the better choice. But there was one more applicant for him to consider.

The doorway to the third room was narrower than the others, attesting to its prior incarnation as a broom closet. Peter stopped short in the open doorway. He'd expected the third candidate to be similar to the other two, but instead, a young woman sat on a stool only a few feet in front of him.

Miss Hollingsworth hardly looked twenty years old, let alone the twenty-seven years she claimed in her letter of introduction. This *girl* had a slender build, blonde hair curled around her face, a graceful neck, and light-blue eyes. She stood from her chair and smiled.

Good heavens, she's nearly as tall as I am. And far too young.

Peter put a polite smile on his face and stepped into the room. He'd closed the door for the other two interviews, but he left it open this time — propriety was suddenly important. The two chairs barely fit between the shelves on one side and the buckets and mops pushed to the other. Peter waved for her to return to her chair. When Peter sat, his knees brushed against hers, and he pulled them back immediately, tucking his feet under his chair.

"Miss Hollingsworth," he said, extending his hand. "I am Peter Mayfield. Pleased to meet you."

She took his hand — hers was warm and soft — and he shook it quickly before pulling away. Such soft hands could mean she was lazy and unused to hard work, though a governess's duties generally did not cause the development of many calluses, he supposed. "So, um, tell me about the family you worked with in London." The closet smelled of lye and dust and . . . lilies? She must be wearing a fragrance — neither of the other women had. One candle in a sconce on the wall and no windows created rather intimate lighting. Peter shifted in his chair, feeling cramped and uncomfortable in the small space. What if their knees touched again?

She cleared her throat. "I worked for the Cranston family in London. There were three children — two boys and a girl. Gerald, the youngest, shall go to Eton next fall and is spending the next six months with his aunt and uncle in Surrey. You read Mr. Cranston's letter of recommendation I sent with the application?"

"Yes." The letter had made a strong impression, but Peter had naively assumed that an unmarried woman of twenty-seven — a spinster by all rights — would not look like a fresh-faced girl who had never lived away from her parents' home, let alone in London.

She met his gaze with cornflower-blue eyes, and the direct look startled him enough that he forced words from his mouth. "Your father raised dogs." He didn't mean for his words to be clipped, but maybe that was best. Neither of the other candidates had looked at him this way, had they?

"Springer spaniels."

"And involved you in the care?" Peter would never expose his daughters to the care of his pack. It was a man's work, and barely a gentleman's. Never mind that he'd been intrigued by this girl's letter in which she mentioned her experience with dogs. He wished she had all the attributes that made her stand out but looked like Miss Lawrence. He'd assumed all governesses were rather homely. Lydia was no great beauty, and the other two candidates were equally plain. It seemed . . . inappropriate to have an attractive governess.

"My father said I had a gift with dogs." She blushed, and he felt warmth wash through him as surely as it did her cheeks. What was that reaction on his part about?

She was looking at him expectantly. What

was it she'd just said? Oh, yes, that she had a gift with dogs, but then she'd been embarrassed at having said it and seemed to be looking at him as though he might save her, which, as a gentleman, was his job, really.

Speak, man! "I have found that people either have a natural accord with dogs or they don't."

It was not meant to sound like such a compliment, but Miss Hollingsworth's smile turned from polite to sincere, and in an instant, he was back in time to his youth and flirting and . . . *Sybil.* Remembering his late wife was exactly what he needed to get him through the rest of this interview.

"And would you say you have an equal gift with children?"

"I hope my gift with children is more than it is with dogs, sir. I have seven nieces and nephews."

"Seven?" he said, staring at the paper. "You don't say." Uncle Elliott had seven nieces and nephews. Peter remembered the folder he'd left in Uncle Elliott's office and still felt no curiosity about what was inside. He had no need for his uncle's gift. He had two healthy daughters, fourteen fine dogs from the best bloodlines in Europe — with two litters due next month — an estate large enough to be comfortable but small enough that he could manage it himself, and an inheritance that secured his future comfort.

Miss Hollingsworth continued speaking, drawing Peter out of his distracted thoughts. "My oldest brother has two children — a boy and a girl — and my sister has five. I was formally educated through the age of seventeen and then stayed on at the parish school as an assistant teacher for two more years."

"Very good," Peter said helpfully while looking for faults in the woman. She was more nervous than the other two had been. And younger, he noted again, which translated into inexperience. Though he'd been impressed with her application letter, a more critical review revealed that the loops of her *L*'s were not perfectly symmetrical. That was nothing but laziness.

Peter hadn't realized silence had fallen again until a few seconds passed. He hurried to fill the space. When was the last time he had been this close to an attractive woman? Not that he was *attracted*. Certainly not — he was just taken off guard since he had not been in the company of an attractive woman in a very long time. Not that she *was* attractive. Well, he'd already accepted that she was attractive, but not to *him*. That's what he meant. Attractive generally, yes, but not to him. Not at all.

"What prompted you to apply for this position in particular?"

"Your situation."

"*My* situation?"

"Well, your family's situation — you and your daughters. Mrs. Cranston was in poor health when they hired me, and she died a year later. Mr. Cranston often said that I had helped them through the worst of it. When he remarried, I believe I eased that transition as well by assisting the children to find comfort with their new mother. I am very sorry for your loss, sir. Losing someone you love is a heartbreak without much comfort."

He stared at her.

She continued. "My father passed when I was young, and while nothing can make up for something as important as a parent, being loved and supported and encouraged to move forward can at least help."

Peter was desperate to move past this particular topic. "And you would not miss London? Norfolkshire is a very different place than the city."

"I would not miss London, sir," she said, following his change of subject without a pause. "I am eager to live in the country again and have only applied for such positions that would allow as much."

"Did you grow up in the country, then?"

"Feltwell," she said. "Some thirty miles from here."

"Hmm," he said. Silence descended yet again. Had the interview lasted long enough that he could put a stop to this without her feeling as though he had cut it short? Peter counted to ten before standing. "Well, thank you for your time, Miss Hollingsworth."

She followed his lead and stood, reminding him again how tall she was. Nearly eye level with him. He must have showed his surprise because she smiled sheepishly. "I promise that my height does not affect my work."

He responded to her humor and smiled automatically. "Of course not. Neither does mine." They stood facing one another for a moment until he remembered himself — again — and inclined his head. "A pleasure to meet you, Miss Hollingsworth."

"The Cranstons called me Miss Julia," she offered. "Hollingsworth was rather long for the children."

"Oh, well, Miss, eh, Julia, then."

She smiled. It made him feel out of place again.

He turned to leave but paused at the doorway. "I shall be sending word through

Mr. Hastings as to my decision within a few days."

She nodded her understanding, and he left the tiny room. Once in the hallway, he rolled his shoulders in hopes of easing the tension that had settled at the base of his neck. Had he been in there for an hour or fifteen seconds? After taking a moment and a breath — the gravy smell helped to restore his senses — he headed toward the foyer of the office. *What an uncomfortable meeting,* he thought. She would never do.

"Ah, there you are, Mr. Mayfield." Mr. Hastings pushed himself to his feet. "The other two applicants have departed. When might I expect your decision?"

"I have decided upon Miss Lawrence," Peter said, striding past the man to the rack where he'd hung his coat upon arrival. It was a relief to be finished with this business, and he was more eager than ever to return home.

"Oh?"

"Yes, yes, Miss Lawrence is *exactly* what I am looking for. Perfect, in fact." He put his arms through the sleeves of his coat and turned to say goodbye to the agent only to meet the light-blue eyes of Miss Hollingsworth, who was standing in the hallway behind Mr. Hastings. Their eyes met over the round man's head, and her shocked expression struck him like a physical slap. Their eyes locked for the longest second of his life before she ducked back into the broom closet without a word. His face flushed with embarrassment.

He hated to be the cause of her distress, but in the next moment he wondered if he should even want to make it right. He knew she would not suit, and to go after her and apologize would only extend the discomfort that already had him feeling so unraveled. Perhaps it was not very gentlemanly, but ignoring it still seemed the better course.

He straightened. He'd done nothing wrong by making a professional decision he believed would be best for his household. That she'd overheard him was unfortunate but not intentional.

Miss Hollingsworth would find another position better suited for her, and he would be all the more grateful for Miss Lawrence and her dour looks because he would be comfortable having her in his home. Peter thanked Mr. Hastings a final time before leaving the office without looking back. He ignored the sick feeling in his stomach and forced his thoughts toward home and all that awaited him there. Routine. Purpose. Focus.

Chapter Three:
Julia

Julia stepped back into the broom closet so she could have a moment to recover. She took a deep breath and squeezed her eyes shut against the overwhelming humiliation.

Why did I follow him out?

If she had stayed in the room she'd have never known that it had been her interview that had made up his mind to choose another candidate. But as he'd left the closet, she'd realized she'd said nothing about her proficiency at both the pianoforte and flute. She'd hoped that mentioning the additional abilities would further recommend her for the position she felt certain was perfect for her. The country setting was familiar and enticing; there were two little girls to care for and dogs to enjoy — she missed being around dogs. Additionally, Mr. Mayfield seemed like a steady man, and his home was close enough to Mother's house for visits, but not so close that Mother could

41

manage Julia's life.

The interview had seemed to go well, and yet Julia was apparently wrong about everything. She would have to return home and tell her mother that the interview had come to naught, which she feared was exactly what her mother wanted.

Mr. Hastings came to fetch her. "I shall let you know Mr. Mayfield's decision before the week is out," he said. "I will send word to the address on your application." It was a kind lie.

Mr. Mayfield had *looked* at her, met her eye as she stood in the hall, yet he'd made no attempt at reparation for what she'd overheard.

You are only a servant, she reminded herself.

"Yes, thank you."

It was only a few minutes' walk to the inn where she'd engaged a room for the night, an expense justified by her belief that she would be offered the position. Now it was a waste of money. It wasn't until she was behind the bolted door of her room that she realized she hadn't ordered a dinner tray, though that was another expense she could not afford, especially now. Her options were either to eat in the dining hall with the other guests or return to the front desk and request the tray. Neither option felt worth the effort. She had a packet of walnuts in her bag; they would sustain her until morning when she could go down for an early breakfast before she caught the mail coach back home at seven o'clock.

She wanted nothing more than to crawl under the unfamiliar covers and stay there the rest of the afternoon, evening, and night, and since she had nowhere else to be and nothing else to do, she decided to do exactly that. There were not many chances in life to give into self-pity; she would take full advantage of it now that she could.

It was noon the next day before the coach pulled up in front of Leery's Pub in Feltwell. She was glad to be amid the safe and comfortable, but the village of her youth was not "home" anymore, and she felt as though she were returning after having lost a battle. Julia waited for the other passengers to exit the carriage before she stepped down, wishing the tightness in her chest would loosen. She would be facing Mother in a few minutes and needed to put a positive light on the interview. Otherwise Mother would ask too many questions or offer comfort that, more and more often, made Julia feel small and incapable.

"Your bag, miss?" the driver asked while

another man began pulling the luggage from the underside compartments. Julia pointed to her valise — an old leather thing that had once belonged to her father. The driver handed it to her, and she thanked him. Her back and head ached from the jarring roads, her stomach hurt from hunger — she had not gone down to breakfast after all — and one would think she'd walked the whole way with how fatigued she felt. Was it too much to hope she might be able to climb under the covers two days in a row? Probably.

Julia made her way down Millborn Road and over the bridge. The apple orchard — planted where the dog yard had been when Papa was alive — filled the back half of the lot, which was larger than most. Mother managed an herb garden on one side of the flat-fronted house, and a row of irises served as a living fence around the whole of it, but it was the row of primroses bordering either side of the walk to the front door that drew her eye.

They had begun to bloom a week or so earlier, and the bursts of yellow and pink were increasing each day. They reminded Julia that all was not lost, joy would come again, but they did not entirely dispel the gloom she felt. She bent down and broke off one pink bloom at the base, twirling the round little blossom in her fingers. There was nothing sensational about a primrose, but there were also no thorns.

Julia looked from the bloom to the house again and felt the gloom darkening even the power of the primrose. Mother kept a very fine house and grew a lovely garden, no one would argue the point, but the longer Julia stayed in this house, the more she feared she would never leave. Instead of tucking the bloom behind her ear as she would have when she was young, she dropped it back onto the mound of color and leaves she'd plucked it from. Primroses could only be brought in the house in groups of thirteen — some folklore Mother had heard once — and Julia did not think Mother would appreciate her picking a dozen more.

Upon opening the front door, Julia inhaled the smell of yeast and fire that had forever been the scent of her childhood. The familiarity brought the first measure of calm Julia had felt since yesterday's interview. Mother's bread was as much a part of the household as was the porcelain tea set she'd inherited from her mother and the portrait of Papa that hung over the mantel in the front parlor. Footsteps from the kitchen preceded the swinging door that divided the home from the kitchen and, more importantly, the bake room at the back of the house. In the Hollingsworth house, the kitchen was not an out of the way room that the family rarely saw. Rather, it was a gathering place where Julia had spent her youth observing, more than participating in, the interactions of her family. There had always been enough people with something to say that Julia had been content to listen. Papa had been like that too.

Mother, with her bright eyes and a kerchief tied over her hair, smiled widely at her youngest daughter while wiping her hands on her apron. "Julia, dear, I am so glad you returned safe." She pulled Julia into an embrace without bothering to stop talking. "I swear I did not sleep a wink all the while you were gone. I wish you'd have let me go with you." She looped her arm through Julia's and fairly dragged her into the kitchen, barely pausing for breath between her chatter. "I've just finished some bread, so your timing is exceptional."

Once in the kitchen, Mother released Julia's arm and moved toward the sideboard, where she picked up a towel and used it to cover her hand as she flipped the still-hot bread from the first pan. Mother liked bread baked in rectangular pans that created uniform slices rather than the typical tray-baked loaves that were higher in the middle than at either end. There were three loaves this afternoon, which meant Mother would be going out in order to give away two of them. Mother had been raised a gentleman's daughter, but marrying Papa — a banker — had led her to learn how to be useful in ways beyond the drawing room.

Julia sat at the table and went about removing her bonnet.

"How was the interview?" Mother removed the other loaves of bread from the pans and placed them on cooling racks. "What was the father like? When will you know if he chose you for the position?"

"He did not choose me." Julia hoped her voice sounded even. She placed the bonnet on the table and smoothed her hair, worn in a twist with tendrils on either side of her face because that was how Mother preferred it, and it was easier to avoid Mother's advice by simply doing things her way.

Mother looked up, an upside-down loaf of bread in one towel-covered hand and the empty bread pan in the other. "You were told already? I had thought the agency would send a letter? Is that not usually how it is done?"

Julia brushed away nonexistent crumbs

from the tabletop. "I know already." She kept details of the positions she applied for to herself so that her mother could not be critical of them. She still hoped Julia would stay in Feltwell, find a husband, and give her pretty grandbabies as Julia's older sister and brother had done. Mother set down the bread and the pan, then came behind Julia and wrapped her arms around her shoulders. Julia did not want or need her mother's comfort. Well, maybe a little.

"I am so sorry, Julia. And after you traveled all that way."

Julia lifted one hand to pat Mother's arms that encircled her shoulders while wishing she could feel just her *own* regret. To have to carry Mother's as well was too much.

"It is all right," Julia said, keeping her tone light and unconcerned. "I shall be better prepared next time."

Mother released her embrace. "Hmm." She moved back to the bread as her focus shifted from compassionate to problem-solving. Her solution would be predictable, and Julia readied her response — equally predictable. "Will you still not consider going to Louisa instead? You were such a help for her, and you would be nearby."

Julia had spent two weeks with her sister Louisa, who lived two miles west of town.

She had enjoyed the children — all five of them — but Louisa's home was too small to afford any privacy, and Julia felt the same obligation to meet expectations as she felt when she was at Mother's.

"I want a paid position, Mother. I enjoy my independence." Not for the first time Julia wondered if she ought to write the words on her forehead so that every time her mother considered advising differently, she would be reminded of Julia's opinion. But, then, Mother would likely ignore words written on Julia's forehead as easily as she ignored the words that came out of Julia's mouth.

As the youngest child in her family, Julia was prone to be parented by her mother, her sister, and her brother; even Simon's wife had taken to clucking over Julia like an overanxious hen. Julia must seem incapable — it was the only explanation. That, and the fact she had so often let others make decisions for her in her youth. Perhaps it was simply a habit for them to continue to do so.

At seventeen, she'd begun assisting the teacher at the school she attended with Louisa. Julia had loved teaching, and Mother was willing to let her take some time before she entered into the business of finding a husband.

By the time Julia turned twenty, she had decided she wanted to be a teacher. Mother wouldn't have it and had pulled her from the school, taken her to a dressmaker, and put her in the shows. Or at least that's how Julia had felt about the dances and dinner parties and garden teas that were all about making the right connections in hopes of making a match. The process brought out her worst anxieties, and after two years, Julia decided she'd had enough. There must be better things to do with her life than say the right thing and wear the right thing and do the right thing — all the time. There were few options for Julia to have a different future than the one expected of her, but she liked teaching children and had been well educated herself.

To apply as a governess was the first decision Julia had ever made completely by and for herself. When she announced to her mother that she'd taken a position . . . oh, the fury had been unprecedented, but the freedom of taking a coach alone for the first time the next day had been everything she'd hoped it would be.

In London, no one asked why she was not married or told her what colors to wear or how best to style her hair to complement the shape of her face. She socialized with her own class when she wanted to, attended church when the mood suited her, and wore her hair however she liked. She'd enjoyed the children in her care, read books, walked through the parks, and enjoyed her own company. Now, however, she was home again. The unmarried daughter who had gone into service — the worry of her mother, the project of her siblings. Not quite right. Not good enough.

Julia hadn't realized her mother was talking and became attentive in time to hear again of the benefits of Julia going to Louisa's home — all things Julia had heard before. She would be nearby. She would be connected to her family. She would have the opportunity to socialize.

Julia kept her expression attentive and listened politely as Mother cut two slices of bread and spread them both with butter that melted immediately. Mother made the very best bread in town — everyone said so — and Julia's stomach rumbled in anticipation. If she were not so hungry, perhaps she would not have been so patient with this tired advice.

Julia took a bite of bread and chewed slowly, truly trying to savor it appropriately, then swallowed and smiled at her mother.

"It is delicious."

Mother grinned, her cheeks plumping up, but her eyes — the same light shade of blue as Julia's — showed concern. Julia ate the bread while her mother's smile lines fell back into worry ones.

"My poor girl," Mother said, reaching out to press her hand against Julia's cheek.

Julia pulled away, startling her mother . . . and herself. "I am all right." Her words were as tight as her chest, and she looked away from the hurt that sprang into her mother's eyes. She laid the slice of bread on the table, not hungry enough to prolong this conversation. She placed a hand on her mother's arm and smiled without trying to hide her fatigue. "I am tired, Mother. Forgive me. I think I shall rest until supper, if that is all right."

Julia stood and turned from the bread, the table, her mother, and the pity. In London, she'd been confident and comfortable with herself, but as soon as she'd come home, she was "poor Julia" again. At Louisa's, she was "Julia, dear." Why could she not just be *Julia*? Why did her accomplishments not count in the minds of the people who were supposed to love her best? How had five years of living away not served to change her family's opinion of her ability to

52

make her own decisions?

As Julia climbed the narrow stairs to her bedchamber, she thought again of Mr. Mayfield. He'd been disappointed in her too — disappointed enough to hire someone else and dismiss Julia without a second thought. Maybe it wasn't only her family that did not *see* her. Maybe no one did.

Once in her room, Julia stepped out of her shoes and, for the second day in a row, crawled beneath the covers and wished she could shut out the world completely.

There will be other positions, she assured herself with the blanket pulled over her head. She had applied for three and was waiting to hear back on the other two. *This was obviously not the right one. God has a different path for you to trod.* She'd been so sure she was meant to have *this* place — with *this* family — but it had come to nothing. She would wallow one more afternoon and then accept what was. Her father used to say "Smile it away, come what may." She'd try that tomorrow.

CHAPTER FOUR:
AMELIA

Amelia Edwards Hollingsworth let out a heavy sigh as the kitchen door swung closed behind her daughter. She listened to Julia's footsteps on the stairs, heard the creak of the floorboards overhead, and then the closing of the door to the bedchamber Julia used when she was home — no longer a common occurrence. Amelia loved her daughter, so much she ached inside, but in all the twenty-seven years of having raised this child, Amelia still did not understand her. Why had Julia wanted to be a governess instead of continuing to look for a husband? Why would she rather care for a stranger's children than her own nieces and nephews? Why had she pulled away when Amelia had tried to offer comfort just now?

A mother was supposed to comfort her child — why would Julia not let Amelia do her job?

With a heavy heart, Amelia set about tidying the kitchen, wrapping the partial loaf of bread in a towel and putting the pans away. She'd opened the windows to keep the heat of the baking oven from the rest of the house, but the gray sky was getting darker, so she closed all but one. Then she stood and felt the weight of her empty and quiet kitchen press upon her.

Amelia's life had not turned out as she'd thought it would when she had first entered society in search of finding her future — or, rather, the man who would fill her future. After having her heart broken by the man she'd loved, she had chosen to love a man who moved in circles that were not whispering about her behind her back. She and Richard had been happy. Then he died, and she was alone to raise their children by herself.

Amelia had been determined to educate her children above the usual expectations of the middle-class life she had married into. But such education was expensive, so much of the light household work had fallen to Amelia to do herself. Instead of keeping a gardener and a cook, she hired a woman of all work to come four days a week and do the more laborious tasks.

She'd taken the children to church every week so they would know God, and she'd tried to anticipate their needs before they realized how desperately a thing was needed. All her effort had been targeted toward their destinations of marriage, family, and purpose. Maybe not as gentry, as Amelia had been raised, but as respectable and well-mannered third class. Simon and Louisa had fulfilled those expectations — Amelia had seven wonderful grandchildren between them — and then there was Julia.

Julia, who was her father's daughter. Julia, who was quiet and thoughtful and tall, just like him. Julia, who preferred Richard's smelly and obnoxious dogs over dresses and ribbons. And after Richard died . . . well, everything had changed after Richard died. Julia preferred school to social events. She preferred her own company to that of the other girls in the parish. She took long walks — hours on end — with Richard's walking stick that, honestly, looked silly in the hand of a young girl.

When Julia had announced she'd found a position as a governess in London, Amelia had thought she was joking. How would she even know how to go about applying for such work? Though the Hollingsworths were working class, there was a dramatic difference between having a profession, as Richard had, and working as a servant in some nobleman's household. Once Amelia realized her daughter was serious, she'd tried to talk her out of the decision, but Julia was determined. Amelia had been a little bit proud of that — though she'd never admit it.

Amelia *had* found comfort in how happy Julia seemed with her course once she'd settled in London. But it was a course without marriage. A course without children of her own. A course that seemed, to Amelia, a short-term situation. Certainly, Julia would not enjoy such work for *five* years. And yet she had. And now Julia was intent on finding *another* position.

She was already twenty-seven years old, but she was pretty and didn't *look* twenty-seven. Her marriage prospects were low, but there was hope for her yet. Unless she insisted on going back to work for some noble family who could never appreciate what she was sacrificing for them. She would be invisible to them; they wouldn't care about her. Amelia knew that from experience. Growing up, she'd had a fat governess whom she and her sisters laughed about behind her back and a dozen servants she never bothered to know by name. She was ashamed of her arrogance and disregard now, but to have her daughter working as one of those nameless people who moved soundlessly through aristocratic homes filled her with a different type of shame.

Amelia put her hands on the counter and dropped her chin to her chest, hating how easily the bitterness could rise inside of her when she listed the turns her own life had taken. She tried to push away the temptation to go back to the first time she'd felt such a rejection. It had been more than thirty years ago. She should not even remember the pain of Elliott's rejection, let alone recall it so distinctly. But he had been the first of many losses, and she could not find a way to separate one from the other — her broken courtship and her broken relationship with her daughter.

How can I help her? Amelia wondered. *Why has she never let me in?*

CHAPTER FIVE:
PETER

By day five of Miss Lawrence's employment, Peter was beginning to question his choice.

"Why does Leah not have proper stockings?" Miss Lawrence asked him as soon as he'd left the breakfast room that morning. She'd been waiting in the hallway, nearly scaring him out of his boots, truth be told.

"Because she insists in playing in the mud. Lydia saved the stockings for Sunday. I believe you shall find them on the top shelf of the wardrobe in a red-and-blue-striped hatbox."

Miss Lawrence put her hands on her hips, and her face — already etched with a permanent scowl — puckered even further. "Why is Leah allowed to play in the mud?"

"Because the enjoyment my girls feel when playing out of doors on fine days lasts far longer than muddy knees." He crossed his arms over his chest and expected the questioning to end. Lydia had managed the girls without bothering him with silly details — why could this woman not do the same?

"I have other concerns, Mr. Mayfield." She did not pause long enough for him to suggest they set a time to speak in his study. He was not known to counsel with staff in the hallway. "Why do the girls still share the same bed? It isn't healthy for them to be so attached to one another."

That rankled him. His daughters had no mother, so he would not prevent them from being "attached" to one another. He'd shared a bed with Timothy until leaving for school, and his daughters were far younger than he had been.

"I am pleased with the arrangement, Miss Lawrence. Now, if you'll excuse me." He gave her a sharp nod and turned on his heel. He spent the rest of the day in the dog yard, not only because there was always much to be done but also to avoid his new governess. Surely she was not so prickly with his girls?

He did not return to the house until supper, which he ate by himself at the large dining room table, an arrangement he'd held for the last four years, save for the occasional visits from Timothy or Uncle Elliott or one of Sybil's brothers. He read the day's paper in between bites, making mental notes about what he needed to do before tomorrow afternoon when he would travel to Swaffham to pick up the new dogs.

Until recently, Peter had primarily raised foxhounds, a breed in high demand in England. He was an excellent trainer and took pride in providing the very best hunting dogs. These new dogs, however, were greyhounds — racing dogs, though he felt that their companionable qualities were equally impressive. The breeding pair had cost him a pretty pound, but he was excited to further expand his pack.

This last year he'd begun breeding his hounds and had already seen a great deal of "expansion." He'd had three litters so far, and all had gone smoothly. He'd also purchased a female collie just after Christmas. In a moment of weakness, he agreed to let Marjorie name the dam, resulting in the name Bumbleberry, which hurt a man's pride when he had to tell it.

Bumbleberry had been bred with a sire in Northallerton, however, and was expecting her first litter in a few weeks. The popularity of collies had been growing in Scotland over the last decade, and Peter planned to be at the ready when England fully recognized the dog's unique traits.

61

Queenie, his female foxhound, was also expecting a litter — her third — in another month. With the greyhound pair and litters from both Queenie and Bumbleberry, he would more than double the size of his pack by the end of the summer. Already he had four of Queenie's litter sold. His reputation was growing.

Peter finished his meal, planning to kiss his daughters good night and then read a periodical on canine husbandry he'd had sent from London, but Miss Lawrence was standing in the hallway like a phantom with her bony face and pale-gray dress, and he squealed like a girl. Had she been waiting for him again? He hoped that he'd simply exited while she was walking somewhere else.

"Mr. Mayfield, might I have a word?"

"Certainly. Why don't we meet in my study?" He wanted his daughters' governess to come to him with questions and problems, but he hated being surprised. If only he didn't feel so anxious beneath Miss Lawrence's judgmental countenance and so insecure about how to guide her. Lydia had required so little of him.

In the study, he waved Miss Lawrence toward the chair on one side of his desk. She sat on the edge, her hands folded tightly in her lap. His chair squeaked when he sat down, and she pursed her lips at the sound. The woman seemed particularly . . . sensitive.

"What would you like to discuss, Miss Lawrence?"

"I am concerned about your daughters' prayers. Are you aware that Leah does not repeat the Lord's Prayer correctly? And that both girls then add words of their own?"

"Yes, Miss Lawrence, I am aware." Leah still said "woebegone" instead of "will be done." Peter found it adorable. He did not strictly follow the daily focuses outlined in the Book of Common Prayer as he felt the girls too young to understand them. This was something he and Sybil had agreed on years ago, not wanting to indoctrinate their children with rote practice that often eclipsed the meaning of the whole. He knew Lydia had not fully agreed with the more relaxed approach to the devotions, but she had supported him and Sybil.

"It is inappropriate," Miss Lawrence declared. "Why, it is almost . . . heathen for them to insert their own words. If I had known that these girls were being raised without the basics of good Christianity, I —"

Peter lifted a hand, interrupting Miss

63

Lawrence. "My daughters are being raised with a belief in God and a devotion to Christ's teachings. We attend church every Sunday; we pray every morning and evening. They are well versed in Bible stories." He could thank Lydia for that, too. She had a deep love for the Bible.

When Miss Lawrence had first arrived, he had told her that he would like the stories to continue, and she had said she would prefer to read straight from the Good Book. Peter had agreed, thinking it a good idea for his daughters to become familiar with scripture. But the girls had begun complaining that the words were difficult to understand and that Miss Lawrence did not change voices to fit the characters. They especially missed Lydia's representation of Goliath. He'd asked the girls to be patient with Miss Lawrence but wondered if he'd acquiesced to her suggestion too quickly.

Miss Lawrence opened her mouth, but he continued before she could speak.

"And, yes, we add some personal words at the end of our prayers. That does not make me, or my daughters, heathens. Have you any other concerns?"

"I need some time to organize my thoughts." Her face looked even more puckered. "I shall return tomorrow at ten

64

o'clock, if that is acceptable to you." She stood and left the room.

Peter leaned back in his chair and let out a heavy sigh. Should he have chosen Mrs. Grimshaw? She likely would not have been so militant in her religious devotion. The image of Julia Hollingsworth came to mind. He imagined she would have been gentle and loving with his daughters. Like Lydia. *Like a mother.* He shook that thought out of his head. They had no mother — *would* have no mother.

When he reached the door to the girls' bedchamber, he took a few moments to improve his expression from irritated employer to loving father. Then he turned the knob and poked his head into the room.

"Are the ladies receiving?" he asked. The girls thought this a great game he played with them every night when he came in for kisses.

"Yes, Papa," Leah called out.

Peter stepped fully into the room and smiled as his daughters, dressed in their nightgowns with their hair up in rags, hurried to get beneath the covers so as to make him believe they had not been bouncing on the tick.

"There are my bugs, snug in their rugs."

The girls giggled. He lay down across the

65

foot of the bed and propped himself up on one elbow so he was facing them. "What shall you dream of tonight, do you think?"

Marjorie frowned. "Miss Lawrence made us practice sitting still for half an hour before bed."

"For *two* hours!" Leah added.

Marjorie scowled at her sister. "One half of one hour." She turned back to Peter. "It felt like two hours, however."

"Sitting still?" He tried to keep an open mind. "Let us think of some ways that sitting still can be a benefit."

They listed church and carriage rides and for when they got older and had visitors. Then Leah added, "When watching frogs," and they all dissolved into laughter and began planning their next frog-catching adventure. Sometimes on a Saturday afternoon the three would go on "Papa picnics" that included a variety of activities. It had been several weeks since they had managed one, what with the new dogs arriving and Lydia leaving. Peter wondered what Miss Lawrence would think if he brought home a bucket of polliwogs.

The next morning at precisely ten o'clock, Miss Lawrence knocked on the door of Peter's study. He steeled himself before calling for her to come in. She had engaged Colleen, a maid, to watch the girls in the nursery during her conference with him. Miss Lawrence sat in the same chair she'd occupied the night before and listed additional grievances for the next forty minutes. Marjorie should not be able to choose her own frock. Leah was too young to wear her hair in braids. Marjorie laughed too loudly, Leah whined too often, and both girls refused to eat kidneys with breakfast.

Peter said nothing, just let her vent and stew and vent some more in hopes that allowing her to purge all the negative observations she'd made during this first week might allow her to better see the positives. When she finished, he smiled at her stiffly.

"Was it not your understanding that you were hired to look after these girls, Miss Lawrence? You are supposed to be *teaching* them the manners and acceptable behaviors expected of girls of their class."

He didn't want his daughters to simply be told to sit up straight and hold their fork just so and not laugh so loudly, but they did need etiquette, and most of Miss Lawrence's complaints seemed to center on that aspect. If the girls could learn the skills they were obviously lacking, perhaps Miss Lawrence would have less to complain about.

"Do you think a bit more patience is warranted on your part as they learn what is expected of them? Miss McCormick was a nursemaid more than she was a governess. My children are in need of instruction, which is why I chose you."

Surprisingly that seemed to stop her flow of irritation. "So I have leave to teach them these things?"

Peter sighed and stood. "Yes, that is your job. Now, if you'll excuse me, I have business in Swaffham."

When he arrived to pick up the greyhounds, they were frightened — not surprisingly. Even more so when he put them inside the crate already loaded in the back of the wagon. By the time he returned home that evening, the dogs had calmed, and he spent some time testing their obedience with pieces of liver as a reward. It was gratifying to see for himself that they were everything the breeder had claimed them to be — in excellent health, well trained, and responsive to praise.

Eventually he settled them into their own pen on the opposite end of the yard from the hounds, who were far too excitable for the new additions. Greyhounds had difficulty maintaining body heat, so he'd had Gregory — the hired handler — prepare an enclosed structure and fill it with old blankets so the dogs would be able to stay warm. The entrance was just big enough for them to get through and covered with a piece of sail that would further insulate the space.

Peter would need to give these new dogs extra attention for the next few weeks as they settled in. Rather than feeling overwhelmed by the increased demands, he felt energized. Peter had always been able to lose himself with the dogs in ways he never did in the other aspects of his life. He enjoyed fatherhood, of course, but what did he know about raising little girls? Running the estate gave him financial security, purpose, and a sense of pride, but it was not particularly satisfying. The dogs were different from everything else. He knew them, they knew him, and they required nothing more than what he was able to give.

It was nearly dark when Peter entered the house through the back doors and took off his muddy boots. He'd told Cook he'd be late and found a bowl of stew underneath a towel along with some fresh bread and a tall mug of ale set at the servants' table. Once his belly was full, he made his way upstairs to kiss his girls good night, though they were certainly asleep by now. He'd dallied too long with the greyhounds. He was eager to fall into his own bed. It had been a long day — good, but long.

"Are the ladies receiving?" He whispered so as not to wake them if they were already asleep.

"Papa?"

Peter heard the strain in Marjorie's voice, and he straightened as he pushed the door fully open. He crossed to her, quickly assessing by the light coming in from the hall that Leah was asleep on the other side of the bed.

"What is the matter?" The dim light reflected off her tear-streaked face, and he felt his chest grow tight. She took a deep, gulping breath while Peter smoothed damp tendrils of hair from her face. "What's wrong, little bits?"

Three minutes later, Peter stormed down the servants' stairs in his stocking feet and burst through the door that led to the servants' quarters and kitchens.

The footman, Jacob, shot to his feet from a rocking chair in the common area.

Peter's nostrils flared. "Where is Miss Lawrence?"

"In her bedchamber, I believe. Shall I fetch her?"

"She is not in her bedchamber," Peter said sharply, his mind moving at a gallop. His first stop after Marjorie had finished recounting her day had been the small room off the nursery, where he'd pounded on Miss Lawrence's door.

Mrs. Allen, the housekeeper, came out of her room, located nearest to the common area, pulling the sash of her dressing gown tight.

Peter barked orders. "Mrs. Allen, please find Miss Lawrence. Jacob, have the groom prepare the gig. Miss Lawrence will be staying at the Inn of the Cross and Bellows tonight."

"Sir?" Mrs. Allen asked, her hands clasped in front of her. "Has something happened?"

"Bruises on Leah's arm and threats that my children will be tied to a chair if they do not use the right spoon." His hands were clenched into fists at his side.

Mrs. Allen gasped just as Mr. Allen joined them. He'd been asleep, apparently, as his hair was pushed up on one side, but he had taken the time to throw his coat over his bedclothes.

"What can we help you with, Mr. Mayfield?"

Mrs. Allen put a hand on her husband's arm. "I shall explain it." She turned back to Peter. "Why don't you retire to your study, Mr. Mayfield? We will find Miss Lawrence and bring her to you."

71

Peter nodded, his jaw aching from clenching his teeth so tightly. He went to his study on the second floor, drank a glass of scotch in one swallow, and began pacing in front of the cold fireplace. He reviewed what he'd said to Miss Lawrence in their meeting and felt sick. He'd told her to do what she felt was best and acted as though his involvement were an irritation. What kind of father was he?

There was a knock at the door, and Mr. Allen entered, Miss Lawrence behind him. Her expression, as always, looked like pasty old leather, but the mixture of fear and defiance in her eyes showed that she knew exactly why she'd been summoned. He pushed aside his regrets for having handled her so poorly until now. He need to be the father his daughters deserved now that he understood the threat against them.

"Mr. Allen, please remain in the room to serve as a witness."

Miss Lawrence's eyes widened slightly.

Peter did not wait for Mr. Allen to answer before he rounded on Miss Lawrence. "You hit my child? You threatened them and pulled a five-year-old girl from the window seat."

Miss Lawrence folded her arms across her chest, seemingly unaffected by his anger.

"You said I was hired to curtail their behavior. You shall spoil a child if you spare the rod, and it did not take long for me to realize why they were so ill-mannered." She turned as if she were the one to decide when this discussion was finished.

Peter's blood was at a full boil, and he spoke through clenched teeth. "You will pack your things, and Stephen will take you to town. I will pay you for your work thus far and cover the cost of your room at the inn tonight, but you will *never* return to this house, and I will send a letter to Mr. Hastings to make certain he never recommends you to another position."

She turned back to him, her eyes flashing. "You have no right —"

"No!" he bellowed. Mr. Allen startled, but Peter hardly noticed. He'd never yelled like this. He'd never *felt* like this. "*You* have no right, madam, and I will not tolerate your presence in my household a moment longer." He crossed his arms over his chest and glared at her. "I will watch you pack your things and escort you to the carriage, and then I shall never see you again."

CHAPTER SIX:
JULIA

During her time in London, Julia had enjoyed walking the city before her day began with the Cranston children. Despite the smog and noise, London had lovely parks, and as morning was not the fashionable time for the *ton* to go out, the streets were nearly empty at seven o'clock in the morning.

Julia had kept up the habit of her morning walks since returning to Feltwell, remembering how much she'd enjoyed walking the countryside when she had been young. The familiar landscape was nice, and encountering people she'd known all her life was enjoyable enough, but she'd sent off four additional letters through Mr. Hastings for new positions. More and more, Mother talked as though Julia were going to stay:

"Simon's children will be coming to stay for a week in June while Simon and Clara attend a wedding in Gloucester. I so look forward to having them here with us."

"Would you prefer spending Christmas with Louisa or Simon? Simon has more room, but there is nothing like Christmas with children, and Louisa has more by half."

When Julia returned home from her walk, Mother was out, likely visiting Mrs. Harris, whose husband had passed last week. Mother had made soup and, of course, bread, and had warned Julia she would be gone for several hours in hopes of helping set Mrs. Harris's house to rights. The woman had kept to her bed for days on end and did not have a servant or any children to help her through. Beth was out back, doing the week's laundry; she would only come inside to return the linens and copper tub. Any inside task was for Julia or Mother today. Julia did not mind. There was only so much walking and reading a body could do in a day, and she enjoyed having purpose. That was one thing she and Mother had in common.

Julia tied on an apron and set about tidying the kitchen. Mother must have run out of time to do it herself. While she cleaned, Julia thought about each new position she had applied for, calculating how soon she could expect to hear back based on when the position began. One position was set to start in just over a week, and the fact that she hadn't heard back led her to think they had chosen another candidate.

Was she somehow so off-putting that no one wanted to hire her? Or perhaps she had been spoiled by the Cranstons; they were the only position she'd applied for five years ago, and then the arrangement had been so well suited for all of them. Perhaps that was an unusual circumstance, and this applying and waiting and feeling rejected and applying and waiting and feeling rejected was typical. How depressing.

Julia was wiping down the kitchen table when she heard a knock. She dried her hands on her apron as she walked to the front door and opened it, expecting one of her mother's friends to have come calling, though it was early, to be sure.

"Mr. Hastings?" she said after a moment of shock, then looked past him and felt her face flush. "Mr. Mayfield?"

"Good morning, Miss Hollingsworth," Mr. Hastings said. He fiddled with his cravat. It was clearly tied too tight by the way his neck bulged around the edges. "Might we have a word?"

Julia untied her apron, embarrassed and flustered to be anything less than properly situated to receive such unexpected and intimidating guests. "Please come in," she said as she ushered them toward the parlor while balling the apron in one hand behind her back. "I shall join you in a moment."

In the kitchen, her heart raced as she prepared a tea tray, grateful that she had her mother's bread, a pot of marmalade, and a kettle that was always kept on. She did not take the time to check her appearance. The main floor looking glass was within sight of her unexpected guests.

Julia returned to the parlor within five minutes and apologized for the delay. From the modest home and amount of time she'd been gone, she suspected they knew she had prepared the tray herself. Normally, such knowledge would not cause her any embarrassment, but seeing these men again — Mr. Mayfield, especially — summoned those feelings of inadequacy that had consumed her after their last meeting. She'd never expected to see him again.

She poured the tea, not having a cup herself for fear that her shaking hands would betray her anxiety. She hoped Mother would forgive her for serving the Darjeeling, which she reserved for favorite guests. When she finished pouring, Julia sat back against the chair and waved toward the tray. "My mother is renowned for her bread; it is always what we serve with tea."

"Thank you, Miss Hollingsworth," Mr. Hastings said as he sipped his tea.

Mr. Mayfield had yet to speak and seemed as uncomfortable as she was. He took a sip of tea, turned his cup as he set it down, then picked it up for another sip, and turned it yet again. For a moment, she wondered if he had come to apologize for his rudeness. Though why would he care? He was a gentleman; she was a servant. He owed her nothing, and they both knew it.

Mr. Hastings set down his saucer and cleared his throat. "My apologies for not warning you of our visit. I'm afraid the situation is urgent, and there was no time to waste."

She looked from him to Mr. Mayfield, who held her eyes while Mr. Hastings continued. "Mr. Mayfield is in need of a governess, as soon as possible, and wondered if you might still be interested in the position."

It had been almost three weeks since the interview that had left her feeling small and discarded. "I understood that Mr. Mayfield had hired one of the other candidates, Mr. Hastings."

The rotund man shifted in his chair and pulled at his cravat again. "Well, yes, but

78

then . . . well, things did not work out, and he is in need of a governess again."

Julia wanted to stand up and shout "It would be my greatest wish and pleasure to take the position!" But she could still hear Mr. Mayfield's voice when he said he would hire the other woman. He'd been so resolute, so certain. Instead, she said, "What of the other applicant? I imagine she would have been Mr. Mayfield's second choice."

Mr. Hastings shifted again. Mr. Mayfield looked into his cup.

So the second candidate had *not* accepted the position, leaving only Julia. A lifetime of sermons about pride and humility flowed through her mind. It was difficult to sort through her feelings. She looked around the parlor, feeling trapped.

Mr. Mayfield cleared his throat, drawing her attention back to him. "I am sorry to put you in such a difficult position, Miss Hollingsworth."

Julia met his eyes and could read the apology there. And the desperation. She said nothing.

"Our interview ended . . . badly, and I offer my apology for having acted so poorly. I believe my daughters would benefit very much from your care, and I hope you will accept this unconventional offer."

Mr. Hastings looked confused, but then he didn't know she had overheard Mr. Mayfield's dismissal that day. But Mr. Mayfield knew, and he'd apologized to her — sincerely, she thought. There was something soft about Mr. Mayfield when his guard was down. She'd seen it during their interview, and she could sense it now, though his discomfort was clear.

I could work for such a man, she thought. Part of her liked the challenge of proving herself the better choice all along. The rest of her simply wanted to find a new *place.*

"I accept the offer."

Mr. Mayfield smiled, a bright, wide smile that lifted his eyes and lightened his whole face. She could not help but smile back.

Mr. Hastings cleared his throat. "Might it be possible for you to leave, uh, now?"

She broke eye contact with Mr. Mayfield and looked at the other man. "*Right* now?"

"As soon as you have had a chance to pack your things. Mr. Mayfield's former governess and a maid have been assisting with his daughters, but the arrangement is not ideal for any of the parties. If you are willing, I can review the contract during the journey to Mr. Mayfield's estate. We could arrive by this afternoon if we can leave quickly enough."

Right now? Julia repeated in her mind. Mother was not home, but she would discourage this course to be sure. If, however, Julia left before Mother returned from her visit . . .

Julia stood, and the men followed suit. "I shall need half an hour to ready my trunk."

"We shall return in a *full* hour, if that is all right, to give you a bit more time," Mr. Mayfield said. "We can help with your trunk when we return."

That is a better plan, Julia thought. *And Mother will not be back before then.* "That would be much appreciated, thank you."

Mr. Mayfield smiled, softening his face again, and inclined his head. "Very good, and . . . thank you, Miss Hollingsworth."

"Call me Miss Julia, please, and feel free to wait here in the parlor if you like. I shan't be long, and my mother's bread really is remarkable."

Julia walked with decorum from the room, but as soon as she was out of view, she ran up the stairs to her room. She opened her trunk and began throwing dresses and shoes onto the bed from her wardrobe. She would not take any of her fancier dresses as she would not need them as a governess, and she stuffed all her toiletries into a canvas sack, which she threw into the trunk as well.

Once she had packed her clothing, she folded her quilt — made by her mother years ago — and placed it on top.

Only then did she consider if she were doing the right thing. After a few moments, she sighed. She was *not* doing the right thing, but leaving now would spare a negative parting with her mother. Julia's sewing bag and three of her favorite books went on top of the quilt before she latched the trunk. Then she sat down at her desk, removed a piece of paper, and wrote a note to her mother despite the tightness in her chest. Every word on the paper included a prayer that her mother would not be too angry. Or hurt.

Chapter Seven:
Amelia

"Julia," Amelia called when she returned to the house that afternoon. She tugged at her bonnet ribbons with one hand as she closed the door behind her. "I ran into Mrs. Partridge, and she's invited us to supper. Her nephew is visiting from Dover, and . . . Julia?"

The house was still. Had Julia gone out? Amelia had stayed too long at Mrs. Harris's — it was nearly four o'clock — but the woman was not coping well with her husband's death. Amelia could not fault her; nothing prepared a person for such a loss. She had folded some laundry — washed by another neighbor the day before — and tidied the kitchen while Mrs. Harris recounted the horror of finding her husband cold after coming home from church.

"It is because he doesn't go to service, I'm certain of it," Mrs. Harris had said.

Amelia offered words of comfort while

remembering how difficult it had been for her to accept Richard's death. He had contracted pneumonia, and she'd known a few days before he took his last breath that he would not survive the illness. There had been a measure of peace in attending him those last days, administering — as it was — to his final moments.

One night, she'd crawled into bed beside him and, though he was not aware of her, cried into his shoulder for the last time. The heartbreak of that moment — knowing that every future challenge she faced would be faced alone — was something she would never forget. How she missed him. How different things would have been if he had not died. He made her better, and sometimes she felt as though she'd been floundering ever since, though no one would guess it from watching.

Julia was certainly floundering. The fear Amelia felt for her daughter's future was exhausting them both. If the girl would just settle down . . .

Or maybe it was time Amelia accepted that Julia was going to find her own way. She'd had to manage everything after Richard died — was she trying too hard to manage her daughter?

Amelia hung her bonnet on the peg in the

hall and continued into the kitchen, taking note of the copper tub set on the shelf inside the door, which meant Beth had finished the wash. Perhaps some of Amelia's noble blood still influenced her from time to time because if there was one task Amelia could take no pride in doing herself, it was washing, though she often felt guilty for not helping. She put on her apron and hoped Julia would return soon. They would need to be to the Partridges by five o'clock. Mrs. Partridge's nephew was on his way up the ranks in the King's Royal Navy, and he would be in attendance for dinner. Julia would hate the effort at matchmaking, and Amelia was feeling embarrassed for creating the situation now that it was done. Maybe the first step to backing off would be telling Julia of the collusion and letting her skip dinner if she would rather.

Amelia was halfway across the tidied kitchen when she spotted the paper, folded and propped against her clean and stacked baking pans. The note had not been there when she'd left for Mrs. Harris's, and she and Julia were not in the habit of writing notes to one another. She picked up the note, confirming Julia's handwriting across the front before unfolding the paper.

Dear Mother,

Mr. Hastings from the employment office came to the house with an offer for a governess position that needed to be filled immediately. I had to leave within the hour. The position is exactly what I hoped for and much closer to Feltwell than the London position was. I will be working for a man by the name of Mr. Peter Mayfield. His estate is located outside of Elsing, where he lives with his two young daughters, who sadly have no mother as she passed away some years ago. I shall write to you with the exact address as soon as I am settled. In the meantime, know that I am safe and happy to have had this turn of events. Be glad for me, Mother.

Much love,
Julia

Amelia stared at the letter, her chest hot and her hands cold. The newly born thoughts of letting Julia choose her own course crumbled like ash as the floor tilted slightly beneath her feet. "Mayfield," she whispered in disbelief to the empty house. Elsing was not far enough away from East Ashlam to allow her to think that it could be a different Mayfield family than the one that had come immediately to mind. Of course, Amelia had heard the name from time to time, the scandals and dissidence of the family were well known, but those things were secondary to the true hook of that name in her heart.

Old memories and unforgotten heartbreak filled her to the brim as though she were eighteen years old again. Elliott had broken her heart into a hundred pieces with his letter of farewell, but as gossip had abounded about the family, she had come to see herself as lucky to have avoided saddling herself to such a reputation. Nobility did not equate with morality, and no family exemplified that more than the Mayfields.

Amelia laid the letter on the counter and slumped into a kitchen chair. For years, she had wondered what might happen should her path cross Elliott's again, but in time her life grew bigger than her memories and she had let it go. Or so she thought. Now, confronted with the family and the memories, she felt frozen and . . . sad.

"It can't be," she whispered, the slightest tremor in her voice. She imagined Julia in a Mayfield house. Teaching Mayfield children. Eating Mayfield food. She closed her eyes and took a breath. *There has to be a way to fix this!*

Her feelings were rising toward panic to think of her daughter in one of their households. But perhaps this Peter Mayfield was not connected to Elliott — *Lord Howardsford* — at all. She would find out, to be sure, and if it wasn't *those* Mayfields, then . . . well, she didn't know. And if it *was* those Mayfields? *Gracious.*

CHAPTER EIGHT:
ELLIOTT

Elliott was halfway through breakfast when the butler at Howardhouse brought in a note on a silver tray. Brookshire — Brookie, for short — was nearing eighty years old and had been the household's butler for the last forty years. The hand holding the tray shook slightly, but Elliott had no plans to replace him.

"Thank you, Brookie," Elliott said, wiping his hands on the napkin in his lap and lifting the card from the tray. The script was unfamiliar, though feminine, and he frowned in suspicion. Despite being sixty years old, Elliott was considered an eligible bachelor now that he was making his home in England, and too many women had made it plain to him that they would be happy to become his countess. Elliott had responded to the feminine attention by avoiding social situations and church — the two prime places of attack — but now and then, someone would invite him to an event in hopes of catching his eye themselves or introducing him to their sister, neighbor, cousin, friend, daughter. Lady Aberline had sat him next to her eighteen-year-old *grand-daughter* at a dinner party last Christmas. The girl had flirted with him all evening. Humiliating.

Accommodating another person into his lifestyle seemed exhausting at his age. The idea of marrying someone *young* — impossible.

Elliott snapped the wax seal and unfolded the paper, already planning the polite refusal of the invitation. When Mr. and Mrs. Clemington had invited him to their annual garden party in April, he'd lied about a trip to London, then felt guilty enough that he'd *actually* gone to London.

Elliott wearied of having to come up with another matter of business in a town far away just to make certain he was unavailable for whatever this event might be.

Dear Lord Howardsford,

I would very much like to meet with you this afternoon to discuss the employment of my daughter, Julia Hollingsworth, as a governess for your nephew Peter Mayfield. I am staying at the Inn of the Cross and Bellows and shall present myself at your estate at two o'clock so that we might discuss this matter of business.

Mrs. Amelia Hollingsworth

Amelia?
He shook his head. Not *his* Amelia, certainly. Not that she was his, nor had she ever been. She'd married that banker — *her* banker, as Elliott often thought of the man who'd taken his place. *It is not her,* he told himself, feeling ridiculous for even thinking of Amelia Edwards. It was not as though there were only one Amelia in all of England.

Elliott set the card aside and cut into the ham steak on his plate while further contemplating the odd letter. Peter *had* been in the process of hiring a new governess when he'd left their interview for Norwich a few weeks ago. The former governess, some relation to Peter's late wife, had gotten married or something like that. So Peter must have hired this Hollingsworth woman's daughter. Why on earth was that any business of Elliott's?

He should simply send a return message explaining his ignorance of the matter and encouraging this meddling woman to leave him out of whatever concerns she had. Yet he hated the idea of her bothering Peter, who had so much responsibility already. And he was curious about why this woman had come to *him.* He took another bite of ham and decided to allow her visit, though it might be awkward. He'd be pleasant and well-mannered and hear her out and try to deflect her concerns. He hoped it wasn't his family's reputation that had soured her against Peter. The boy did not deserve such prejudice, and Elliott was prepared to tell this woman as much should that be her motivation.

Do I know anyone with the last name Hollingsworth?

There was enough ring of familiarity to make him think he may have known a man by that name before leaving for India, but he couldn't be sure. And why would this woman come without her husband? Surely her husband knew of her visit, didn't he? Or perhaps Mr. Hollingsworth had told his wife not to be a busybody, and she was coming here without his blessing. Or she could be a widow and therefore had no one else to represent her concerns. His chewing slowed, and he looked at the letter as another idea barreled into his thoughts.

Could this be some kind of ploy to secure

an interview with him? The type of situation with Lady Aberline's niece was one sort of irritation, but not the only way in which female wiles had caused him discomfort. A few months after his return to Howard-house, a woman and her daughter had knocked on his door, claiming their carriage had thrown a wheel and asking if they could come in from the rain. Uncomfortable with their effusive thanks, Elliott had taken a groom with him and put the wheel — suspiciously removed, not thrown — back on the carriage. He did not offer the woman or her daughter tea, preferring being remembered as a boar if that meant they would not attempt such a trick again.

He had another woman trip right in front of him when he was in town a few weeks ago, requiring that he catch her. She invited him to dinner as a way to thank him; he flatly refused. He was rich. He was single. That was all some women needed to behave poorly. What if this Mrs. Amelia Hollingsworth were one more woman on the list who cared not a fig for him but only for his money and status?

By the time Elliott finished his breakfast, he had decided not to wait until two o'clock for Mrs. Hollingsworth to darken his doorstep. It was not as though he had anything of importance to do today, so he could give this matter his full attention. The sooner he informed this woman that he had no authority over Peter's household and she had no reason to object to her daughter's position there, the sooner he could push all worry from his mind.

The Inn of the Cross and Bellows was located a few miles south of Howardhouse, on the outskirts of East Ashlam. A proper English gentleman would take his horse or a carriage, but Elliott enjoyed physical exercise, and his knee ached less on days he went walking. He could walk to the village and intercept Mrs. Hollingsworth before she came to him. It was more proper for him to meet her where she was staying than for her to come to his home anyway.

An eligible man who did not want to be caught by some conniving woman had to look out for himself.

CHAPTER NINE:
AMELIA

Amelia left the inn at ten o'clock. She was nervous about her afternoon visit to Howardhouse and had not been to East Ashlam in some time. Life did not require her to travel north very often, which kept her away from the area of the country where most of the various Mayfield estates were located. But she was here now, so she took the opportunity to reacquaint herself with the area while hoping the self-guided tour of the village would distract her from her nerves.

There was not much to see, however. The ribbon in the front street shop was no different than the ribbon she could buy in her own village, and she had no need for a tailor, solicitor, butcher, miller, or blacksmith — which made up the remaining places of commerce. The parish church was simple and modern, with clean lines and large windows. After touring the church, and sitting for a spell in hopes that she could meditate some of her growing anxiety away, she left through the side yard, which put her in the churchyard where the rows of headstones made her heart ache. So much loss.

She followed the narrow gravel path, reading headstones and allowing herself the melancholy of remembering the many people she'd loved and lost. Her parents had both passed, and Richard had been gone almost as long as they had been husband and wife. She missed his steadiness, his security, his arms around her in the dark. When they had been married, she'd become part of a set, a whole. When their children came, it had connected them even further. And then he was gone. Knowing her children needed her more than ever had made the pain bearable, and after a time, parenting alone became ordinary. Only once since Richard's death had Amelia entertained another man's attention.

Vincent Arrington had been a yeoman farmer and a client and friend of Richard's. He'd done well for himself, and when his wife passed some five years ago, he became a widower. For more than a year, they had attended socials together, and he had walked her home from church more than once. And then he'd had an accident on his farm and a portion of his leg had been amputated. His son took over the farm, and Vincent saw himself as a broken man. Amelia had visited, brought him bread, and told him rather boldly that his injury had no bearing — she had gotten used to the idea that they would marry — but he closed himself off to her, and he eventually moved to Manchester to live with his spinster sister.

After the initial sorrow, Amelia made peace that it was not meant to be, but when the days got lonely and the nights got long, she wished that what might have been could have been. Other men had paid her some attention since then, but none had struck a chord.

Richard had provided well for her, and she did not worry for her future — aside from Julia. If that girl would stay closer to home and give Amelia grandbabies to fawn over, Amelia would want for nothing. For Julia to work for a Mayfield — Elliott's heir, no less — well, that broke any remaining consideration to let Julia find her own way.

Reminded of her purpose, Amelia exited the churchyard and returned to the street. As she passed shop fronts, she glanced at her reflection in the wavy glass. Stood straighter. Lifted her chin. Shoulders back.

I am certain you feel the same as I, she said

in her mind, practicing how she would broach this highly awkward conversation. *The idea of my daughter working for your nephew is unacceptable to me, and you owe me your help in putting an end to the situation.* Could she really say that out loud to him?

She would have to, if it came to that.

It was nearly noon when she returned to the inn, which would give her plenty of time to change into the rose-colored gown she'd brought. Richard had always told her she looked exceptional in that color. Though she was not the beauty of her youth, there was no reason not to present herself as well as possible, especially in the halls of the home she had once thought she would call her own. The thought sent a shiver through her, and long-buried questions popped their heads over the surface of her contentment.

Why had Elliott cut off their courtship so suddenly? Had she done something to chase him away? Or had inheriting his title improved his prospects so much that she was no longer a consideration? Had it been a game all along?

She had let him kiss her more than once — with far more ardor than a young woman should allow. At the time, she'd been certain she would become his wife, and she wanted to leave no question as to her level of interest in assuming that role. When he'd left, she'd felt like a fool who had been played by a master. And now she was going to meet with him face-to-face after more than thirty years. Was she rash in having made this plan? It was too late to entertain regrets. She had already sent the note requesting they meet to discuss this business between them.

"Mrs. Hollingsworth?"

The clerk said her name, and she moved toward the desk, wondering what this issue might be. She'd paid for the room upon her arrival last night, meals were included, and she would be leaving first thing tomorrow morning. No one knew she was here, so she could not have received correspondence . . . *Wait.*

"Yes?" she asked, hiding both her eagerness and anxiety rather well, she thought. Had Elliott responded to her note from this morning? What had been his reaction when he'd seen that it was from her? It would not surprise her if he did not remember her at all, though that would be humiliating.

"Lord Howardsford is awaiting you in the parlor."

Amelia raised a hand to her hair, which would be frizzy once she removed her bon-

99

net. A flush crept up her neck, intense enough to strangle her. She looked down at her dress, a simple blue-and-gray-striped walking dress with a high collar. She looked like an elderly widow in a frumpy frock and untidy hair. As though she'd given up on life, herself, and —

"Mrs. Hollingsworth?"

Another voice said her name, and Amelia spun around, too fast and too sharp to give the impression of casualness she would have preferred. But that voice, and that face. They stared at one another across the expanse of twenty feet and thirty years, and all the feelings — good and bad — rushed through Amelia like a northern wind.

He blinked.

She blinked. And then she reminded herself that she was mature and centered and there was no reason to let emotion overcome her. They had outgrown one another years ago. But her mouth was dry, and her mind was swirling. He was right there! Standing in front of her. Older, but still handsome and still . . . Elliott. Kind eyes, straight posture, broad shoulders. She had been afraid of what her reaction might be to seeing him and was disappointed to realize how strongly her whole body had responded. Why could Julia have not found a different position? Then Elliott could remain a part of Amelia's past and the Mayfields could continue to be a faraway family with no connection to her own.

"It *is* you," Elliott said, his eyes wide.

He didn't know?

The shock receded, reminding Amelia of reality and truth and the strength she needed to hold on to. If he hadn't known the message was from her, then he hadn't come because he was eager to see her. But then she did not want him to be eager to see her. She closed her eyes for a moment so she could pretend he was not there. She found her center and her strength, let go of the desire to look her best, remembered her reason for being there, and opened her eyes with her defenses back in place.

"Might we speak in private, please, Lord . . ." She paused because she'd never called him by his title, had struggled to think of him as anyone other than Elliott. Her Elliott. Or so she'd once thought. "Lord Howardsford?"

She walked past him before he answered. She could not let down her guard. He turned to follow her, and she was aware of every move he made and breath he took. She was tempted to smooth her hair and check her hem as she entered the private parlor located off the foyer of the inn, but it was too late for vanity, which was immature in the first place. She was here to protect her daughter. Nothing more.

Chapter Ten:
Elliott

Elliott followed Amelia — *his* Amelia, or rather her banker's Amelia — into the inn's shabby parlor. There was a dark stain on the rug, and the chairs did not match the settee. Amelia did not sit but instead turned to face him when she reached the cold hearth that smelled like wet ashes.

"I did not expect you to come here," Amelia said, her expression tight.

"I did not expect that the woman who sent the note was you."

Her cheeks colored. "I thought you would recognize my signature."

"If I ever knew your married name, I had forgotten it. My apologies."

She was attempting to look stoic — like she'd represented herself in the note — but her neck was red, and he could read her nervousness in the set of her shoulders and the way she shifted her weight from one foot to the other.

He was staring, but he couldn't help it. Amelia was standing right in front of him! It was remarkable how much she looked like . . . herself. Her gray hair was pulled away from her face and pinned up to show off her graceful neck. Her skin showed the years that had passed since he'd last been able to study her face, but it looked soft and clear. Her eyes were the same, the shape of her face, the full lips that had sent his heart racing . . .

He forced himself to stop, and he looked at the faded and dusty curtains to refocus himself. Was she the least bit affected by this meeting? Probably not. She'd lived a full life without him — marriage, children, community. Whatever connection they had once had was likely infantile in comparison to the other connections she'd made since.

"I presume you came because of the topic I introduced in my note?" she said.

Was she disappointed? Had she hoped he would have known it was her and come, eager to see her? "Yes, I thought I would save 'Mrs. Hollingsworth' the trip."

Amelia is standing right in front of me! He felt he needed to repeat it a dozen times before he could believe it. As to determining what he felt about seeing her, well, that would take far more work. He had never anticipated seeing her again, and certainly not under circumstances such as these. Unexpectedly, words from Napoleon — of all people to come into an Englishman's head — came to mind: *It is sometimes better to abandon one's self to destiny.* Napoleon's destiny had sent him to an island where he lived out his miserable days. Elliott's destiny had sent him to India . . . and then brought him back. And now he was standing before Amelia. And she was beautiful.

She parted those lovely lips enough to take a deep breath. "Well, that was kind of you, Lord . . . Howardsford."

She seemed to struggle saying his title, and it sounded strange on her lips. "Please call me Elliott, Amelia." He smiled and looked her over once more. "It is remarkable to see you again. You are as beautiful as ever."

She swallowed. "Thank you, Lord Howardsford, but I must address you as is appropriate, just as you should call me Mrs. Hollingsworth."

Elliott took a mental step back. What did she mean? Were they not friends?

She cleared her throat. "As I stated in my letter, Peter Mayfield, your nephew, has

recently taken my daughter into his household."

Shift, think, focus. He needed to match her
mood so as not to be distracted. He took a
breath and tried to settle his thoughts into a
line of professional considerations. "He
hired her as a governess, you mean."

"Yes, that is her official position, but she
is a young woman in a household of a
widowed man. That, in and of itself, is
improper. That he is your heir makes it an
impossible situation, and I would like your
help in remedying this situation."

Remedy? "I do not know the details
of . . ." He trailed off and waved toward the
chairs. "Would it better for us to have this
conversation seated?" Perhaps they could
order tea, relax, speak slower. She could lose
her tightness, and he could listen without
feeling as though she wanted to rap his
knuckle with a ruler.

"No, thank you."

Elliott felt the sting, intended or not, and
the shock and wonder of seeing her after all
these years began to fade. She did not want
to be comfortable nor extend this interview
any longer than she had to. The carefree girl
from London whose eyes had lit up when
he entered a room and who had kissed him
behind hedges was becoming harder to see

in the woman before him.

"Very well," he said. "As I mentioned, I do not know the details of Peter's household, and it is certainly not within my rights to dictate to him how he should manage it, but if he hired your daughter, then she must have *applied* for the position. I see no reason why either you or I should interfere, though I am sorry that you are against it."

Amelia let out a breath and shook her head, crossing her arms over her stomach. "She does not know who he is."

Elliott frowned, and his defensiveness increased. "He is Peter Mayfield, a widowed father of two girls, respectable, and God-fearing. I daresay your daughter is fortunate to work for such a man. I can confirm his good character."

She narrowed her eyes at him. "And why would your confirmation give me any peace?"

He blinked. "I beg your pardon?"

She swallowed, showing her discomfort. "Speaking plainly, I do not want my daughter to have any connection to your family, Lord Howardsford. I can see that you do not share my concerns, but I hope you will be considerate of mine."

"Considerate of the fact that you do not want your daughter connected to me even in some minuscule way? You are being ridiculous."

Her nostrils flared, and she dropped her arms to her sides. "How dare you say such a thing to me."

"How dare you lob such an accusation at my nephew."

"I made no accusation."

"You are accusing him of being some kind of threat to your daughter," Elliott returned. "That is ridiculous."

Her eyes flashed, and her chest heaved with indignation even as he mentally reprimanded himself. He put up his hands to signal a pause for both of them. "Forgive me. That was ungentlemanly of me."

She glared at him, and he thought that if he did not know this was Amelia Edwards, he would not recognize her for the tightness of her face and the fury in her eyes. She was still lovely, but she was hard and . . . ridiculous, though he would not say so again.

"You obviously have some serious concerns," he said diplomatically. "Could we please sit so that we might discuss them in a calmer manner?"

"No."

He all but threw his hands in the air.

"You owe me this, Lord Howardsford."

He stared at her a moment, waiting for her to clarify or elaborate, but when she didn't, he had no choice but to respond. "I am supposed to interfere with my nephew's household because I *owe* you?"

She nodded once. And crossed her arms again, her stare unwavering. In another situation, he would find the flush of her cheeks and confidence of her expression rather impressive. But not now.

"Forgive me, Mrs. Hollingsworth, but why on earth do I owe you such a thing?"

She swallowed and looked toward the window as though reorganizing her thoughts.

He'd caught her off guard, which only confused him further.

"We had a connection once, Lord Howardsford, and it ended . . . poorly, for me at least. Because of that history between us, and in light of the scandalous nature of so many of your family members, I do not feel confident having my daughter living beneath a Mayfield roof." Her mood softened, and a hint of pleading appeared in her tone. "She is young, and I fear for her future positions if she is linked with such scandal. Please understand that I mean no offense to you and yours. I am only protecting the security of my child. I am asking for your help in this."

"Because I owe you." He felt rather stuck on this part but forced himself forward when he saw her jaw tightening again. "I am the last to condone the actions of members of my family, I regret their choices, but Peter does not deserve your censure. He is as respectable a man as I have ever known. Those responsible for the reputation you are concerned with are gone."

Something hateful flashed in her eyes. "Not all of them."

Elliott felt as though he'd been slapped. She meant *him*? It took a few seconds for him to recover. "Even so, Peter does not deserve your prejudice. He is a good man."

Amelia walked to the window. She pulled back the curtain, but he sensed she was not looking at anything specific on the street. He hoped she was thinking about what he'd said and how unfair she was being.

"I assume you have already asked your daughter to leave his employ and she refused?" It didn't explain why Amelia had come to him, necessarily, but perhaps it would clarify some aspect of the situation. Obviously Amelia felt strongly about this, but he still did not fully understand why. If her daughter was employed by Teddy, or if

Peter had even the slightest lack of moral character, Elliott would understand, but neither of those was the case, which made her position feel prejudicial and punitive.

She took a breath and let it out, still looking at nothing through the dirty window. "I have no wish to burden my daughter with her mother's childish fears or spread gossip about your family. I am certain she is, so far, ignorant of those things for now. But I do not want her working in that household." She turned back to him and, though her expression was again determined, she lowered her voice a touch. "If you ever cared for me, Elliott, help me. Give me the peace of mind I need."

Elliott had not realized how much he'd hurt her until this moment. All these years and she was heartbroken enough to go such lengths to keep herself separated from not only him but his entire family. Elliott could not separate his shame from her prejudice. He also could not look away from her as she held his eyes. There was a time when every thought and feeling had showed on her face, but not anymore. That carefree girl had grown into a fearsome woman.

Regardless of how she felt she'd been treated by him, what she was asking was unfair — to her daughter as much as to Peter. To agree to any part of Amelia's request felt like an agreement with her bias. But Elliott could not find the words to tell her no. Perhaps he did owe her. Or perhaps he simply didn't want to break her heart again. She was different, and he mourned the parts of her that she'd seemed to have lost in the years since they had last met, but there was still some kind of connection between them — a curiosity of just how much might be left beneath the mask she'd worn for this confrontation. *Thirty-six years.* If he gave her what she wanted, might he have the chance to see her again?

"I can speak to Peter and share your concerns with him."

She didn't look particularly pleased with this solution.

"Surely you do not expect me to walk into my nephew's home and order her out of the house. Handled badly, it would be a disaster for everyone involved. But I will talk to him and see if there might be . . . something." He had no idea what that something was. Amelia seemed to only want her daughter out of Peter's house, and yet she was not willing to go to her daughter in person, so she too was mindful of some considerations. "That is all I can do, though I am unable to go until next week. I have matters to attend to before I can get away." This part was not *entirely* true.

Peter's brother, Timothy, was coming up from London so Elliott might introduce him to the marriage campaign, but Elliott could be to Elsing and back before Timothy arrived. Rather, he wanted time to craft the right approach that might allow him to see Amelia again. Perhaps after a few days of reflection, she would reevaluate. Maybe she would even withdraw her objection.

"Thank you," Amelia said, sounding relieved but still cautious.

"After I've spoken to him, may I contact you?" Did his tone sound casual and professional? He hoped it didn't reveal his ulterior motives of wanting a second opportunity to see her.

"Yes, that would be all right. Perhaps the clerk has a pencil and paper we might use."

He inclined his head and then stepped aside in order to allow her to exit the parlor. As she strode past him, a memory of leading her down a garden path and taking her face in his hands became so real for a moment that he forgot time and place. Amelia had not shied away from his attention back then, but she could not even look at him now.

What might have been different if I had

stayed here instead of going to India?

He followed her to the desk, where she requested a pencil and paper from the clerk. She did not look at Elliott as she took the items and wrote out her address. When she finished, she thanked the clerk and turned, paper in hand. She must not have realized how close he had been standing behind her as she startled slightly before taking a step back. He took the paper and glanced at it. "You live in Feltwell?" It was not close — some fifty miles away — but neither was it far.

"Yes."

"That is where your husband is from, then?" He'd already noticed she had not included her husband's name in the address.

"Yes." She did not expand on her answer. Was she estranged from Mr. Hollingsworth? Was she a widow? Or did she simply not want to invite the familiarity of sharing any details of her life with him? Because he could not be trusted. Because his entire family could not be trusted.

Elliott folded the paper and tucked it into the inside pocket of his coat. They stood in the middle of the foyer for a moment, waiting for the other person to speak, while the desk clerk looked on with curiosity.

114

"It was good to see you, Am — Mrs. Hollingsworth," Elliott finally said. Impulsively, he reached out his hand and touched her arm. She pulled away as though he'd used a hot poker and took another step away from him. The glare she gave him caused his own cheeks to heat up. "My apologies," he said, embarrassed at having been so forward. He wasn't sure what he'd expected her reaction to be, but he hadn't thought she'd be so repulsed.

"I shall look forward to your letter," Amelia said, her expression wary. "Good day, Lord Howardsford."

"Good day, Mrs. Hollingsworth." He held her eyes another moment, frustrated with her prejudice, and yet something told him she hadn't changed as much as she seemed. He'd hurt her, and this was her reaction. He inclined his head and turned away from her.

So help me, I hope to see you again.

CHAPTER ELEVEN:
JULIA

Julia arose Monday morning of her tenth day at Peter Mayfield's house firmly convinced that she'd been right about this position from the start — it was *perfect* for her.

She took her morning walk. The country was lovely, and the estate backed a wooded area threaded with a variety of footpaths she hoped to one day have memorized. When she returned, she looked in on the dogs for a moment, brushing Bumbleberry's long coat and then petting the long, sleek backs of the greyhounds, head to tail. Fortified for the day, she went inside and woke the girls at exactly eight o'clock.

They spent the morning as had become their routine: dressing, breakfast, reading, a short walk, then playing in the circle yard until Cook rang the outside bell to announce lunch. Usually she served sandwiches and lemonade, but yesterday she'd served a lovely salad of different greens, including dandelion and yellow primrose petals. Cook had been surprised that Julia recognized the flowers, and they'd had a short discussion about edible plants. She hoped it helped their relationship a bit. This was only the second household she had ever been part of the staff for, but it had taken some weeks for the staff at the Cranstons' house to warm up to her. She hoped the transition would be faster here, though everyone was so busy with their responsibilities there hadn't been much time to get to know people.

"Can we check on Bumbleberry before we go inside?" Marjorie asked.

"Certainly," Julia said, reaching out one hand to each girl. She loved the warmth of their soft hands in hers as they headed toward the dog yard, where Mr. Mayfield kept his foxhounds on one side and the pregnant dams and new greyhounds on the other. Julia was glad for the foresight of separating the breeds; the hounds' bouncing energy made the girls anxious. However, they were quite taken with the calmer animals.

Bumbleberry was a beautiful black-and-white, long-haired female collie — the only collie Mr. Mayfield owned — and nearly to term with her first litter. Marjorie was excited to meet what she thought of as "her" puppies, and Julia did not dare break the girl's heart with the fact that the puppies would likely be sold. For a good price, if Julia had to take a guess.

The periodical Julia had borrowed from the study a few nights ago — Mrs. Oswell had told her she was free to read anything from Mr. Mayfield's collection — had an entire article on future expectations of dog ownership in Great Britain. Collies were one of the breeds specified as growing in popularity, yet Mr. Mayfield had made the decision to bring on collies months *before* the periodical had been published. She would have loved to discuss the addition with him, but the man only spoke to her when he was coming and going from visits with his daughters, which were infrequent.

Mrs. Oswell had explained that Mr. Mayfield was too busy with the dogs to regularly attend children's hour — from five to six at night — and often, the only time he saw his girls was when he came to kiss them good night. Leah was usually asleep by then.

When the three of them reached Bumbleberry's pen, the dam did not come to greet them like she usually did. Julia scanned the enclosure until she saw Bumbleberry lying by the side of her shelter. Her tongue was out as she panted heavily, although the day was not so warm as to warrant it.

Bumbleberry had been fine when Julia had checked on her that morning. "Oh, dear," she said under her breath.

"What?" Marjorie said.

Bumbleberry heaved herself to her feet at the sound of their voices, whimpering slightly as she lumbered towards them. Julia looked around for Gregory, the handler. Had he not recognized that Bumbleberry was in labor? Surely Mr. Mayfield would not have left the dam alone if he knew.

Bumbleberry put her muzzle through the fencing, and Julia rubbed her ears. She looked past the dog to the empty water bowl and felt heat rise up in her chest and neck with irritation and concern. A whelping dam with no supervision and no water?

"It's going to be all right, Bumbleberry," she said soothingly, forcing a calm tone and a smile. "You're going to be a mama."

"She's having her puppies?" Marjorie asked with delight, eyes wide and hopeful.

"Today?" Leah exclaimed.

"I think so." Julia visually assessed the dog as best she could. The physical changes she observed showed that the dam was well through the first stage of labor. Julia stayed calm, for all their sakes, and gave the dam a kiss on the nose, then took each girl by the hand and quickly led them out of the yard toward the house.

"We need to get your father," Julia said, concern mingling with bubbling enthusiasm in her chest. Caring for their dogs with her father had been one of the most enjoyable times of Julia's life, and it had been fifteen years since Julia had enjoyed daily interaction with dogs of any kind, let alone being nearby when a new litter of puppies was born.

As soon as the three of them entered the kitchen, the girls let go of her hands and ran for their father's study with such energy that Julia winced. Mrs. Allen, the housekeeper, did not like it when the girls ran in the house, but it was too late to call them back, and Mrs. Allen was not in sight. Cook, however, was stirring something on the stove, and Julia turned toward her.

"Have you any idea where Mr. Mayfield is, Mrs. Burbidge?"

"He has not yet returned from the village. Went to put in notice for a new handler."

"But Gregory —" Julia began.

"He turned Gregory out yesterday. Mr. Mayfield don't tolerate dissolute behavior."

Julia had no time to ponder Cook's words. She thought of Bumbleberry. No water. No handler. No Mr. Mayfield. Her anxiety rose even higher. "Oh, dear."

"Miss Julia?"

Julia looked back at Cook. "Bumbleberry is delivering her pups." The sound of pounding feet rumbled above them. The girls would not find their father in his study as expected and would return soon. "Where is Mrs. Allen?"

"She's to town on Monday mornings to buy for the upcoming week."

Julia clasped her hands together. "The dog should not be alone, Mrs. Burbidge, but I am not sure what to do. I could supervise until Mr. Mayfield returns, but I would need someone to watch Miss Leah and Miss Marjorie."

Cook eyed her skeptically. "You've experience with whelpings?"

Julia nodded. "I would not presume to step in if anyone else were suited. Do any of the other staff work with the dogs?" She held her breath in anticipation of the answer. She wanted to be the one to supervise the whelping, but it was important not to presume to have more right to the task than anyone else. She did not yet understand the intricacies of the household staff.

"Not so much that we would want to be responsible at a whelping. Those dogs are

Mr. Mayfield's pride and joy, they are."

"Have you any suggestions on someone who might watch over the girls in my place, then? I am not sure what else to do."

Cook's face softened as she tapped her spoon on the side of the pot. "I'll see that the girls are cared for." She moved the pan off the stove and walked toward the servants' quarters on the other side of the kitchen. "Colleen! Miss Hollingsworth needs you to watch the children."

Julia did not stay long enough to hear the maid's complaints — Colleen had been the slowest to warm up to Julia thus far — pausing only to take a stool from the kitchen and grab a handful of rags from the bucket beside the door.

Likely Bumbleberry would be fine, dogs were incredibly instinctive in matters of birthing, but Julia's father had always attended deliveries. "Nine times of ten, everything goes perfectly," he'd told her the first time she'd been allowed to watch a whelping. "But I want to be on hand that one time it doesn't."

It just so happened that the first delivery Julia had witnessed had been that one time of ten. The dam had begun seizing after the third puppy was born. Papa had tasked Julia to break the sack on the most recent pup while he attempted to deliver the others. In the end, they lost the dam and two of the pups. Julia had cried for hours but then helped her father feed the puppies until a suitable surrogate — a farmer's dog with a two-week-old litter — was able to manage them.

Papa had helped her come to terms with what had happened, and the next time there was a whelping, Julia had begged to attend. Her parents had argued, but in the end, Papa convinced Mother that if Julia felt capable of being there, they should not make the decision for her.

That delivery had gone smoothly, as had half a dozen afterward. When another whelping went badly, Julia had been a calm assistant for her father, rubbing the last puppy for fifteen minutes when the mother was too exhausted to revive it herself. That was the last litter they'd had before Papa became ill. The puppy Julia had kept alive had been sold along with the rest of her father's pack after he died, despite Julia pleading that they keep at least one.

Bumbleberry was in the corner of her pen again when Julia returned. She let herself in and whispered encouragement as she crossed the space, watching for any sign that Bumbleberry did not want her to come closer. Bumbleberry's tail thumped against the dirt, but she did not try to stand. Julia soothed the collie for a few minutes, then stepped out to explore the shed situated between Bumbleberry's pen and Queenie's. The foxhound dam was due to whelp her litter in a few more weeks.

Inside the shed, Julia found a stack of old grain sacks and some long boards with pegged ends she thought might be the sides of a whelping box. There were small doors on either side of the shed that she assumed allowed controlled access for a dam on either side. She turned the latch and opened the door that led to Bumbleberry's pen before assembling the whelping box, about six feet square, inside the shed.

Though the day was not warm and no fire burned in the small iron stove in the corner, the shed was stuffy, and Julia had trickles of sweat making trails down her face and back by the time she finished laying the grain sacks along the bottom of the box. She laid the largest blanket over the sacks and then went back to the pen to encourage Bumbleberry into the shed.

The dog did not want to move from her place in the dirt, but Julia was persistent, and finally the dog complied — after Julia crawled through the door to show Bumbleberry how it was done. She could not understand why the shed had not been readied for the dam long before now. Canine gestation following a scheduled breeding was easy to predict.

The collie had only just collapsed inside the box when the first sack-encased puppy made its debut. "You've done it, Bumbleberry!" Julia said softly so as not to excite the dam.

Bumbleberry laid her head down instead of attending to the pup, so Julia used one of the rags she'd brought from the kitchen to lift the tiny pup and move it toward the mother's head.

"Come on," Julia said, anxious for Bumbleberry's instincts to kick in. "You know what to do."

Bumbleberry stared at the pup lying before her a moment before leaning forward, sniffing, and then licking her first-born. Julia smiled as the sack broke open and the puppy wriggled with life.

Bumbleberry pulled back, then looked at Julia as though for confirmation that this normal.

"You're a natural," Julia whispered.

Bumbleberry began licking the puppy more intently. Julia stroked the mother's ear a few moments before fetching the stool from where she'd left it outside and bringing it in the shed. She wanted to be able to keep an eye on the process without distracting Bumbleberry from the very important work ahead of her. She propped the shed door open to encourage a cross breeze, though it did not ease the increasing heat of the shed as much as Julia would have liked.

Julia had to move the second puppy toward Bumbleberry as she had the first, but by the third puppy, the dam seemed to know her job. Puppy number six had just arrived when Julia heard running feet outside the shed mere seconds before Mr. Mayfield pulled the door open with a great whoosh of air that fluttered the hair around Julia's ears.

Mr. Mayfield wore no hat or coat, and his hair was tousled as he stared at Bumbleberry and the mewling newborn puppies, then turned his wide eyes to Julia, who forgot to be nervous in his company. "She's doing very well, Mr. Mayfield." She attempted to smooth her hair that had fallen out of her bun. What a sight she must be. "Six puppies so far."

"Six!" He was still breathing hard. He looked at the puppies again, and then looked at her as though still not comprehending what was happening. "Have you assisted a whelping before?"

Julia couldn't help but feel pride in reaction to his surprise. "Several times, Mr. Mayfield. Bumbleberry needed a bit of help in the beginning, but all is well now."

"If you had not been here . . ." He paused to catch his breath, his attention focused on the collie again.

"I *was* here," Julia said boldly. "There is no need to worry."

Mr. Mayfield finally stepped into the shed, looking around the small space which Julia had managed to set up perfectly despite the limited time she'd had. Another surge of pride rushed through her.

"According to my charts," Mr. Mayfield said, "she was not due until the seventeenth."

Bumbleberry shifted and whimpered at the sound of his voice, trying to turn to see him and ignoring the newest puppy.

"You're exciting her," Julia said, raising her hand to signal him to lower his voice and steady his breathing. "Wait until you're calm. She needs to focus on the work, not your anxiety." She nearly choked on the last few words. She was advising *him* on how to care for his animal? Her cheeks flushed with embarrassment. The man had barely spoken to her since she'd joined his household, and she was ordering him about?

"Yes, right, of course." He stepped back but remained focused on the dam.

Julia was careful not to look at him, expecting that at any moment he would take belated offense at her cheekiness. She moved the sixth puppy closer to the dam's head and noticed a tear in the hem of her dress. Likely it had happened when she'd crawled through the dog entrance. Thank goodness Mr. Mayfield hadn't returned in time to witness *that*.

Bumbleberry calmed, and she set to work on the newest pup. After a few minutes, Julia heard the floor creak behind her. Mr. Mayfield had moved forward, but someone else was outside the doorway of the shed. She stood up slowly and stepped out of the whelping box, intercepting Mr. Mayfield halfway across the floor and putting a hand on his arm. His eyes snapped to her face in surprise, and she dropped her hand.

"Marjorie," she whispered in explanation, then nodded over his shoulder.

He seemed confused, but then turned to see his daughter peeking around the doorway. "Marjorie, go inside," he snapped.

"Sir . . ." Julia trailed off.

Mr. Mayfield turned back to her and raised his eyebrows.

The memories of her time with her father were so thick she couldn't hold back her words. "Is not Bumbleberry Marjorie's dog?" The girl must have somehow slipped away from the maid's attention.

"You think I should allow my *daughter* to watch this?" He sounded shocked, and slightly revolted, reminding Julia that she herself had not been protected — or, rather, prevented — from knowing the natural world the way a gentleman's daughter would be. Most young women of quality did not know how offspring were created, let alone the way they were birthed. Julia thought that a silly thing, especially since it was female bodies that provided such miraculous matters of biology to take place, but her opinion mattered little.

"My apologies." Julia looked at the floor of the shed and stepped around Mr. Mayfield, embarrassed to have spoken out of turn. Though she had enjoyed every bit of her time with Bumbleberry and her precious new pups, Julia could not afford to forget that her responsibility was to the Mayfield children. "I shall take her back inside, Mr. Mayfield."

"Yes, that would be best."

Marjorie looked up pleadingly as Julia closed the door to the shed behind her and reached out her hand to the girl. Marjorie took it with a sigh and turned away from the dog yard.

"I just wanted to see my puppies."

"We'll come see Bumbleberry and the new puppies when your father allows it, but you should not have run off."

Marjorie frowned. "We were playing hide-and-seek."

"That is an unkind thing to do — slipping away during a game. When Colleen is watching you, she is taking my place and deserves your respect. You shall need to apologize to her."

Marjorie nodded, and Julia smiled and gave her hand a squeeze. This was the first time she'd had to be stern with either of the girls. She needed Marjorie to understand the lines she could not cross, but she did not want to create a distance with the girl. "The puppies are messy and boring right now, anyway. Tomorrow will be a better day, once Bumbleberry has made them present-able."

"Why are they messy?"

"Well, never mind that." Julia opened the gate and ushered Marjorie through before fastening it behind them.

Colleen was frantically searching for Marjorie when they entered the kitchen.

130

The maid narrowed her eyes and let out a breath.

Marjorie apologized, and Colleen accepted it, but still seemed frazzled.

"Thank you, Colleen," Julia said.

Colleen turned without a word. Julia made a mental note not to ask for her help again if it could be avoided.

She left the door open between her room and the nursery while she refreshed herself, listening to Marjorie read to Leah in the other room. It was hard to focus on their lessons after the afternoon's events, and she introduced quiet hour earlier than usual. They all needed time to relax.

The girls played in a corner of the room with quiet toys and books while Julia set about straightening the rest of the nursery. It was incredible how two little girls could introduce chaos into a room in such a short time.

She was pushing the benches underneath the half-high table when she saw a letter on the small table set beside the door. Julia moved to the letter and picked it up. Her entire chest prickled when she recognized her mother's script across the front. Guilt snarled at her. She'd promised Mother she would write once she was settled, but she had talked herself out of that promised letter a dozen times. Even yesterday, Easter Sunday, when she had plenty of time and no excuses, she hadn't taken up a pen. What a terrible daughter she had become.

Julia looked toward the windows where the bright sunlight seemed to have dimmed along with her mood, wishing she could pretend the letter hadn't come. But it had. She avoided reading it for a few more minutes as she finished tidying, then settled in the rocking chair by the east windows, took a breath, and unfolded the paper.

Dearest Julia,

I will not pretend that I was not heartbroken when I returned to find your letter, but I suppose you must make your own decisions. I hope the new position is all you wished for, but I worry a great deal for your safety. Know that you are always welcome at home. I do hope you will write to me and tell me more about the position. I am glad it is not too terribly far away. I shall include you in my prayers.

Much love,
Mother

Julia breathed easier. Mother wasn't angry. She wasn't demanding that Julia

132

return home. She even sounded as though she understood Julia's reasons for leaving the way she had. Had they finally crossed the line of being mother and daughter to a place where they could both be women with their own paths in life? Julia read the letter again before moving to the writing desk to pen her response.

Dear Mother . . .

She smiled to herself as she wrote about her first week. Perhaps she had underestimated her mother all along. Wouldn't it be wonderful if this was the start of a better relationship between them?

Chapter Twelve:
Julia

"When can I see the puppies?" Marjorie asked as she slid beneath the covers that night. Julia was as eager as Marjorie but careful not to show it.

"I hope we shall see the puppies tomorrow," Julia said, brushing the hair off the girl's forehead. Her mother must have had these same melted-chocolate-colored eyes since Mr. Mayfield's eyes were green, like Leah's. Julia looked to the other side of the bed the girls shared and smiled. Leah had fallen asleep before the first story had finished. All but one candle had been put out so that all Julia could see was the girls and the bed.

"When tomorrow?" Marjorie pressed.

"Perhaps after breakfast. Maybe we can get an extra sausage from Cook to give Bumbleberry as a celebration." She would need to ask Mr. Mayfield when they could visit the dogs, and the idea made her nervous. He was an imposing man, and then today she'd been so bold in directing him during the whelping. Yet he'd been so obedient and helpful. It was a strange interaction to have had, and she wasn't sure how to handle it. Should she apologize for being bossy? Or pretend that none of it had happened?

"Why would Papa not let me see them today?"

"Bumbleberry needed to focus on birthing her puppies. Pretty little girls who ask too many questions could distract her from such an important job." Julia tapped her on the nose.

Marjorie did not smile, and she had that thoughtful expression that so often creased her brow. "How did the puppies get into Bumbleberry's belly?"

Julia bit back a smile, remembering her own confusion when she was a girl. It seemed no one wondered until they were part of a birth, then the questions came faster than answers. When Julia had asked that question, however, Papa had told her. It wasn't until Mother found out that Julia realized it was something she should be embarrassed to know and never talk about.

"That is a question your father must answer, when he thinks you are ready. For now, just marvel at the miracle Bumbleberry has facilitated today."

Unappeased, but willing to let it go, Marjorie relaxed into the pillow.

Julia planted a kiss on the girl's forehead, then stood and turned, startling when she saw Mr. Mayfield leaning against the door-frame. Julia's hand flew to her chest, and she fell back a step as her cheeks instantly caught fire. He was backlit by the light from the hall, and his arms were folded across his chest, making his shoulders seem broader than she remembered — though she re-membered them to be quite broad. The shoulders of a working man.

His eyes moved from her face to his daughters' bed as he strode forward, nod-ding at Julia as he passed her. She continued out of the room, glancing back long enough to see him kneel beside the bed. Her heart hitched a beat in her chest as she remem-bered Papa coming to tuck her in at night. Today had been filled with such sharp memories of her father. Bittersweet.

Julia took the servants' staircase to the servants' quarters on the first level where Cook always left her a plate of dinner. She'd suppered with the girls at five o'clock, but the meal had been light. She wanted to check on Bumbleberry more than she wanted food but felt as though she had overstepped her bounds too much today already.

The servants' hall consisted of a large room off the kitchen. One end included a collection of chairs set round a fireplace, while the other side of the room had a rough-hewn table with benches. A few staff members sat by the fire, talking, reading, or sewing. Some of them smiled or nodded at her as she passed. Colleen stood up from the group, sewing basket in hand, and walked away as though to make a point. Everyone watched her, then looked to Julia, making it clear that Colleen's dislike of the new governess was no secret. Julia tried to ignore the embarrassment she felt at the maid's abrupt reaction.

At the dining table, she removed the cloth that covered her meal, which consisted of a slice of ham, mashed turnips, and a quarter loaf of bread that she knew would not be as good as her mother's.

Julia had made her way through half of the meal when Mrs. Allen bustled around the corner from the main hall. She paused a moment, saw Julia, and came toward her. "Oh, good, I did not have to go searching for you, Miss Hollingsworth."

Mrs. Allen was still dressed in her

charcoal-colored dress — a version of which she wore every day — with her gray hair twisted at the base of her neck.

Julia dabbed at her mouth with the serviette and stood as Mrs. Allen reached the head of the table.

"Mr. Mayfield requests you meet him in the dog yard."

Julia was wonderfully surprised at the request. "Yes, ma'am. Thank you." As she stepped away from the table, however, a rush of concern washed through her. What if there had been complications with the puppies? Surely he would have said as much when they crossed paths in the nursery, but she did not know the man anywhere well enough to know. For all she knew, his quiet hulking mood as she'd told Marjorie good night was due to his anger with her. She could be turned out before the night was through if he chose to.

"I hope all is well with Bumbleberry," Mrs. Allen said, looking concerned. "If you need me, I shall be in my office finishing the daily log."

Julia wanted to retrieve her shawl before she went out into the cool evening, but she was anxious about keeping Mr. Mayfield waiting. That same anxiety would likely keep her warm enough that she would not miss the shawl.

Mr. Mayfield was in the shed with the door open, sitting on the stool Julia had used during the whelping, though he'd moved it closer to the doorway. Julia dared not presume to let herself in without invitation.

"Mrs. Allen said you wanted to see me, Mr. Mayfield."

"Yes, please come in." He did not look at her.

She swallowed and stepped inside the shed, having to cross closely enough to smell the day on him, which was not altogether unpleasant. But then she didn't mind the smell of the dog yard either, so she might be a strange female. As soon as she'd passed him, her eyes focused on the whelping box. A lantern hanging from the hook showed Bumbleberry resting on her side, a mass of squirming black-and-white pups fighting for milk. Julia smiled down at the little miracles.

"All of them survived delivery," Mr. Mayfield said from behind her. "Bumbleberry did very well."

He did not scold her, and Julia felt she could breathe a little easier. "I am so glad. May I pet her?" She glanced back at him, and he held her eyes a moment with an

139

expression she could not read before he looked back at the dam.

"If she will let you."

Julia moved closer to Bumbleberry and squatted down so she could rub the dam's head, tentatively at first. Some mother dogs were anxious about humans getting too close to their puppies, but Bumbleberry nuzzled into Julia's hand. Julia spoke in a soft, nearly reverent voice. "Well done, Bumbleberry. What an accomplishment." She counted the puppies — eight in total. Only two more had been delivered after she'd returned to the house with Marjorie.

"She was early," Mr. Mayfield said.

"First litters are unpredictable," Julia said, wanting to scoop up all the puppies at once. "The pups seem full term." One was smaller than the others and, after moving slowly to make sure Bumbleberry would not mind, she moved it closer to Bumbleberry's head, where he would get more attention. Julia then shifted the other puppies around so they were more evenly distributed.

"Queenie has had two litters since I acquired her, and both were on the predicted day."

Mr. Mayfield leaned forward on the stool with his elbows resting on his knees. He looked comfortable and . . . handsome, though Julia looked away as soon as she admitted the thought and tried to forget that she'd noticed.

"My father's best dam, Guinness, always delivered four or five days early."

"And it was not a concern for your father?"

Julia shook her head, liking that she had the answers he wanted. "So long as the puppies were healthy, he did not concern himself, but he kept a whelping journal, in addition to his own stud book. Over time, he could predict when a dam would deliver with frightening accuracy. He once skipped church because he was sure that a dam would deliver before noon. She always seemed to go into labor in the mornings, and her deliveries were fast. When we returned from services, there were five puppies waiting for us."

"Remarkable."

"Yes, he was."

Mr. Mayfield was silent for several seconds, watching her, and Julia, feeling suddenly exposed, looked away.

"Your father — was his whelping area similar to this one?"

Julia shifted into a sitting position, careful to keep her ankles covered as she adjusted her skirts. "My father was a bit unconventional. The dams always whelped in a back room of our house." She kept scratching Bumbleberry's head but looked up at Mr. Mayfield, who reacted with raised eyebrows.

"Inside your house?"

She felt like a bumpkin and looked back at the pups so he would not see her embarrassment. "Papa was a working man and did not want to risk the dam being alone. He would brag that our survival rate was exceptionally high because of this attention, which was a difficult point to argue." She looked around the shed. "This place, however, is perfectly situated for the task."

Mr. Mayfield nodded distractedly and ran a hand through his hair. "I'm grateful you were able to get her to come inside — and set up the shed — though I apologize that you had to do so."

That reminded Julia of something. "I understand that Gregory is being replaced?"

Mr. Mayfield's jaw tightened. "Yes. I was in town today to find another handler."

"Ah," she said instead of asking additional questions. Cook had said Mr. Mayfield had no tolerance for dissident behavior. Julia wasn't entirely sure what actions would fall into such a category, but it must have been something extreme for Mr. Mayfield to turn Gregory out with two whelpings so close together. Queenie was due in a few weeks.

Julia looked around the shed, but then remembered the dog brush was in the outside pen. The new mother deserved a little pampering. "May I fetch Bumbleberry's brush? I have been brushing her when I visit in the mornings and would like to continue the routine as best I can tonight."

"You have been brushing her?"

"Oh, should I have asked your permission?"

"No, not at all. I am only surprised I had not noticed." He seemed a bit disappointed in himself. "I shall get it for you."

After he left, she took a breath and let it out, though her heart continued to race. Would she ever feel comfortable around the man?

He returned, brush in hand, and approached her, still seated next to Bumbleberry. As he crossed the shed, Bumbleberry lifted her head and thrust her muzzle forward, growling low in her throat.

Julia startled, but put her hand on the dam's head. "It is all right, Bumbleberry," she soothed, stroking the dog's head until Bumbleberry laid back down, though she did not take her eyes off Mr. Mayfield. Julia looked up at her employer, who had stepped back and looked concerned by the aggressive reaction. "She's exhausted, that is all."

"She has not let me near her since you left us. She nipped at me earlier."

"Oh." Julia did not know what else to say. She stood and crossed the small room to him. He held out the brush to her by the bristles, and she took hold of the handle.

Bumbleberry continued to stare intently at Mr. Mayfield, her body tense.

"Yet she responds to you just fine," he said, sounding as though he took Bumbleberry's rejection as a personal failing.

"You have only had Bumbleberry a few months," Julia reminded him, shifting her weight from one foot to another. It was strange to be offering reassurance to a man. Never mind that this man was her employer and had said more words to her in the last few minutes than he had in over a week. "My father always felt that new mothers responded better to women." She shrugged, embarrassed to put herself above Mr. Mayfield in any way.

She had told him in that first interview that her father had felt she had a gift with dogs. After regretting having said it then, she certainly wasn't going to say it again. But she believed it was true all the same. Dogs were usually calm with her, wanting her attention, willing to be obedient.

She returned to Bumbleberry's side and began brushing the dam's head and shoulders. The dog relaxed; the puppies were beginning to still.

"I'll have Jacob put a fire in the stove to ensure they stay warm overnight," Mr. Mayfield said.

"That is a wise idea."

He left, and Julia continued to brush out Bumbleberry's coat. At one point, Bumbleberry rolled onto her back, scattering the puppies. Julia laughed while helping the dam find a better position and then replaced the puppies.

When Jacob arrived, he asked her about the whelping, and she explained what had happened, careful not to make herself sound overly heroic, though it was a very flattering story for her part.

"Brilliant," he said, smiling at her. "Mr. Mayfield surely appreciates your willingness to assist."

Julia felt her cheeks heat up. "Thank you."

After Jacob tended to his task and left, she adjusted the damper so as to keep the shed from getting too warm. After staying as long as she felt she could — though she'd gladly stay all night if the rest of the household would not think her completely addled to do so — she said good night to Bumbleberry and let herself out, taking the lantern with her. She closed the door and turned to find Mr. Mayfield leaning against the exterior wall of the shed. She stumbled back a step.

Mr. Mayfield took the lantern from her hand without a word, then turned and moved toward the house. Julia walked an appropriate distance behind him, but once they had left the dog yard, she realized he had slowed. Was he angry with her? Did he want her to catch up with him?

"You talk to Bumbleberry as though she can understand you," Mr. Mayfield said when she was nearly beside him.

"She *can* understand me," Julia said. "Or at least, she can understand my tone. A calm manner is the first step towards a calm dog."

They took a few more steps in silence.

"How old where you when you watched your first whelping?"

"Six."

"Six!" His tone was judgmental and surprised and perhaps even disgusted. "Was it not a disturbing thing to witness?"

She swallowed, her confidence waning as it so easily did with him. "Well, yes, but only because the dam had a seizure. She and two pups did not make it. I ended up having to

146

help my father, and it was . . . extremely intense."

"Good heavens."

"I have no regrets," Julia said, turning towards him so he would see the truth of it. "Yes, it was difficult, but I am not scarred by it. My father helped me come to terms with the loss, and most whelpings since have seemed quite easy in comparison."

He was quiet another moment. "How many whelpings have you been involved with?"

"A dozen or so, though it has been years."

He nodded, thoughtful. "Did not participating in such things raise . . . delicate questions?"

"Certainly." She made sure her tone remained level. The biological processes of reproduction did not embarrass her, though talking to him about it did. "My father answered my questions appropriately for my age."

"I see."

They continued in silence until they reached the kitchen door. When he stopped, so did she. "I appreciate your help today, Miss Julia."

"I was glad to do it, though I think Bumbleberry is a natural." She hadn't realized just how much she wanted his thanks and validation until that moment. "Caring for my father's pack was one of the greatest joys of my life, and today was a wonderful reminder of those years."

"He passed away when you were young." Not a question — she'd told him as much when they had first met in the broom closet of Mr. Hastings's office.

"I was thirteen," Julia said, realizing Papa had been gone longer than he had been in her life. "I've had little interaction with dogs since."

Mr. Mayfield gave her a thoughtful look. "I have never known a woman interested in canine husbandry."

She turned her head to smile at him. "Well, neither have I."

The slightest smile quirked the edge of his mouth in return, and her chest warmed to know she was the cause of it.

"If you need my help in any way, I am happy to do so. Good night, Mr. Mayfield. Congratulations on a very fine litter."

She reached for the door.

"I found a new man to help with the dogs," he said quickly. She turned back, but he was looking at the ground, his shoe smoothing out the ground at his feet. "He will begin training on Friday, and I hope he will be able to take over the bulk of the care by the end of the next week, but he does not have the experience I would have liked."

Why was he telling her this? She didn't mind, she even liked it, but it was out of character from the man she'd known so far. Not that she *knew* him. Not really. "I am glad the situation was managed so quickly."

He looked up but said nothing for several awkward seconds. Then he cleared his throat and spoke quickly. "Would you be willing to assist me with Bumbleberry? I can manage caring for the other dogs with some help from the groom until the new handler starts, but I want Bumbleberry to be comfortable, and . . . she is not comfortable with me. It should only require the basics: food, water, and brushing. Checking on her and the puppies a few times a day. I hope in a week or so she will be less . . . particular."

Julia opened her mouth to say she would absolutely love to help, then paused. She thought for a moment, and, after a few seconds, she was glad she'd restrained her quick response. "May the girls assist me?"

He did not wince physically but she felt sure he did inside.

"They love spending time with the dogs and seem excited to be involved with something you enjoy so much. Additionally, I am uncomfortable leaving them while I perform the necessary tasks for Bumbleberry." Colleen would likely be the one who would need to step in for her, and she obviously resented the responsibility.

Mr. Mayfield weighed her request for so long that she nearly rescinded it, but then he spoke.

"I do not want them involved in any . . . delicate tasks." What he meant was that he did not want them to have the same advanced education Julia had received when she was young.

"Of course."

"Then, yes, they may. And thank you. If you would be so good as to meet me in the dog yard at eight o'clock tomorrow morning, I'll show you what you need to know."

"Yes, sir."

He nodded, then reached forward to open the door for her.

She smiled, feeling shy about him offering such courtesy, but he smiled back, and though their eyes connected as she passed him in the doorway, she looked away as soon as she realized it. He stepped in behind her and closed the door, then headed toward the family portion of the house.

She watched him go before giving in to the bubble of joy rising up in her chest. He had recognized her efforts! He had asked her to help with the new puppies! He would allow the girls to participate! She would dance all the way to her room, if she were the dancing type. Which she wasn't, but if she'd ever felt like dancing it was now.

"You best watch yourself."

She looked up to see Colleen standing in the shadows of the hallway that led to the servants' rooms.

"Pardon?" Julia asked, swallowing her joy.

"Mr. Mayfield will turn you out at the *slightest* provocation."

"Provocation?" Julia pulled her eyebrows together. Provoking of what?

"He's no tolerance for dalliances between staff, and he won't be entertainin' advances from the likes of you."

Advances? Julia's face immediately turned hot, which she realized might look as though she were guilty of such expectations. "I can assure you I have no such intentions, Colleen. I am here to care for Leah and Marjorie. And he has asked that I help with the new litter."

Colleen narrowed her eyes, bright blue glinting from her overall rigid expression. "He only hired you because the crones did not work out. No other reason."

Crones? "I am sure I don't know what

you are talking about," Julia said, confused and offended.

"His first pick was cruel to Leah, and the second had another place by the time he had turned out the first. He even asked a woman from church, but she be leaving for a London position next month. You were his very *last* option."

Julia swallowed, stung that her suspicion had been proven true, but did not know what to say. She was unused to being so determinedly disliked.

"You best watch yourself," Colleen said again, then turned back to the hallway.

Julia reviewed the maid's words as she took the servants' staircase to the third level. Did Colleen think Julia had designs on Mr. Mayfield, her *employer*? Did Mr. Mayfield have a history of inappropriate relations with previous staff and Colleen's words were a warning? Julia was not naïve enough to believe such liaisons did not happen in aristocratic households, but she had never been the recipient of an untoward advance, and Mr. Mayfield had never been anything other than completely appropriate.

There was only enough space in her small room off the nursery for a narrow bed, a mismatched wardrobe, and a vanity with basin. She had to stand to take down her hair, and then washed her face by the light of the oil lamp. She slid beneath the cool sheets and closed her eyes against Colleen's warning, knowing that in the hours ahead she would be reviewing every interaction she'd had with Mr. Mayfield to be sure that nothing she had done or said could be misconstrued by anyone.

CHAPTER THIRTEEN: PETER

"Uncle Elliott," Peter said as he came into the drawing room, adjusting his cuff. He'd changed his coat and boots in order to be presentable for his uncle's unexpected visit. Uncle Elliott had sent a message, but Peter had not read it until after running the hounds in the rain that morning. The men had not spoken since the awkward parting in Elliott's study nearly a month ago now, but Peter bore no ill will and wanted this meeting to be a positive one. "What a pleasure it is to see you. What brings you to Elsing?"

"Oh, I was in the area and thought I would stop in and see how you are getting on." The men clasped hands.

Peter sensed his uncle's nervousness, but he wanted none of that between them. "I should have sent a letter before now assuring you that though I left your office in a huff, I no longer feel any offense. It is very generous of you to create such an opportunity for each of us. I know it comes from a place of kindness."

"Oh, you mean the wedding campaign."

Peter furrowed his brow. What else would he mean?

Uncle Elliott continued. "I should have brought your folder with me from Howardhouse."

"No need for that." Peter was careful to keep his tone light. "I still have no interest for my own sake, but I do hope to hear happy news for my brother and cousins."

"You and me both," Uncle Elliott said. "Know that should you ever be curious, you only need request your folder and I shall have it sent straightaway."

"You may as well find an out-of-the-way place to store it, then. I shall have no use for it. Ever." He was glad they could speak in light tones, but the topic was deepening. Though he did hope happiness for the others, he felt that marrying for profit wasn't right. What kind of woman would want to know that her husband made money from wedding her?

Uncle Elliott laughed, perhaps too loudly, further raising Peter's suspicions as to the reason for his visit.

"So, how are things with you and the

155

girls?" Uncle Elliott asked after a few seconds of uncomfortable silence.

"We are well. We are all enjoying the spring, and I am able to be out with the dogs nearly every day. My first collie litter was delivered earlier than expected. All are thriving."

"I am glad to hear that the expansion into companion dogs is going well for you. And your household? Running smoothly?"

My household? "Yes," Peter said, feeling a niggling caution. Had Uncle Elliott ever asked after his household?

Uncle Elliott rubbed his thumb over the satin armrest and shuffled his feet on the rug before making eye contact again. "Last month you said you were interviewing new governesses. Did you fill the position?"

"Ah, yes, I have hired a new governess. Miss Hollingsworth. She's been caring for the girls nearly a fortnight now. It was a bit tricky to find the right woman for the job — my first choice was a rather poor one — but all is well now."

"The first choice was poor?"

Peter nodded, not wanting to discuss details. His stomach still burned whenever he remembered the bruising on Leah's arm.

"And the girls have taken to the current governess?"

156

"Very well. Her father raised dogs, which makes her a good fit for the household. She is even helping with this new litter." Though he'd been hesitant in the beginning to have his daughters involved with the dogs — afraid of anything that might stain their status or reputation — the girls had regaled him with stories about the puppies for several nights now, and their enthusiasm only increased his own. Much of what they said started with "Miss Julia showed me how to . . ." and "Miss Julia said that if I . . ." He smiled to himself at the thought.

"How fortunate to have found a woman so well suited for your household."

There was something contrived in Uncle Elliott's interest, but for the life of him, Peter could not make a single guess as to what his uncle's motivation might be. And then he could. He straightened in his chair. "Uncle," he said with careful deliberation, "if you are asking after my new governess because of this campaign of yours, you best leave right now."

Uncle Elliott pulled back. "What? No!"

The sincere reaction calmed Peter some, but his body remained tense, and his tone was hard when he spoke. "I would never marry a servant."

"Of course you wouldn't," Uncle Elliott

said, then shook his head. "My visit today has absolutely nothing to do with the campaign, which requires that you make a match of someone of equal class anyway. Why on earth are you being so defensive?"

That was a good question, and one Peter could not answer. The initial attraction he'd felt to Miss Julia in that broom closet was not the only unsettling notice he'd taken of his daughters' governess. He told himself it was just part of being a man; it was not as though engaging with her more often now that she was caring for the girls had driven him to some mad fantasy, as perhaps he had feared in the beginning. *I am not my father.*

Mrs. Allen brought in a tea tray, and both men sat back as she attended to their cups. Peter took the time to consciously relax the muscles in his neck and shoulders. Once his housekeeper had left them to their privacy, Peter looked at his uncle. "If you are not here on marriage campaign business, then why the interest in my household, Uncle?"

Elliott took a breath, then a sip of tea, then a bite of the mince tart on his plate. With deliberate movements, he set his cup back on his saucer and balanced it on his knee before meeting Peter's eyes. "I fear your suspicions might be less offensive than the truth."

Peter felt himself tensing again.

Uncle Elliott took another sip of tea and let out a breath. "I've had a visit from Mrs. Hollingsworth from Feltwell."

Peter stilled. "A visit? To what purpose?"

Uncle Elliott moved the cup and saucer to the tray, as though whatever he had to say next would require his full attention. "Mrs. Hollingsworth does not have a very good opinion of the Mayfield family and is concerned about her daughter's reputation after being employed by one of them."

I will never be free of what my parents have done. Peter put his own cup and saucer down and then gripped the arms of his chair. "Then I shall turn her out by the end of the week."

Elliott startled. "I think that is a hasty conclusion, Peter. I —"

"I will not be the cause of anyone's concern for a daughter's reputation." He made to rise, refusing to acknowledge the sting, and instead mentally listed what he needed to do, starting with writing yet another letter to Mr. Hastings. Then a discussion with Mrs. Allen regarding how they would arrange care for the girls until a new governess could be found. Colleen had been willing to help here and there, but she was a maid, not a governess. Could Lydia come in the interim as she had after Miss Lawrence's turning out? His heart rate was increasing. Why could nothing be simple? His poor girls, having to transition yet again.

"Sit down, Peter."

Peter had all but forgotten his uncle was there but did as he was told.

Uncle Elliott leaned forward. "This has nothing to do with you and does not require such a hasty decision." He paused, sat back in his chair, and let out a breath. "I'm afraid Mrs. Hollingsworth's prejudice is mostly my doing."

"What?"

Uncle Elliott relayed his story — one Peter had never heard before.

Though Peter was aware that Uncle Elliott had gone to India to help with the financial circumstances that followed his father's passing, Peter's grandfather, he had not known that his uncle had been on the verge of proposing marriage when the burden of his family debts came to him, or that Peter's conception had coincided with the misery of that time.

"When it became clear that I was in no position to marry financially, nor that her family would smile upon the match once Teddy's scandal became known, the only option was for me to beg patience from my father's creditors and go to India in hopes that I could salvage some scrap of the life I had taken for granted for so long. I could not bear to see Amelia again, and so I wrote her a letter and then stepped on that ship to Bombay. I did my best to put the whole of the situation behind me.

"When I returned two years later with the necessary means to pay off the debts, Amelia was a wife and a mother. I had no reason to think she had sat out for even one country dance pining for me." Uncle Elliott shrugged in a casual way that Peter did not believe for a moment.

"Amelia citied her awareness of our family scandals — we've certainly had more than our share — as her reason for objecting to her daughter associating with our family, but I know it was my treatment of her that is driving her objections, and for that I am very sorry. You do not deserve to be affected by the poor way I handled my relationship with her. However, my apology should in no way be misconstrued as my agreeing with her prejudice. But I am not sure how far she might take this complaint."

Peter stared at the rug between them and let the understanding fully settle. "My father ruined your chance for marriage." In his mind, he added, *I ruined your chance.* Peter closed his eyes as a wave of anger washed up from his stomach until it overtook his whole body. "I am sorry, Uncle."

"You have nothing to apologize for, and I have no regrets. I take pride in the honor and security I've been able to restore to our family, something you have also done. Perhaps without all that happened, I too would have fallen into dissipation." He shrugged. "The past is the past."

Peter was not so quick to forgive his father or himself but did not argue.

Uncle Elliott continued. "My concern at this point is for you. I do not want Ameli— Mrs. Hollingsworth — to make accusations against you or question your honor. I told her I would speak with you, but I would like to find a way to convince her that her fears are unreasonable."

"I shall find a new governess."

Uncle Elliott let out a frustrated sigh. "Peter, you are as moral a man as God ever put upon the earth, and it sounds as though Miss Hollingsworth is well suited for your household. Let us discuss other possibilities."

"There are no other possibilities. I shall find a replacement." Peter was already drafting a letter to Mr. Hastings in his mind. "I shall not bear even the smallest whisper of scandal, Uncle. Just last week I turned out my handler because I learned he was having a liaison with a woman in the village."

Uncle Elliott paused. "Surely your staff's behavior away from your household is beyond your scope, Peter."

Peter shook his head, holding tight to his determination. "I pay them well and offer tenant cottages if they marry so they might remain in my employ, but I forbid any fornication. I will not keep Miss Julia under my roof if her mother is concerned for her reputation."

"I did not come here to advise this drastic an action, Peter, only to discuss the conversation I had with her mother." His tone was hard, frustrated. Peter was not swayed.

"I had concerns about Miss Julia from the first interview, truth be told. But the other two candidates did not work out, and I was in a desperate situation."

"What was it about her that made her such a poor candidate?"

Peter took a breath, shifted uncomfortably, but did not speak. He stretched his arm along the back of the settee, tapping his fingers on the wood and debating whether to admit the truth. Perhaps if he confessed his weakness, it would help his uncle better understand Peter's reasons for being so willing to turn out an absolutely fantastic governess.

"Is your reason so hard to say out loud?" Uncle Elliott pressed. "You've just told me what an excellent fit she is for your household — was that untrue?"

Peter brushed nonexistent dust off the back of the settee. "Honestly, Uncle, she was too young and pretty to be considered. It felt . . . inappropriate, and so I chose another candidate. When that did not work, I attempted to hire two other women, one I had also interviewed and a woman in the parish."

"Too young and pretty, you say?"

"Since Sybil died, I have not . . . noticed other women." He felt heat creeping up his neck and wished he hadn't said anything. It sounded as though he had intentions toward Miss Julia, and he did not.

"Ah," Uncle Elliott said, nodding.

The knowing tone in his uncle's voice made Peter cringe and feel like a schoolboy caught peeping over the bushes at a woman in her knickers. "Yes, well." Peter cleared his throat. "Perhaps her mother's concerns are another sign that this is not meant to be. Perhaps removing her from my household will be a protection for all of us." He imagined telling Miss Julia that she could

164

not stay, and let out a heavy breath. He felt sure she was as happy here as he was to have her. And the girls . . .

"You should think on this, Peter. That Miss Hollingsworth is attractive is not a fatal flaw. Neither is an overbearing mother who is attempting to take her anger with me out on you. Let me talk to Amelia and try to help her understand. Perhaps your *willingness* to turn Miss Hollingsworth out will be enough to show her mother that you are upstanding and trustworthy. Especially if she knows how well suited Miss Hollingsworth is but that you would sacrifice anyway."

Peter clenched his jaw, wishing to heaven he could say that he trusted himself as much as Uncle Elliott did. It had been different with Lydia. She was family and older and . . . homely. *Gracious, am I so shallow?* Miss Julia's mother may very well see probabilities he had allowed himself to become blinded to.

"Do not turn her out just yet," Uncle Elliott pressed. "Let me talk to her mother. See if I might smooth her ruffled feathers a bit."

There was something in Uncle Elliott's tone — eagerness? *Did he want to meet with Mrs. Hollingsworth again?* Peter tried to see past his uncle's innocent expression. He'd said that he had no regrets and had put Amelia behind him as soon as he went to India, but were there deeper issues at play? Had seeing this woman after so many years brought to life feelings Uncle Elliott had buried? Gah, Peter could not countenance such speculation.

"It will take me some time to find a replacement," Peter admitted. "But I cannot afford to wait. It took me more than a month to find Lydia's replacement, and three more weeks to hire Miss Julia." And she had been here for only a week and a half. The idea of starting the process all over again was exhausting. And telling Miss Julia that he no longer needed her . . .

He felt sick.

"I suggest you keep her on until you hire a replacement, at least, but I still feel you are being hasty. Appealing to her mother's reason may be an easier solution."

Peter took a breath and let it out, tired and overwhelmed and frustrated and . . . sad. Miss Julia was perfect in every way but one, but it was enough.

"Miss Hollingsworth does not know of the connection between her mother and myself," Uncle Elliott continued. "Amelia would prefer that she never know; however,

I am not convinced that is fair."

"Miss Julia should not learn of it if it can be avoided," Peter said, shaking his head. "I know too well what it is like to be embarrassed for your parents' actions, and I do not want any part in her learning something that might make her think ill of her mother."

Uncle Elliott watched him a moment, then shifted in his chair. "You understand that my relationship with Amelia was appropriate, don't you, Peter? I did not compromise her or break any promise I'd made. She was hurt, yes, but we were both young, and she went on to make a respectable marriage. I did not cause her any sort of ruin."

"I did not think any such a thing." But as he said it, he realized that perhaps he had assumed the worst. Peter's father and aunts had lived by poor moral standards. Maybe he'd jumped to the conclusion that Amelia Hollingsworth had been Elliott's debauchery.

"I am glad to hear it." His tone betrayed that he had followed the trail of Peter's thoughts and felt an offense he would not bring to debate.

They fell into silence — awkward and heavy and filled with frustration.

"So," Uncle Elliott said when the silence had become wholly uncomfortable. "You will not turn her out until I have spoken with her mother?"

Peter hesitated but then nodded. It was sensible to keep Julia on until he had a replacement, even if it made him feel horrible to be so conniving. If he thought she would stay and that they could continue to get on well if he told her the truth about looking for a replacement, he would. But she would be hurt, and things would be difficult, and she could very well leave anyway.

"Good," Uncle Elliott said. "Well, would you introduce me to this young woman before I leave?"

"Oh, Uncle," Peter said with a sigh, closing his eyes. "What good could that possibly do?"

Uncle Elliott leaned forward and slapped Peter's knee. "Humor an old man, my boy. I would like to meet Amelia's daughter."

Peter did not stand immediately but stared at his uncle while trying to think of an excuse. Several seconds passed without his being able to think of anything. "Very well," he said in surrender, pushing up from his chair and giving his uncle a severe look. "But you had best school your expression and keep the topic of this conversation to yourself."

Uncle Elliott's face sobered in an instant. "Of course."

Chapter Fourteen:
Julia

"Miss Julia?"

Julia looked up, then scrambled to her feet, nearly tripping on her skirts in her haste. It was a wet and cold day, and so she and the girls had stayed indoors during their usual outdoor time and were building a city using nearly every possible article they could find in the nursery — blocks, books, shoes.

Mr. Mayfield never came to the nursery during the day, and the man next to him was a stranger. She immediately worried something was wrong with the puppies. It was the only reason she could think that he would track her down, though even then he would have sent a member of staff rather than come himself.

She bobbed a curtsy. "Good afternoon, Mr. Mayfield."

The girls barely looked up from their road building, which currently consisted of laying out socks top to toe. Why could Mr. Mayfield not have come when she was teaching letters or etiquette?

"Miss Julia, I wanted to introduce you to my uncle, Lord Howardsford."

Julia glanced at the man and bobbed another curtsy. "Pleased to meet you, Lord Howardsford."

"The pleasure is all mine." He put out his hand, and she belatedly realized he was requesting hers. She lifted it to him, and he took it, then kissed the back of her hand. It was the act of ballrooms and society, not being introduced to his nephew's governess. She tried not to withdraw her hand too quickly, but once he let go, she clasped her hands behind her back. She was used to being overlooked, as though she were a necessary piece of furniture, but this man seemed to be taking in every detail of her face.

"Peter says you are from Feltwell."

She glanced at Mr. Mayfield, remembering that his Christian name was Peter. It fit him. He did not seem inclined to add to the conversation, so Julia looked at Lord Howardsford.

"Yes, though I have been in London these last five years." She wanted him to know that she was an experienced governess, not some country girl who knew nothing of the world.

"Five years?" He lifted his black-and-gray peppered eyebrows. "You do not look as though you could be a day over twenty."

She answered him with a nod, not liking to be told she looked like a child. She was a proper spinster of twenty-seven years and deserved recognition for having accomplished such a feat.

"That will be all, Miss Julia," Mr. Mayfield said with a polite, if not cautious, smile. "You may return to your . . . games."

Did she hear judgment in his tone? Was he displeased?

"The rain has prevented our usual time out of doors, so we studied letters and numbers in the morning today. We've also attended to the dogs already," Julia said, hoping she didn't sound as defensive as she felt.

His jaw tightened, and she wondered what she'd said wrong. *The dogs,* she thought. She should not have mentioned that she and the girls worked with the dogs in front of his uncle. Mr. Mayfield had made it clear that he was concerned about the task being below his daughters' station. Not hers, though.

"This looks like a very clever use of time

and space," Lord Howardsford said, waving his hand over the haphazard city.

She appreciated his attempt at rescue, but his focused attention made her want to back up a step.

"Yes," Mr. Mayfield said, then put a hand on his uncle's arm and turned him toward the nursery door. "I shall return tonight for the girls' bedtime stories."

Julia nodded, then watched the two men leave. She let out a breath and returned to the girls, wondering at the tension she felt during the exchange.

She'd been caring for Bumbleberry and her pups for several days now, and she and Mr. Mayfield had interacted several times when they were both attending to animals in the dog yard. She was careful to keep their exchanges professional; Colleen's warning was still loud in her ears. His visit to the nursery just now had been different, however, with a different tension as though she'd done something wrong. And his uncle, why was he so . . . interested?

"You cannot put a house there, Leah! It's in the middle of the road."

Julia looked over in time to see Marjorie throw a boot to the side — presumably Leah's house.

"Too much road," Leah pouted, crawling

after the boot.

Julia returned to the floor and moved the socks slightly. "This would be a good place for a square, I think."

Leah returned with the boot and set it in its new place. "We need more buildings."

Marjorie jumped up and returned with a basket, two more shoes, a bonnet, and a small jewelry box. Once the box was placed in Julia's hand, she realized it was rather fine for a nursery toy. A scrolling letter *S* was carved into the inlaid top. She ran her finger over the letter.

"What is this?" Julia asked Marjorie.

"Papa says that was my mama's, but now it's mine."

Julia looked back at the box with new interest. No one in the household talked about the late Mrs. Mayfield; Julia did not even know her name. The girls would tell her something about their mother now and again, but always prefaced it with "Miss McCormick said . . ." Leah would have been only two when her mother died, but Marjorie would have been four, and Julia hoped she had memories of her mother separate from what their former caretaker had told them.

Curiosity got the better of her, and Julia pulled back the delicate clasp on the jewelry box that was not much bigger than her palm. Inside were a lovely silver ring and a ruby pendant, both of which only just fit in the box. She didn't dare touch either item. In fact, she felt as though she were intruding somehow and closed the lid. She turned her gaze to Marjorie but kept her expression soft. "I do not believe this is meant to be played with, Marjorie."

Marjorie gave her a quick but guilty look. "We needed buildings."

"Where was this?" Julia asked.

"I will show you!" Leah jumped to her feet and ran to the small desk set below the middle of the three windows and lifted the top, revealing a lid Julia had not realized was there.

Julia took Marjorie's hand and moved forward. Inside the desk was an inexpensive beaded necklace, a handkerchief with the monogram of SMK in the corner, and a small portraiture of a lovely woman with brown curls piled on her head and chocolate eyes like Marjorie's. There were also some rocks, shells, and what looked like a dried-out cricket. A child's treasures, though some were far too fine for such storage.

"You keep your mother's things here?"

Marjorie said nothing, her eyes sad and somewhat confused — as though she did

175

not understand why she had put those things there. But Julia knew, and it made her nose sting with tears she would not indulge. She sat down on the floor and pulled both girls onto her lap. She did not tell them her thoughts — about her father and the way she'd treasured the remnants of his life after he passed — but she rested their heads on her shoulders and rocked them gently, like a mother might. There was nothing she could say to ease such a loss, but she could remind them that there was still warmth and love in the world.

CHAPTER FIFTEEN: PETER

After seeing his uncle to his carriage early the next morning after breakfast, Peter changed into his work jacket and shoes and went out to the dog yard. It would be another cold and wet day — what passed for spring in this part of England — but he did not want the hounds to get lazy, and if he didn't run them on days with rain, he would rarely run them at all. Henry, the new handler, would arrive at noon to begin his training, which Peter would oversee.

The muddy ground sucked at Peter's boots with every step as he made his way to the whelping shed. He looked in on Bumbleberry every morning, but she still growled if he came too close and would not let him handle the puppies, whereas Julia and the girls could hold them in their laps. It wasn't fair, but only a schoolboy would say as much. He made a point of practicing that soft tone of voice Julia always used with the dam even though it made him feel silly — he was far more accustomed to sharp commands. But he wanted to earn Bumbleberry's trust the way Miss Julia had; the way his own daughters had.

Aside from brief visits from the outside of the pens, the girls had never had much interaction with the dogs before Julia arrived. Allowing Marjorie to name his first collie — a favor he had already accepted as a grave mistake on his part — had been his attempt at involving the girls more, but that hadn't made much difference. Then Miss Julia had come and started taking them to see the dogs every day, and now they were holding the puppies before he did and giving them ridiculous names he refused to consider — Lollydrops, Butterfly, and Sultana Pudding. Sharing his love of the dogs with his daughters was something he had not realized he wanted so much until Miss Julia had made it happen. But he wanted to hold the puppies too!

Peter opened the door of the shed and stepped onto the mat, only to find Miss Julia already there. She stood from where she was sitting on the stool from the kitchen, cradling a black-and-white puppy in her arms while the dam and the other pups slept.

"Good morning, Mr. Mayfield." She spoke in a whisper.

He removed his dripping hat. "Good morning, Miss Julia. I am simply checking on Bumbleberry. It looks as though all is well." He nodded and turned to exit the shed.

"Wait."

She had still only whispered, but her tone was commanding. Julia crossed the space between them and held the puppy out to Peter.

He did not take it, even though he wanted to so badly. "Bumbleberry has growled at me every time I've tried to touch the pups."

"It is time she got used to you, then," Miss Julia said, extending the puppy further. The little creature — equal to a squirming loaf of bread, really — mewled, and Bumbleberry's head instantly came up. "Do not look at her," Miss Julia said in that same soft, soothing voice. "Take the pup, hold it close to your chest, and calm it while she looks on."

Peter removed his gloves and put them in his coat pockets, then took the puppy, feeling ridiculous that he needed Julia's guidance and yet eager for the opportunity. He stroked the puppy's silky head, and the tiny thing nuzzled into his chest. Bumbleberry watched him steadily from the whelping box, but she did not growl. The pup began rooting around, and so Peter put his pinky finger near the puppy's mouth. The pup instantly began to suck on the tip of his finger. Peter chuckled, then realized Miss Julia was watching him, and forced his expression closed again. It would be wise to keep from feeling too comfortable in her presence.

How on earth will I turn her out?

"You can return the puppy to Bumbleberry, now," Julia said, waving toward the dam.

Peter hesitated, then wiped his boots on the mat as best he could before doing as Miss Julia had instructed. He knew Miss Julia kept the shed clean, despite him telling her she did not need to perform such tasks. She'd put in nails to hold hats and coats, reorganized the bits and bobs that had been added to the shed in recent years, and folded the old blankets into a crate.

A woman's touch, he thought. *In a whelping shed.*

"After you return the puppy, try to pet Bumbleberry."

Peter nodded his understanding as he laid the puppy gently into the box. Bumbleberry watched him but did not react. He paused, then moved his hand slowly to Bumbleberry's head. She growled, and he instantly pulled back his hand. A smaller, softer hand took hold of his wrist, keeping him from withdrawing fully. Julia had come up beside him without his notice, and suddenly he could not breathe. The touch was not intimate, he told himself, and yet it somehow was. He swallowed, unsure what to do.

"No, Bumbleberry," Miss Julia said in a firmer tone than usual. "It is time you remembered who your master is."

Julia shifted her hold until her palm was against the back of his hand, then she moved both of their hands forward. Bumbleberry growled deep in her throat again, and Julia paused to chastise the dog again, but she did not pull back.

The shed was cool enough that Peter could feel warmth radiating from Miss Julia beside him. He swallowed and, despite his better judgment, turned to look at her. Her face was near to his own, but her attention was centered on the dog. He'd never looked at her so closely before, but the smoothness of her skin and perfect shape of her nose and chin impressed upon him just how beautiful she was. Her blonde hair was pulled back in a braided bun that shined in the muted morning light coming through the window.

The sudden desire to touch her hair took him by surprise, and he inhaled deeply, only to fill his lungs with the scent of her perfume. Some spice, he thought. Sybil's vanilla scent had remained on her pillow for months after she'd died but was long gone now. Sometimes he would smell something baking from the kitchen and be transported to those easy days when spending the rest of their lives together had been an expectation they could take for granted.

Peter looked back to Bumbleberry while shifting away from Miss Julia as best he could, which was only an inch. Not enough. Miss Julia guided his hand forward, and he tried very hard to focus on the dog. Aside from hugs from his daughters, he didn't think anyone had been this close to him since Sybil's death. Certainly no one had made him feel so aware as she did. Did he feel guilty for the awareness? No. But should he?

His hand touched fur. The dog was not growling, but still watched him.

Miss Julia said softly, "Leave it there a moment."

Her hand — her small, delicate, and feminine hand — remained over the top of his as it rested on Bumbleberry's head. He

182

could hear her breathing, and for an instant, he imagined turning his hand over so their palms touched and their fingers fit together. She would look at their hands, then look at him with a question in those eyes the color of a summer sky, and everything would change between them.

Just as her mother feared.

Just as it had for his parents once upon a time.

The back of his neck began to sweat.

Peter jumped to his feet, startling Julia, who pulled back sharply, causing Bumbleberry to bark, just once. He offered no apology and turned on his heel. This would not happen!

He'd been disheartened by his uncle's words yesterday, but now he saw Mrs. Hollingsworth's prejudice as a blessing. The Mayfield men had proved themselves unworthy stewards for the gentler sex.

He marched to the stable and readied his horse. He needed to run the hounds — no, the foxhounds and greys together, he decided in the moment. The rain in his face and the cold wind whipping at his coat while his pack ran with their tongues hanging out was exactly what he needed to distract himself. And Henry would need to take over Bumbleberry's care as soon as possible. Miss Julia needed to stay in the nursery where he could more easily avoid her.

He'd promised his uncle he would not turn her out immediately, but he *would* turn her out as soon as he found a replacement. He had to. He would write to Mr. Hastings that afternoon. That his heart clenched in his chest was certainly for the sake of his daughters, who had taken to her so well.

"Mr. Mayfield."

He spun around from where he was fitting the bridle. Miss Julia stood in the doorway of the barn, wearing a hooded coat against the rain. "What is it?" he said gruffly. *What on earth will I say if she asks why I bolted from the shed?*

"I wondered if I could speak to you for a moment about your girls — Marjorie, especially."

If it were any other topic, he likely could have come up with an excuse to avoid having this discussion when he felt so vulnerable. But mention of his oldest daughter slowed his heart rate and drew his attention.

"I can schedule a time to meet if you prefer."

Goodness, no, he thought. The anticipation of a more formal meeting would be

184

miserable. "Now is as good a time as any. What was it you wanted to speak with me about?"

She took a few steps into the barn and pushed back the hood so that he could better see her face — he'd have been fine if she'd kept it in shadow. She told him about the jewelry box and the other items she'd found in the desk. She did not say they were Sybil's, but he could tell by the delicate way she spoke that she knew the items had belonged to his late wife.

"Last night, after the girls were asleep, I moved the items to the top of the bookshelf in their room, where they would not be able to see them. I thought you could fetch them and put them where they belong."

"Thank you," he said, the discomfort seeping away as he imagined Marjorie sneaking into his room, finding the drawer where he had kept the few things of Sybil's that meant something to him. For months after she'd died, he would lay the items out on the dresser and remember: the ruby pendant he'd given her the day after Marjorie's birth, her grandmother's earrings Sybil had worn on their wedding day. He hadn't looked at the mementos for some time, and apparently Marjorie had taken on the task of remembering her mother for him.

"I did something similar," Miss Julia said, drawing his attention back to her. "After my father passed, I would find things of his — a buttonhook, his cuff links, and a black leather sketchbook that had rows of numbers I didn't understand. I hid them under my bed, afraid that if I lost them I would lose . . . I don't know, my memories of him, I suppose."

"I don't believe either of the girls remembers her." They'd never said as much, and since talking about Sybil made him miss her even more, he avoided doing so.

"But they know *of* her," Miss Julia said. "They know they had a mother and that she is not here anymore. Marjorie is a wonderful girl." She said it with a soft, warm smile as though she had known and loved his daughters all their lives. "And I sense that her desire to have these items of her mother's close to her was stronger than her knowing that it was wrong for her to take them."

Peter's chest tightened with . . . regret? Fear? Sadness? His throat felt thick, and he was suddenly tired, as though he'd been thrust into a weeks' worth of thoughts in a single morning. He cleared his throat. "Is that all, Miss Julia?"

"Well, there is one more thing," she said, looking at the floor of the stable, then up again. "Your daughters have missed spending your hour with them after their supper."

He was confused. "My hour with them?"

"Children's hour?"

He tightened his jaw.

Julia continued, though her words were quick, betraying her anxiety at having to say them. "Mrs. Oswell told me that sometimes you were too busy, but, well, I have been here two weeks, and you have only ever come to kiss them good night."

"That is not true," he said defensively. "I attended them after their supper just . . ." He tried to remember. "Last week."

She looked doubtful.

Had he truly not attended to them except for bedtime? At most he stayed with them for a quarter of an hour when he looked in on them at night, not wanting to keep them awake too long and often eager for his own bed. He might also have been avoiding the new governess. "It has been a busy few weeks."

"Oh, yes, I know that," she hurried to agree. "And I do not mean to say any of this as a reprimand. I just worry that Marjorie's behavior is perhaps a reflection of missing both her parents." She cringed slightly as she said the last, which was the only reason he could hear it for the truth it was. If she were being accusatory, he'd be hard against it. But there was no way for him to justify that what she said wasn't sincere and focused on what she saw as a way to help his daughter.

"I shall do better," he said finally. In truth, his hour with the girls had become less and less a priority over the last year as the dogs demanded more of his time. Lydia had never made a complaint against it.

"Thank you, sir." She curtsied and turned to leave, pulling up the hood of her coat.

Peter opened his mouth — but why? To call her back? To thank her for telling him? To ask her advice on how he should handle this?

She disappeared through the door before he decided what to say, let alone if he should say anything. He stared at the place she had been, then returned to saddling his horse.

He tried to pin down the memory of the last time he had spent more than fifteen minutes with his girls at the end of the day and was disappointed to realize it had been the night before he'd turned out Miss Lawrence, when they had talked about catching frogs. They had never caught those anticipated frogs, had not had a Papa Picnic for some time. When he listed his priorities in his mind, he always put his girls first, but apparently that did not translate to where he spent his time. He needed to do better by his daughters, both with his time and with talking about Sybil now that they were old enough to need such things.

But he would still write to Mr. Hastings. The events of this morning had convinced him that, for the good of all of them, Julia could not stay in his household. No matter how much any of them wished that she could.

Chapter Sixteen:
Elliott

Elliott took off his hat and knocked on the door, glancing around the modest neighborhood. It was surreal that this was Amelia's house, where she'd raised her children, tended her garden, lived her whole life. Had she ever thought of him through those years? Even a little bit?

It was wrong for him to hope for such a thing. She had moved forward with her life, and he wanted to be supportive of that. But . . . *had* she thought of him? Had she ever wondered, the way he had? Especially since seeing her again last week? What if her father had agreed to their marriage? What if she'd come to India with him? What if they'd had children together, shared experiences and adventures, and he'd come home from the field to her bright-blue eyes and welcome arms?

The sound of approaching footsteps from inside prompted him to straighten as the door was opened by a woman in a gray dress, dirty apron, and mobcap.

"Yes?" she said flatly.

"Lord Howardsford to see Mrs. Amelia Hollingsworth."

The woman's expression changed in an instant. "Oh. Yes, of course." Elliott was familiar with the transformation that took place when someone realized he was a nobleman. "Do come in, my lord." She curtsied before moving quickly down the hallway.

She did not take his hat or his coat but showed him into a nicely appointed parlor. There was a pianoforte in front of the window — did Amelia play? Elliott couldn't remember — and a settee with two matching chairs set before a fireplace. A decorative rug stretched almost wall to wall, and an array of paintings filled the vertical spaces. Everything was neat as a pin, dusted, perfectly arranged, and comfortable.

A portrait, painted in profile, above the fireplace caught his eye, and he walked toward it. Richard Hollingsworth — it had to be him — wore a dark suit befitting his occupation as a banker. Elliott had done his research this last week and learned that Mr. Hollingsworth had passed away fifteen years ago. Elliott refused to ask himself if he were glad to know the man had died. It was a question he could not answer with both charity and honesty.

Julia favored Amelia so much that Elliott feared he had made her uncomfortable with his attention yesterday. She had her mother's eyes — bright and clear. Dare he say, entrancing? Yet he could see in the portrait those aspects she had inherited from her father.

Her father.

Elliott turned away from the portrait of the man who had made vows to Amelia, fathered her children, and lived the life Elliott had briefly believed would be his own.

Footfalls caused him to turn toward the doorway, hat still in hand. Amelia stopped just inside the room, wearing a simple green-and-white-striped dress with a square neckline that framed a locket she wore about her neck. Had it been a gift from her husband? Did she cherish it as a token of the life they had shared? Perhaps the man's miniature was inside. Amelia's hair was pulled up in a loose twist, and her expression was wary.

Even so, he felt a thrill in his veins to see her again. He spoke before she could. "You look lovely, Amelia."

There was a flicker of something in her eyes — softness? Regret? But then she schooled her expression with a formal air. "Please address me as Mrs. Hollingsworth." She did not step farther into the room. "What can I do for you, Lord Howardsford?"

"My apologies for both the casual address and my coming unannounced," Elliott said, inclining his head. "I had planned to write a letter, but then Feltwell was not so far out of my way. I hope I have not taken too much liberty." He hadn't considered her comfort and realized with a stab of embarrassment that he would never had made an unannounced or uninvited call on a noblewoman. He was above her in station, but that did not mean he had any right to treat her with less respect. "If you would prefer, I can come back another time. I should have let you know I was coming."

She seemed to consider his words, then looked at the hat in his hand and let out a breath. "Forgive our lack of manners. Beth is not always clear on the way things are to be done. The focus of her work is keeping the house, not managing callers." She finally crossed the room toward him, pausing only a moment in front of him before she took his hat and then indicated for him to remove his coat. Once he handed it over, she turned away and left the room.

He wanted to ask if it had been hard for her to step below the level of her birth. Was Beth her only servant? Was it Beth who kept things pristine, or did Amelia dust and polish and garden herself? Who managed the lovely border of yellow flowers that lined the walkway to her front door? The day was gray and brisk, but those little yellow flowers had almost glowed with their own sunshine. Of course, he said none of these thoughts aloud.

Amelia returned a minute later without his things, and he imagined his hat resting on a hook next to her bonnet. Amelia crossed to one of the chairs and sat down, waving him toward the settee.

Elliott complied, then glanced up at the portrait again. "Is that your husband?"

She did not look up and instead adjusted the folds of her dress. "Yes."

When she finally met his eye, he wanted to ask, *"Did you love him?"* But of course she had. Maybe what he really wanted to know was if she'd loved Elliott. Perhaps the feelings he thought they'd shared had not been love at all and would have wilted and died if he'd stayed. He cleared his throat as a reminder to himself to stay on topic. He

194

was too old a man to give any credit to "If only . . ." when there was absolutely no way to know what the potential outcome would have been.

All he had were facts: He'd left. She'd married her banker. And she'd made it quite clear to him that she had no feelings for Elliott now. Which was good. Right. Fair. He had no feelings for her either — why would he? He wasn't the same man he'd been back then any more than she was the same woman. Why was he even letting his thoughts ramble over such ridiculous territory?

"I spoke to Peter, uh, my nephew."

She sighed in relief, and her shoulders relaxed. "Oh, wonderful." She wriggled forward in her chair, and her face lost some of its tension. "How did he respond?"

"Favorably, I suppose," Elliott said, though it made him sad to report it. "He has no wish to cause any damage to Julia's reputation. He offered to turn Julia out as soon as he could find a replacement."

Amelia blinked. "Turn her out?"

"Well, yes. Is that not what you wanted?"

Amelia was quiet a moment, then nodded, though slowly. "I suppose it was, but . . ."

"You did not want her working in a Mayfield household," Elliott reminded her, taking advantage of this first sign of her insecurity. "That is what you'd told me."

"Yes," she said, lifting her chin in a fresh display of confidence. "That is what I wanted. It will be better for all of us in the long run. Turning her out simply sounds . . . drastic. Perhaps Mr. Mayfield could say he had only hired her temporarily."

"That would be untrue."

Amelia nodded, her neck slightly pink. "How much *truth* will she be told?"

"I suppose that shall be up to you. Peter will replace her, but he does not want to do anything that might interfere with your relationship with your daughter. Whether or not she knows the decision was your choice, not Peter's, will be up to you. I find it generous on his part that he so quickly agreed to bend to your interference."

She looked up at him, a flash of anger in her eyes. She'd apparently seen through his thin attempts at hiding his disappointment. He continued before she could add words to the withering look she directed toward him.

"It is a shame, though." Elliott settled back against his chair. "Your daughter is very well suited for the position, and I imagine being turned out will be very difficult for her. She gets on very well with Peter's daughters."

"She is excellent with children." Amelia's tone held regret. "I don't know why she is so determined to use that gift toward other people's children instead of her own."

Why hadn't Julia followed the prescribed course? Elliott wondered. She was pretty, loved children, had been raised by good parents — as far as Elliott could tell. So why hadn't she married some local boy and made her mother happy? He doubted Amelia knew the answer. Perhaps Julia did not know either.

"She is also very good with Peter's dogs," Elliott added. "She has been helping Peter with a new litter of puppies. Apparently the dam responds to Julia better than she does to Peter."

Amelia sighed and shook her head. "Dogs," she said under her breath, then added, louder, "Your nephew has dogs?" There was an odd edge to her tone, as though raising dogs proved some additional flaw in Peter's character. A sort of "I should have known," which made very little sense.

"He trains foxhounds, mostly, but has recently taken to breeding as well," Elliott said, surprised that Amelia did not know this. "He became very passionate about raising dogs after his wife passed. I believe it keeps his mind occupied and his hands busy. He also manages nearly two hundred acres and stays up-to-date on the Howardsford estate, which will someday be his. He's an ambitious man, Mrs. Hollingsworth, and determined to make more of what he has than the three generations before him ever did."

Amelia did not seem to be listening. "Julia should not be caring for dogs. She is a governess."

"Apparently she volunteered to help with the litter and seems to enjoy the work. She's a very capable young woman. It's a shame that she cannot stay on with a position so well suited to her interests and abilities."

"Well, she cannot," Amelia said strongly, sitting up straighter. She reminded him of a cat, the way they would puff up to look bigger to an opponent.

"Yes, so you've said." He watched her closely, trying to make sense of what was defense and what was true concern, and which was the stronger motivation of the two. "I asked Peter not to make a final decision just yet. I had hoped that perhaps I could help you reconsider."

Amelia shook her head, her lips pressed tightly together. "I did not come to you on a whim, Lord Howardsford."

"She will be turned out from a position that suits her," Elliott summarized, hearing the edge in his voice and not caring if she heard it too. "Because of your prejudice. Does that sit easy upon your shoulders?"

Her eyes widened. "My prejudice? As her mother, it is my job to protect her."

"But that is not what you're doing," Elliott said, her reaction only proving his growing hypothesis. "You are orchestrating a circumstance that will hurt her, personally if not professionally, since she will have to explain to any future employer why she stayed such a short time in this position. Heaven forbid Julia finds herself in some household you approve of with an employer who does not respect her as Peter does."

Amelia's already pink neck colored deeper red, but he could not tell if she was angry with his comments or embarrassed by her own — he could live with her feeling some of both. After several seconds ticked by on the mantel clock, she looked up, her expression composed.

"I know you do not agree with me, Elliott, but I cannot allow my daughter to remain in a situation that I feel is unsafe. She is young, and for all her belief that she knows the world, she does not. I will not see her hurt."

Hurt? And then, in an instant of clarity, Elliott understood. Her prejudice was not about the Mayfield family scandals or even Elliott's poor treatment of their relationship all those years ago. "This has nothing to do with reputations, does it, Amelia? You're worried about her having her heart broken. You think she will fall in love with Peter."

She stiffened. "That is not what I said!"

A triumphant sort of irritation rose in Elliott's chest. "It is *exactly* what you said. You think she will fall in love with Peter the same way —" He stopped himself, but it was too late. The words he didn't say sounded in the room as loudly as if he'd yelled them: *The same way you fell in love with me.*

He sat very still. He felt as though his mind was slogging through a muddy riverbank as he tried to piece together the bits of conversation.

Amelia closed her eyes as though to hide from this exchange, then looked at her hands in her lap. Everything went silent for the space of three breaths on Elliott's part.

"I do not want my daughter under your nephew's roof," she said, pulling her shoulders back and lifting her chin. "A young governess in a widower's household is inappropriate."

Elliott could no longer see the girl Amelia had been through the closed expression of the woman in front of him. Had life made her hard? Was he responsible for some part of that? He wanted to pull apart the past one year at a time to see when she had changed from a happy, carefree girl to this calculating woman who would go to such lengths at the expense of her daughter. Perhaps the draw he had felt to Amelia since seeing her last week in Ashlam was nothing more than nostalgia. Perhaps he did not want to know the woman she had become, willing to hurt her daughter for her own vengeance, which she tried to promote as peace of mind.

"I am so sorry I hurt you, Amelia. I was in an impossible situation and —"

"You did not hurt me," she bit back. "And you *will* call me Mrs. Hollingsworth."

Elliott took a deep breath to keep from asking her to drop this mask and let them talk as adults. "Perhaps if I could explain the circumstances that led up to my leaving all those years ago."

She laughed. Hard and dismissive. "I do not need you to explain anything to me. All of that is in the past. My focus now is the present and my daughter's best interest. I would do this very same thing if she were in a different household with the same reputation as yours."

"But you would not have gone to the titleholder and asked for their help to orchestrate it."

"If I knew them and felt they owed me the consideration, I most certainly would have."

Elliott stood as Beth came into the room with a tea tray. He stepped aside while she set the tray down, but he did not return to his chair. If he stayed, he and Amelia would continue to argue. She was too hard against him to hear what he had to say, and he could not endure her bitterness much longer without losing his temper. The maid glanced at him uncertainly, then left the room. Amelia did not pour the tea but only looked up at him from where she sat.

He held her gaze for a moment, trying again to see the girl she'd been. "Let us consider the favor I owe you paid in full, then, Mrs. Hollingsworth. I did as you asked me to, and Peter will turn Julia out for your sake. I hope that your decision in this will not damage your relationship with your daughter, though I do not see how it could not — assuming you tell her the truth of your involvement. Good day."

CHAPTER SEVENTEEN:
PETER

Peter stood at the window of his study, looking over the grounds of his small but sufficient estate, drawing his eyes from the horizon to the area surrounding the house. To his right was the dog yard. To his left were the carriage house and stables. Directly below him was an area of grass encircled by a pathway rimmed by rose bushes and then taller evergreens. Sybil had named it "the circle yard," and their daughters played there whenever the weather was fine enough for them to escape the house.

Today, Miss Julia had brought Bumbleberry and the puppies to the circle yard. Not quite two weeks old, the puppies were still blind and clumsy, but the girls held them in their laps, nuzzling and kissing them, while Bumbleberry rested in the grass and soaked up the sun. He watched Julia show Marjorie how to lift a puppy, both hands underneath and keeping the pup

204

close to her chest.

It had been a week since she'd told him about Marjorie stashing Sybil's things away and suggested he be more attentive to children's hour. He'd hardly spoken to her since, but he'd retrieved Sybil's things from the top of the bookshelves and had only missed one children's hour on a day when he'd had to go to town and had not returned until the girls' bedtime.

Last Saturday, they'd commenced their first Papa Picnic in months and taken a lunch to the old millpond, where he had tied up the girls' skirts so that they could all walk in the mud of the pond and catch a bucketful of polliwogs, which was now in the shed waiting for the slimy little slugs to turn into frogs. The girls had enjoyed themselves immensely, and for a few hours, Peter forgot everything except them.

In the process of spending focused time on his daughters, he'd realized how comfortable he had become with the amount of responsibility he left to their caregivers — first Lydia and now Miss Julia. To a certain degree, he had been functioning more like a figurehead than a father. What would Sybil think of that? He'd wondered it a dozen times, each time answering himself with the truth that she would be so disappointed.

For all of their sakes.

So during children's hour on Monday, he'd brought out each of the items Marjorie had hidden, telling the story behind each piece of jewelry and when their mother had worn it. The girls had been rapt with attention, convincing him how much they needed to feel connected to their mother, and to him. Each subsequent day was easier, and he enjoyed the time more and more. Without Miss Julia, he may never have realized the importance of how much he needed it too.

But she would still have to go, regardless of what he — or she — wanted. Or what was best for his daughters. It didn't make much sense when he thought of it that way, but he shook the thought away. He would not allow the merest whisper of scandal to surface. It would not be fair to any of them — especially to Miss Julia.

A week ago, he'd received a letter from Uncle Elliott regarding his meeting with Miss Julia's mother, in which he'd written, "To my grave disappointment, she did not change her position, but I encourage you to think hard about your decision. Mrs. Hollingsworth's fears are not fair to any of you, especially Julia. In time, I believe she will come to realize that for herself. You have my support in whatever direction you choose, of course, but I would be very sorry to see Miss Hollingsworth go when she seems to be such an asset to your household."

Peter was very sorry to see Miss Julia go as well — more so with every passing day — but there was only one direction to pursue, which was why he had sent a letter to Mr. Hastings several days ago. He'd received a reply that morning. Mr. Hastings was disappointed Miss Hollingsworth had not worked out, but he would make it a priority to find new applicants as quickly as possible. Peter hadn't said outright that he did not want someone young and pretty, but he did request a "mature woman of experience."

A glance at the clock unstuck his feet from the floor and his eyes from the scene in the circle yard below him. He went to his bedchamber to retrieve his blue coat. He did not find the cut as comfortable as it was fashionable, but he wanted to look his best . . . for as short a period as possible.

Jacob met him halfway up the stairs. "Mrs. Oswell awaits you in the parlor, sir."

"Thank you," Peter said without stopping. When he reached the doorway, he bowed slightly to his girls' former governess — and his late wife's cousin — before he smiled and crossed the room to her. She bobbed a curtsy, and then they both sat in tandem, across from one another.

"You are looking well, *Mrs.* Oswell. Matrimony seems to suit you."

She smiled. Her long face, prominent chin, and nearly circular eyes were eclipsed by the kindness and self-assurance he had long admired. "I believe it does, Mr. Mayfield. How are the girls? I spoke with Julia after church last week, and it seems that everyone is adjusting. She is a lovely young woman."

"The girls are well," he said. "And, yes, Miss Julia is lovely." As soon as the word had been said, he wanted to specify that he meant her demeanor was lovely, not her appearance, but he couldn't say more without drawing unwanted attention. He cleared his throat and attempted to strike a casual pose that would hide his tension. "Perhaps we can look in on them during your visit. I am certain they would love to see you."

"I would like that," Lydia said, smiling and showing the wide gap between her two front teeth. "I have missed the girls very much, but I have kept my distance so as not to interfere with Miss Julia settling in to your household. Is she doing well?"

"Yes," Peter said, then took a long breath and let it out. "But I am afraid I cannot keep her in my employ, which is why I asked you to come. I am in a bit of a spot."

Lydia puckered her eyebrows as Peter explained that Miss Julia's mother was against her employment and he did not want to create discord between mother and daughter. He had practiced the speech and was quite pleased with how he delivered it. It did not cast ill light on anyone, even Miss Julia's interfering mother, nor did it draw attention to the scandal of his birth or betray the former connection between Mrs. Hollingsworth and Uncle Elliott. It was professional, he thought, and fair.

"I feel that I need to release Miss Julia as soon as possible, but I am without a governess until I can hire another. The staffing service is gathering applicants, but I had hoped that perhaps you could attend to the girls during the between."

"I am a married woman now, Peter, with three children to look after."

"I thought perhaps a parishioner could watch after your new children as was the situation when you assisted me after Miss Lawrence left. It should only take a few weeks for me to find a permanent replacement."

Lydia smiled as though he were an adorable child. "Perhaps you should find a parishioner to look after your children instead."

Peter shook his head. "The girls are comfortable with you, and you know the ways of this household. To bring on a new person temporarily would be terribly inefficient, not to mention upsetting to the girls. I would pay you, of course, and compensate whoever will look after your husband's children." He threw that last part in as a show of his generosity. In truth, he hadn't thought much about what Lydia would do with her children, though he should have.

"Beyond the difficulty your request would be for my new family, this feels very unfair to poor Miss Hollingsworth. Does she know anything of your intentions?"

"I wanted everything in place before I inform her," Peter said. "I shall write her a letter of recommendation, and the staffing service will assist her in finding a new position. I will leave it to her mother to explain her involvement, if she chooses."

"But you will have to give her cause when you turn her out."

Peter hadn't considered that either, but of course it was true. "I shall simply tell her that we do not suit." Unfortunately, their

210

first encounter had ended nearly the same way when she'd overheard him choosing Miss Lawrence. It was horrible to essentially tell her the same thing a second time, but what choice did he have?

"But it is not true that she does not suit."

Peter huffed a breath and let his shoulders fall. "I have few choices, Lydia. I cannot disparage the girl's mother to her directly."

"But you *can* insinuate that the reason for the termination rests solely upon Miss Hollingsworth's shoulders?" She shook her head and pursed her lips. "I have always spoken plainly to you, Peter, due in part to the fact that at times you see only one way of things without considering other aspects. Have you thought about how Miss Hollingsworth will be affected by this change in her circumstances? Have you considered how difficult it will be on her professionally, as well as in her own mind, to be turned out this way?"

"She cannot stay," Peter said sharply, avoiding what Lydia had said. He *couldn't* think about how this might affect Miss Julia. "I have no choice but to believe that this is in her best interest, too. Her mother is right — her professional reputation is at stake if she continues to work in my household."

"I disagree."

Peter scowled at her. "Do you speak to your husband this way?"

She smiled widely. "That is why he married me. A certain portion of men need a woman to talk plainly to them. You and he seem to share that requirement." She leaned toward him. "You forget that I was in Miss Hollingsworth's position for five years. Working for you did not damage my reputation in the least — I married a vicar, for heaven's sake. Her mother is being petty, and you are acting scared."

Truth had a way of sounding harsh to the ear, but Peter attempted to justify his position anyway. The silence lingered long enough to remind him of his goal of this meeting, which was not to convince Lydia that this was his only course. He was the head of this household and therefore responsible for each and every person associated with it. The choice was his, not hers.

"I appreciate your thoughts, Lydia, but you must trust me to do what's best for my family. I shall take care of the particulars and truly believe that all will work out for the best on all sides. But I need an answer from you regarding the care for Marjorie and Leah before I can move forward." He attempted to look pleading but not desperate. "I would very much appreciate your help, for my girls' sake." He held her eyes because he wanted her to see his sincerity.

Lydia studied him for several seconds, then stood abruptly. He came to his feet. "I shall need to think upon this. May I see the girls before I return to the vicarage?"

"Of course. They were playing outside last I saw them." He did not say that she was being coldhearted, that these were her own cousin's children, but then he'd never quite understood Lydia. Or most women, really. They thought so differently from men, and Peter especially, it seemed.

The girls were still in the circle yard when he and Lydia came around the gravel drive. They seemed to be racing from one side to the other, a vastly unfair game since Marjorie was so much older than Leah. As they drew closer, however, he realized they were not racing. Instead, they were moving stones from one side to the other, where Miss Julia was laying the rocks out to form the letters of Marjorie's name. Bumbleberry was still on the grass, but out of range of the children. The puppies were squirming about, some eating, some enjoying the sunshine like their mother. As soon as Peter stepped onto the grass, Bumbleberry lifted her head, but then lowered it without growling. He took that as a good sign.

Leah spotted them first and called out for Lydia before running into her arms. Marjorie was more reserved, but not by much. Miss Julia stood, a smile on her face and her hands behind her back, patiently waiting for . . . what? Acknowledgment? To return to the game? Seeing both governesses with his children made him realize how easy the transition between them had been. The girls seemed as comfortable with Miss Julia in a few weeks as they'd been with Lydia after their entire lives with her. Could he dare hope that finding Miss Julia's replacement would be as smooth a transition? Even *with* that hope, he knew no other governess could be as well suited for his household as Miss Julia was.

After Lydia had greeted the girls, she took each one by the hand and walked toward Miss Julia. He was uncomfortable knowing what he was planning to do while she remained unaware.

"Good morning, Julia," Lydia said.

"Good morning, Mrs. Oswell."

"Oh, do call me Lydia when we are not at church." Lydia smiled at the girls. "And how are Leah and Marjorie treating you?"

"They are remarkable," Miss Julia said with such pure sincerity that Peter winced inside. She loved his daughters. He would turn her out anyway.

"They truly are," Lydia commented.

Leah pulled away and ran for the stones on the far side of the circle yard. She grabbed two and ran back to where her sister's name was being spelled out.

"Excuse me," Miss Julia said and took the stones to make the last portion of the second *R* in *Marjorie.* "We are teaching Leah some letters."

"I can spell my name already," Marjorie said, but she let go of Lydia's hand and went back to moving the stones.

"You are not spelling Leah's name?" Lydia asked Miss Julia as both girls continued to gather stones.

Miss Julia lowered her voice, causing Peter to move forward in order to hear what she had to say. "Marjorie will play if it is her name."

"Ah," Lydia said. "Clever."

The two women continued talking about the girls as Miss Julia placed additional stones. Peter shifted his weight from one foot to the other.

". . . Mr. Mayfield?"

He looked up, quickly determining that Lydia had said his name, but she was speaking to Miss Julia, not him.

Miss Julia glanced between Lydia and Peter before she answered. "I have enjoyed my position here very much."

The look on her face, the honesty and gratitude, struck him sharply. He imagined how her expression would change when he told her that she was being let go. Through no fault of her own. Or his. Instead, it was his parents, his uncle, and her mother who bore the responsibility. It was not fair.

"Even the dogs?"

Miss Julia's face brightened, and she did not seem to notice that Marjorie handed her two more stones. "I adore the dogs." She transferred the stones from one hand to another.

"Bumbleberry had puppies!" Leah exclaimed, also returning with stones in hand.

"Miss Julia," Marjorie interrupted, looking at her name in stones. "There needs to be an *E* on the end."

"Oh, yes," Miss Julia said, holding out the stones. "Why don't you finish it, please? Show your papa how well you can spell."

Marjorie scowled slightly, but Miss Julia raised her eyebrows, and Marjorie's expression repaired. Such command with a single look?

Marjorie knelt on the grass before carefully placing stones at the end of her name.

Lydia looked at Peter. "How many puppies?"

"Eight," he said, though she could very well count them herself as they were right there.

"And everything went well? I know you were concerned for Bumbleberry's first litter."

"The whelping could not have gone better. Miss Julia was there to assist."

Lydia raised her eyebrows at Miss Julia. "This is a story I must hear."

Both Peter and Miss Julia remained silent, each waiting for the other to begin. Finally, Julia bent down to help with the E, advising Marjorie to keep the line straight and explaining what "perpendicular" meant.

Peter began the story, and although he wished he could represent himself a bit more heroically, there was nothing to tell but the truth. In the process, his gratitude for all Julia had done for Bumbleberry settled around him. He watched her help complete Marjorie's name using whispers and a light touch on his daughter's arm. Leah had wandered over to the puppies, but he noted how Miss Julia often glanced that direction, vigilant but allowing Leah her independence. Once the name was complete, Miss Julia stood, holding Marjorie by the hand. She glanced at him quickly, a soft smile on her face before moving toward Leah.

"That is a remarkable story," Lydia said.

She and Peter stood side by side as Miss Julia begin writing Leah's name, the sound of her voice carried on the afternoon breeze like flower petals. He swallowed the rising regret of what was to come even as Lydia's words came back to him — *"You only see one way of a thing."* Was there another way? If so, he could not see it.

"Will you walk me back to the carriage, Mr. Mayfield?"

"Certainly." He looked past her and smiled at his daughters. "I shall see you lovely ladies in the nursery this evening."

"Yes, Papa," Leah said without looking up from the puppies.

Marjorie jumped up to give Lydia another hug, then ran back to the game without giving Peter so much as a look. He shrugged, and both Lydia and Miss Julia laughed. That laugh! Yes, she *had* to go. They said farewell to Miss Julia, and then turned toward the front of the house.

Once they had left the circle yard, Lydia spoke. "I have made my decision regarding the interim position."

Thank heavens! "You will assist me, then?"

What a relief that she was coming around to his way of thinking.

"No." She lifted her prominent chin. "Actually, I will not."

"What do you mean?" he said, flustered and unhappy. He needed her help. There was no other way he could feel good about what had to be done unless she was here to help soothe the difficulty it would cause for his daughters.

"I will not do it," she repeated, not looking at him. She lifted her skirts but did not slow her step as she reached the slight incline of the east drive.

They reached the front of the house, where his carriage waited to return her to the vicarage. He felt somewhat out of breath as they came to a stop beside the carriage door, held open by the groom, who also filled the role of driver when necessary.

"I want no part of this," Lydia said, waving her gloved hand over her head as though to take in his entire household and grounds. There was no edge to her words, but they felt sharp all the same. Lydia leaned toward him and lowered her voice, which merely emphasized her words. "There is not a governess in the world who could be a better fit for your household, Peter, and I refuse to play any part in changing what I think is a perfect situation for all four of you."

"B-but," he sputtered. "She cannot stay here. Her mother —"

"Invite her mother to dinner," Lydia said simply. "The vicar and I will join you, if you like. Let her mother see what I have seen."

"You don't understand," Peter said, tempted to stomp his foot, though he knew it was beyond childish. "There are additional complexities. She cannot stay."

"Explain those additional complexities to me, then." She did not put her actual hands on her actual hips but everything in her posture and tone conjured the pose.

Peter felt his neck heating up. "You shall have to trust me." Not in a hundred years would he tell her that his eyes went to Julia first when he entered a room, and strayed to her too often. He would not say that she was the first woman since Sybil died who had made him feel like a man. Just thinking such things was horrifying. To say them out loud was unimaginable.

Lydia did not press him, thank goodness, but she smiled an oddly sweet, almost patronizing smile. "Here is what I will offer," she said decidedly. "We've an extra bedchamber at the vicarage for guests or parishioners in need. Julia is welcome to stay with us whenever it is deemed appropriate for such an arrangement to be made. She could come here each day to care for the girls; I'm sure you could arrange for her transport easily enough."

Peter pulled his eyebrows together. "That is no solution." Unless, perhaps, it was. If Miss Julia did not sleep at his house, could the arrangement satisfy her mother? He shook his head. She would still be working in a Mayfield household. She would still be young and pretty and . . . disarming. No, she needed to leave his household and take a position in someplace like York. Or better yet, Edinburgh or Dublin. Far, far away. But why had Lydia offered a guest room in the first place? What did she mean by "whenever it is deemed appropriate"?

"It will make sense in time," Lydia said and accepted Stephen's help into the carriage. Before the door closed, she leaned through the opening. "I truly hope you will invite her mother to dinner before you go to all the trouble of finding a replacement. If there is even the slightest chance that it might assure her mother of Julia's safety, do you not think it would be worth the effort?"

Peter let out a breath but said nothing. Having Mrs. Hollingsworth to dinner would only address one increasingly small aspect of the situation.

"I think it about time you entertained again, and I would *love* to meet this Mrs. Hollingsworth." Lydia's eyes seemed to sparkle with anticipation. "You could make a dinner party of it."

Chapter Eighteen:
Amelia

Elliott.

Julia.

Bread for Mrs. Poughtan.

A roast for Sunday — Louisa's family will be coming for supper.

And potatoes.

Amelia did not bake on Sundays, which meant she would need to set aside two loaves from Saturday. One for dinner with Louisa's family and another to send home with her.

Elliott.

Julia.

Elliott.

Julia.

"What can I git for ya', Mrs. Hollingsworth?"

She looked at the butcher. "A one-pound roast and half a rasher of bacon, please."

"Yes, ma'am."

Elliott.

Julia.
Elliott.
Julia.
Elliott.

Amelia had not heard from Elliott since his visit last week. Oh, what he must have thought of her home, which could fit a dozen times into his. He was likely embarrassed for her, and that possibility made her defensive.

She had always lived comfortably, but her lifestyle was so different from Elliott's, and from the one she had portrayed when they were courting. Her father had been a clerk in parliament, and a poor gambler. Sending her to London had been in hopes of her making a match that could save him from his creditors. And, in the end, it had. After she'd left London, heartbroken and humiliated, she'd stayed with her aunt in Feltwell, where she was reacquainted with Richard Hollingsworth, the son of a banker who was the son of a goldsmith who was the son of a goldsmith.

That was thirty-six years ago, she reminded herself. She took pride in the life she had lived since Elliott Mayfield had disappeared from it, and had nothing to feel ashamed of. But it was unsettling to her at how badly they had parted last week. She knew she'd come off as punitive and callous. He'd done as she'd asked him to, and his nephew had agreed to remove Julia from his employ like she'd wanted.

Why didn't she feel better about getting exactly what she wanted?

"Here you be, ma'am."

Amelia took the two parcels and thanked Mr. Boyce. He would add the amount to her account, and Mr. Kendrick, Richard's solicitor, would pay the debt at the end of the month. She put the meats in her satchel and headed for the dry goods store. She needed thyme for the potatoes — hers had been dug up by a neighbor's dog — sugar, cream, and a packet of salt. The door chimed merrily when she entered, and she acknowledged Mr. Bates, who was helping Mrs. Preston. Amelia found her items, added a peppermint stick for each of Louisa's children, and waited her turn.

The topic of Elliott was exhausted for the moment — she hoped — and so her mind turned to her other equally distressing worry: Julia. The idea of her daughter living under a Mayfield roof still caused Amelia to clench her teeth, and yet she knew she shouldered some of the blame for Julia practically running when she had the chance.

Amelia knew she was overbearing and so eager to help that she often bowled people over, especially people who, like Julia, did not always assert themselves. She had tried to curtail such behavior, but being a widow at the age of thirty-eight and having to manage her own life since then had increased these undesirable qualities rather than softened them. And it was driving Julia away. Or, rather, it already had.

If it were any other household, I would accept this as Julia's choice, she told herself in hopes of appeasing her increasingly guilty conscience. After all, she'd supported Julia when she accepted a position in London, and that position had been successful, other than being so far away that Amelia had rarely seen her.

What Amelia would not do to have Julia accept a London position now! Why, she would order Julia new dresses with matching bonnets and pack her trunk herself if it meant getting her away from Peter Mayfield. She was convinced he would be Julia's ruin in one way or another, just as Elliott had . . . no. She shook her head. Elliott had not ruined her. She'd lived a good life. She had no regrets. Just frustration and the desire to protect her daughter.

Elliott had left her with barely a word all

those years ago. Didn't she deserve to live the rest of her life without interference from him or his family? It seemed the least he could do would be to disappear from her world, like he had before, and take his entire family with him. That was all she wanted — no Mayfields. Oh, but she sounded ridiculous even in her own head.

". . . she's decided to rent out her house in Brighton. The return trip was too difficult, and she wants to stay closer to her family year-round now, though I am sure she will miss the mild winters she enjoyed there."

Amelia listened to the end of the conversation rather than mire herself in her own ugly thoughts.

"Well, I think that sounds like a very nice thing," Mr. Bates said as he put the last of Mrs. Preston's packages in the woman's satchel. "I shall put the word out if anyone mentions they are looking for a position. You might also want to talk to the vicar. He's helped find folks a variety of positions in the past."

Position?

"Excellent suggestion," Mrs. Preston said. "Thank you for your help."

Mrs. Preston turned, seeing Amelia for the first time. "Oh, good morning, Mrs.

Hollingsworth."

The women had worked together through the church on a few different projects, most recently making quilts for a foundling home in Manchester.

"Good morning," Amelia replied with a slight nod. She wanted to ask what they had been talking about, but it felt too direct. Instead, the two women discussed an upcoming social both were helping organize; Amelia would be baking a hundred tarts while Mrs. Preston was supplying the decorations. "Seeing as it is spring, I thought primroses in matching pots would be perfect. You know they symbolize youth and gentleness."

"Indeed," Amelia said. "I think that is just the thing. All yellow, do you think?"

"Perhaps some separate pots of violets to coordinate."

"An excellent suggestion," Amelia said. "I could place a primrose bloom on a few of the tarts to coordinate the display. They are edible, you know."

"Are they, really?" Mrs. Preston said. "How wonderful. My mother used to take primrose tea for her headaches."

They spoke a few more minutes about primrose tea, and oil, and wine. When Mrs. Preston's adolescent daughter came in to ask if her mother was finished yet, they said their farewells.

Amelia waited until the bell signaled that Mrs. Preston had left the store before she asked Mr. Bates about the position he and Mrs. Preston had been speaking about. The twinkling of a possibility was hovering in her mind.

"A lady's companion for her husband's mother — Mrs. Berkinshire. The lady has summered in Brandon and wintered in Brighton for years, but apparently she's outgrown it. The woman must be seventy years old at least." He added Amelia's items to her account, which would also be paid by the solicitor by the end of the month.

A lady's companion, Amelia repeated in her mind. Such a position was similar to a governess. Julia could have her independence but be closer to home. They could meet for tea once or twice a week, and church on Sunday. Perhaps Julia would have Sunday evenings off so they could enjoy dinner together — with Louisa and her family, too.

With practice, Amelia could do better than she'd done. She could be a better mother and fix this relationship that was causing her so much insecurity. Best of all, Julia would be out from under the questionable influence of Peter Mayfield, which meant Amelia could forget all about Elliott . . . again. If Julia were not entangled with Elliott's nephew, Amelia could be rid of him for good. If there was a slight regret at that idea, she quickly quashed it. Falling under Elliott's spell again was out of the question. Absolutely.

Amelia added her purchases to her satchel and returned to the street, looking up and down for Mrs. Preston's blue hat. She saw the young Miss Preston standing outside the milliner's shop, talking with some other girls her age. Amelia moved in that direction, arriving just as Mrs. Preston emerged from the store, a hat box in her hand.

"Mrs. Preston," Amelia said, slightly out of breath. "I am sorry for not addressing this earlier, but wonder if I might ask after the position I overheard you talking about with Mr. Bates. Would you have time for tea at Oliver's, by chance?"

CHAPTER NINETEEN: PETER

Peter woke with a start, breathing deeply as he blinked at the ceiling and oriented himself to where he was. In his bed, in his house.

Today is Wednesday, April twenty-seventh. I will do command training with the greyhounds today, then attend the books and —

The details of his dream came back to him, and he pulled a pillow over his face. Was this how his father had unraveled? First, he felt attraction for the young maid. Then he began to dream about her? Had dreams led to fantasy, and fantasy to flirting, and flirting to —

Peter threw the pillow aside and got out of bed. He needed to distract himself. He pulled open the drapes and frowned. The night sky was only beginning to fade into daylight, and rain streaked the windows. He would not be able to train in the yard this early.

"Then I shall work on the books first," he said out loud and set about readying himself for the day. Breakfast would not be set out yet, but once in his office, he rang for tea. Ten minutes later, he was enjoying the warmth of hot tea and warm scones as he set about factoring the crop expectations for the season that was well underway.

The world outside the window came to life as he worked, the room lightening as the minutes ticked forward into the day. Around seven o'clock — some two hours after he'd woken — he stood, stretched, and poured himself another cup of tea, though the pot was cold. Still, the tea alerted his senses.

He turned to the window, looking over the acres of field and pasture that transitioned into tenant farms. He'd inherited this estate through his grandfather, the fourth Viscount Howardsford. The estate had been a bequest for the first son of the second son. That Peter was heir presumptive to his uncle's title had nothing to do with *this* estate, but being the recipient of both inheritances sometimes made Peter feel undeserving. He was all but illegitimate; his mother had been nearly to term with him when she married his father.

A man born of such scandal should not

have so much reward. When Miss Sybil Bordin had caught his eye and returned his attention, he had been astounded. The question as to why he should have been so blessed continued to chase him until five years after their marriage, when he was holding her hand as it slowly grew colder. Sybil's death had felt like an atonement, as though he and God were even. He'd lost the love of his life as penance for the sins of his parents and the undeserved blessings he'd been given.

Life had moved on. Peter managed the land his parents had neglected with an efficiency that made it profitable again. He built up his pack, watched his daughters grow, found joy where he could, and thought himself content.

His dream came back to him — a dream that was not about Sybil but about his daughters' *governess.* She had been walking down the staircase of his house in a champagne-colored dress, smiling at him with a bouquet of pale-yellow flowers in her hand and his daughters following behind her, laurel crowns on both their heads. Remembering made him groan.

Even without her mother's interference, having Julia here was exactly what he'd feared when he'd first met her in that broom

233

closet. She pricked his senses, reminded him of his loneliness, and made him want more than what he had decided he deserved.

He'd began to turn away from the window when he saw movement to the west side of the property. He stepped closer to the glass to better see through the rain and recognized the blue-caped figure walking down the drive. As if his own thoughts had conjured her up like a spirit, he saw Miss Julia turn down the path that ran the length of the stream. He continued watching, seeing the blue through the trees from time to time until she faded completely from view.

He did not move from the window, remembering Uncle Elliott telling him to not be so hasty in dismissing her. And then came thoughts of the marriage campaign that had spurred Peter to tell Uncle Elliott that he believed in marriage, only not for him.

Why not?

Peter didn't recognize the voice he heard in his head. But instead of arguing, he gave himself permission to wonder. Lydia had refused to attend the girls in the interim between turning Miss Julia out and hiring a new governess. The very idea of sending Julia away made his stomach twist. Uncle Elliott had said he did not agree with Julia's mother. Julia did not deserve to be let go.

You are afraid, the voice in his head said.

Yes, Peter *was* afraid — afraid he would never find a governess equal to Julia, afraid she would be hurt, but mostly afraid of the feelings he was not prepared to acknowledge. Peter sat in his chair and faced the window. He steepled his fingers and stared at the gray sky and the misty clouds that flowed over the treetops like wraiths.

A flash of blue caught his attention, and he leaned forward to watch Miss Julia emerge from the path. She had taken down her hood even though it was still raining. He could not see her features, but her hair was a cascade of gold that fell over her shoulders and down her back. He could imagine her smiling — not as she did at him, both polite and wary — but the way she smiled at the girls. A rewarding smile. A smile of pleasure.

She went to the dog yard and disappeared from his line of sight.

Why was he so resistant to his feelings toward her?

She is not a household maid.

You are not your father.

Your intentions are honorable.

He shook his head. *Intentions?* He was not ready to accept that he had any intentions at all. He forced himself to turn away from the window. He put his elbows upon the desktop and dropped his forehead into his hands.

Lydia thought him foolish to turn out Miss Julia. Uncle Elliott agreed. Both understood his abhorrence for scandal, and why. His dream had been more soothing than it had been sensual. Julia was pretty, she was kind, she loved his daughters — and his dogs — and brought light into his home. He wanted to know her better, he wanted . . .

Well, he wasn't ready to pinpoint exactly what he wanted. But he did *not* want to let her go.

What if she could stay?

What if her mother removed her objection? What if he didn't let his fear be the ruling factor in this decision? What if he trusted Lydia and Uncle Elliott — and even himself?

Before he could talk himself out of it, he cut a piece of paper and wrote a note to Lydia that was quick and to the point.

Dear Mrs. Oswell,

I have considered your suggestion of inviting Mrs. Hollingsworth to dinner. Should I act on that idea, and in the end

236

feel that dismissing Miss Julia is still the best course, would you agree to assist me with my daughters' care until I can find a permanent replacement? I must know this before I move forward.

Sincerely,
Mr. P Mayfield

He signed it quickly and rang for Jacob. By the time the footman had arrived, the message was sealed and addressed. Once Jacob left, Peter forced himself back to work on the ledgers. An hour later, Jacob tapped on the door and brought him the reply.

Dear Mr. Mayfield,
I officially agree to your terms. I will await the date and time of the dinner party with great anticipation.

Your friend,
Mrs. L Oswell

He rang for Mrs. Allen while his anxiety and hope swirled and twisted and danced inside him. This was madness, and yet it felt like freedom, too. If Miss Julia could stay . . .

"You rang for me, Mr. Mayfield?"

"Yes," Peter said, looking up at the housekeeper. "I would like to have a dinner party next week — Tuesday, I think."

Mrs. Allen's eyebrows lifted. "A dinner party, sir?"

Peter nodded. "I shall manage the invitations and leave the specifics of the meal in your capable hands."

She blinked at him, and he sensed she was mentally repeating what he'd said to make sure she'd heard him properly. With Sybil ill the last year of her life, it had been five years since anything even close to a dinner party had taken place in his home.

"Yes, of course," Mrs. Allen finally said. "For how many guests, sir?"

Peter counted in his mind — Mrs. Hollingsworth, Lydia and her vicar, Uncle Elliott, and *Julia.* At his table. In his circle. He wished he could ask her how she felt about the idea. Would she be comfortable? Would she welcome the invitation?

Am I mad?

"Six."

CHAPTER TWENTY:
ELLIOTT

Elliott couldn't stay away. He was sixty years old, set in his ways, a determined bachelor, devoted to the security of his wards, irritated with Amelia Edwards Hollingsworth, and yet he had thought of little but her in the week since he'd left her home. He was coming to see her, again. Unannounced, again. But he was on a specific errand this time, one that intrigued him, and he desperately hoped for a different mood to this visit. Each time he saw her, he understood it could be the last time, and while this visit was no different, it *could* lead to at least one more encounter.

On the ride from Howardhouse to Feltwell, Elliott listed all her bad qualities: controlling, hard, stubborn, uncaring for her daughter's happiness, unforgiving, prejudiced, judgmental. But he did not turn back, nor did he stop at Peter's but instead went *past* Elsing by thirty miles. Amelia's home was not convenient. Amelia was not welcoming. They disagreed on a sensitive issue. Eight hours in the saddle would leave him sore for days. He was not a young man; he should have brought a carriage. He should have avoided the trip entirely and sent the information in a message, which Peter had expected and she likely would have preferred. None of it made sense.

Elliott reached Feltwell at just after three o'clock in the afternoon and dismounted at a public stable. He paid the extra coin to buy a bag of oats and fresh water for his horse; who knew how long the water had been sitting in the trough? He had to walk a rather substantial distance to Amelia's house, but it felt good to stretch his legs. He paused in front of her house — immaculately kept — and smiled at the yellow blossoms that seemed to light the flagstone path to her door.

Their exchanges had not been encouraging, and yet he knew there was more to her than what she had chosen to show him. Those hidden aspects drew him like a bee to a flower. Like moth to flame. Like birds to dawn. Like —

A sound stopped him. Humming.

He quietly moved from the walkway to the eastern corner of the house.

Amelia was on her knees, bent over what he thought to be an herb garden. Her face was relaxed, her apron dirty, and she was humming . . . a hymn? She was at her leisure, without tense shoulders and anxious eyes. And she was lovely. Truly lovely. All those poor qualities he'd listed the last forty-some-odd miles were hard to remember, and instead other truths about the years that had passed rose up with greater definition.

She was a widow, forced to find her way alone in a world she was not raised to be a part of, concerned for her youngest daughter, and working hard to make the small corner of the world she lived in more beautiful. She had succeeded at most of those things, and he admired her as a competent woman who had overcome much.

He'd decided long ago he would not marry — first, because he had work to do, and now because he was old and tired — and yet what if he'd met Amelia by accident a month ago and she'd been *happy* to see him after all these years? What if they had met in a way that did not involve her questioning his nephew's honor and Elliott trying to balance what she wanted against what Peter — and Julia — deserved?

A young female voice called out, "Mrs. Hollingsworth," and Elliott ducked around the corner, pressing his back against the bricks.

"Good morning, Clara," Amelia said.

"Good morning. My mother sent round this jar of preserves as thanks for your help with the new baby."

"What a kindness from your mother." Her voice was so soft and easy; she had no pretense with this girl, no pain to hide or history to remember. He envied the young woman on the receiving end of Amelia's easy conversation very much. "And how is your new sister doing?"

They went on to converse about such things as diapers and what type of compresses the girl's mother should use for engorgement, whatever that was. Elliott knew enough to know he did not want to know. They shared their goodbyes a few minutes later, along with a promise from Amelia to stop in after church the next day.

Then Amelia began humming again, and Elliott realized that any minute someone could walk in front of her house and see him pressed up against it like a criminal. So he took a breath and walked around the corner again, standing in full view of her, though she did not notice him right away.

She kept weeding her herbs, cutting some bits to put in the basket beside her, and humming her hymn.

Amelia reached for the basket and caught sight of him. She startled, those big blue eyes bigger and perhaps even bluer. "Elliott!" She scrambled to her feet, but in the process, caught her foot in the hem of her apron and pitched forward.

Elliott quickly crossed the space between them and caught her, but she pulled away from him, lost her balance again, and fell backward into the herb bed behind her.

Elliott froze, his hand still outstretched.

Amelia froze, her eyes and mouth open. They stared at one another for a few seconds, both as surprised as the other at what had happened so quickly.

"I am so sorry, Mrs. Hollingsworth." Taking a chance, he stretched his hand out further to help her up. This time, she took it — dirty garden gloves and all — and he pulled her fluidly to her feet.

The momentum caused her to stumble forward, those wide blue eyes locked on his as she stopped mere inches from his chest. They both froze again. Taken off guard, without her defenses drawn and her agenda before her, she was open and bright and beautiful in her vulnerable surprise. The moment could not last forever, but Elliott would have ridden another eight hours to have had another one.

She dropped his hand, stepped back, and brushed at her skirts before glancing over her shoulder to appraise the extent of the damage done to the back of her dress. When she looked at him, her cheeks were flushed.

"What can I do to amend having startled you, Mrs. Hollingsworth?"

"Well," she said, her tone unexpectedly light. "Perhaps you could pretend it never happened?" She arched an eyebrow at him and gave him an embarrassed smile.

This was the Amelia he remembered. Comfortable, funny, and light. This was why he'd ridden fifty miles. This was what he was longing to see. And she had called him Elliott. By accident, surely, but he locked it away all the same — like pennies dropped on the cobbles, there was value even in the accident. "Shall I present myself at your front door in ten minutes' time? Will that be long enough for the amnesia to set in, do you think?"

She chuckled and swiped a tendril of hair behind her ear, leaving a swish of dirt on her cheek that looked as though it had been put there by a watercolor brush. "Plenty of time, I hope. Thank you."

He turned away so she might make a dignified exit and walked back to the flat-front of her house. When he remembered the preserves and the basket, he returned to the side yard to fetch the items, as well as a small trowel he hadn't noticed before. A tuft of something green with small leaves had been smashed when Amelia fell, and he tried for a moment to right the stems before realizing such work was out of his depth. He wiped his hands on the inside of his coat — his valet would have a fit — and returned to the door with the items Amelia had left behind.

He surveyed the immediate area about her home. On the north side of Milburn Row were thick shrubs and intermittently planted trees that created a natural border and a lovely view. Her home was built from red brick with a pitched roof, and there was an orchard of some sort behind it. Was the orchard hers or did it belong to someone else? She did not live in the more populated part of the village but within a mile of the shops, church, and market — walking distance. He saw no stable.

Her life is so different from mine, he thought uncomfortably. One of the stipulations he'd made in the marriage campaign — as Peter had called it — was that his nieces and nephews marry gentry. Amelia would not qualify under those terms. Neither would Julia; he and Peter agreed on that fact. Elliott had said Julia's station — so far below his own — was reason enough for Peter to feel comfortable with her in the house, but Peter had refused to keep her for any reason. But now he was hosting a dinner party and inviting Amelia to attend. Certainly it was to reassure her that Julia was happy and safe in the household. But what if there were a different reason? Elliott had been disappointed when Peter had said he did not plan to marry again, and Julia's station had nothing to do with anything, really. Peter did not need the wedding gift Elliott had arranged for him. He could marry whomever he wanted.

Oh, dear.

The front door opened, and he turned to face a still-smiling Amelia standing sheepishly in the doorway. She wore a different dress — a nicer one — he noted. He smiled and held out the basket toward her. "These were left in the yard. I fetched them for you."

"Thank you, Lord Howardsford," Amelia said as she took the basket.

Did she remember that she'd called him

Elliott before? He wished he dared remind her.

She showed him to the parlor, then excused herself — leaving him alone with the portrait of Richard Hollingsworth. Elliott wondered if he would have liked the man, had they ever met, or if he would have disliked him on the principle of him having married the only woman Elliott had ever cared for. When he heard movement in the doorway, he stood and hurried forward to take the tea tray from Amelia.

"I am capable," she said as he took the tray.

"As am I."

He noticed her scowl as he made his way to the table but dared hope it was not entirely sincere. A sincere scowl on this woman's face was fearsome, but he did not yet feel icy undertones and dared to be optimistic. "I hope my chivalry does not cause further awkwardness between us."

"I shall let you know."

He looked over his shoulder, and her teasing smile moved through him.

"Though I am sure I do not know to what other awkwardness you are referring since you only just arrived." She arched an eyebrow at him.

He chuckled. "Indeed." Once he'd put the

tray down, she moved around the table, sat, and began serving the tea.

She remembered he did not take sugar or cream and handed him the cup. He took it carefully, watching her, though she was not watching him. After she prepared her tea, she sat back in her chair and took a contented sip.

"I must say I am intrigued, Mrs. Hollingsworth, by your disposition today. At our other meetings, I felt as though you wished you could throw me through the nearest window."

She laughed — gracious, what a happy sound. "Well, perhaps I *did* want to throw you through the nearest window."

"But not today."

She turned her head slightly and gave him a look that could be considered coy. "Not yet." She placed her cup down and faced him fully. "Outside of a certain recent event in my herb garden that shall not be discussed, I have had a particularly successful week that I expect will bear very positive results. I am also hoping that your presence — unannounced though it is yet again — will add to my optimistic expectations. Has there been progress made toward my daughter's situation?"

Elliott's hopes began to fade. Oh, yes, how

could he forget that the bond between them was forged from her bitterness toward him and his nephew. "I suppose whether or not my presence will add to your optimism depends on how you feel about coming to dinner at Peter's house on Tuesday evening."

Her smile fell. She said nothing.

Elliott pretended not to notice how the room took on a shadow. He reached into his jacket pocket and removed Amelia's invitation, which Peter had sent with the one intended for Elliott. Peter had asked Elliott to forward it to her. Instead, Elliott had brought it fifty miles in person. Because he was intrigued by this woman. Because he was insane.

Amelia took the invitation while Elliott explained what she could read for herself. "Peter is having a dinner party, and he's invited you, myself, and his former governess and her husband, who is also his parish vicar. Julia will also be in attendance."

"A dinner party for what purpose?"

"I have no idea." He put down his cup. "He asked me to forward the invitation to you, and I feared that it would not reach you in time, which is why I am here." He knew that she knew he could have sent it by post.

"He did not say why he was inviting me

to this dinner party?"

"No, he simply requested your company."

"I am vastly uncomfortable with this prospect."

"As am I," he confirmed with a nod. "But I plan to attend, if only to satisfy my curiosity as to the purpose of the event." He did not add that, to the best of his knowledge, Peter had never hosted a dinner party.

Amelia picked up her cup and took a thoughtful sip while focused on the invitation beside the tea tray as though if she stared hard enough it would surrender its secrets. After a moment, she met his eyes. "You have already sent your acceptance?"

"Yes. From here, I am going to his home, where I shall stay through Wednesday, after the dinner party is concluded."

"There is something afoot." She pressed her lips together. One would think the invitation was a rodent by the expression on her face. Possibly a dead rodent.

"Yes, likely there is."

She narrowed her eyes. "You are certain you do not know your nephew's agenda?"

"He did not give me a reason, though I can't help but wonder if he is hoping that you becoming familiar with him and his household might lead to your approval. It is the only theory that makes sense." His other theory that had developed during the last several minutes was that Peter and Julia had somehow come to an understanding of one another that went beyond the professional and Peter wanted to inform Mrs. Hollingsworth in person. "Regardless, I have no reason to refuse the invitation."

"That is very well for you," Amelia said, bristling even more. "I have more than enough reason."

Elliott did not ask, as he knew the reasons would be derogatory toward either him, Peter, or both of them. After all, they were Mayfields and therefore untrustworthy. Despite the pleasant beginning to his visit, he could feel the increasing tension creeping up on them.

Why on earth did you come here, old man?

Elliott felt his fatigue funneling into the places left behind from his fading optimism. He took a final sip of his tea and returned the cup to the tray. "I have issued the invitation as I was asked to do. It is now in your hands to decide if you will accept it or not."

He stood, but a shot of pain in his left knee caused him to shift his weight to the right. He had to catch himself on the chair in order to maintain his balance.

Amelia jumped to her feet. "Are you all right?"

Still braced by the chair, Elliott looked across the table at her. Her eyebrows were knit with concern, and she leaned forward slightly as though she would throw herself beneath him if he lost his balance again. *Tempting.* He used his left hand to massage the back of his knee, easing the pain and stiffness but also drawing out the moment. He liked being the recipient of her sympathy.

"I twisted my knee several years ago. It will bite me like a snake from time to time, but it always passes." He put weight on the leg, bouncing slightly to test the recovery. "Likely I have simply spent too much time in the saddle these last weeks. It will be good to arrive at Peter's and rest my old bones." He smiled in a way he hoped was reassuring, then turned toward the door. It would take a few hours to travel to Peter's home. He could make it by evening, and then perhaps take a hot bath before going to bed early with an extra glass of whiskey to ease the ache.

"Wait."

He turned at the doorway. She was holding the note, still sealed. "Please tell Peter that I accept the invitation."

Elliott hid his surprise at her quick change of heart and nodded toward the invitation

252

in her hands.

She looked down as though she'd forgotten she held it. With a sigh of irritation — whether at him or herself, he did not know — she broke the seal and unfolded the paper. He watched her beautiful blue eyes scan the page. "Five o'clock, and because of the distance, he will have a room prepared so that I might stay the night. He has offered to hire a carriage for both directions."

Well done, Peter, Elliott thought. "It should be an enjoyable evening, then."

"Perhaps," she said suspiciously.

"You will have the opportunity to see your daughter, if nothing else," he told her, afraid she might be trying to come up with an excuse. "Perhaps it would be a good time to share your concerns with *her.* I must say I am less and less comfortable with the maneuvering taking place without her knowledge. One way or another, that needs to be remedied, I think."

A calculating look replaced Amelia's concerned expression, which made him uncomfortable. "Hmm," she said, tapping the invitation against the palm of her hand. "Perhaps you are right."

It *was* a good thing he was encouraging her to attend, wasn't it?

CHAPTER TWENTY-ONE:
JULIA

Julia began clearing the supper dishes while the girls tidied the toys strewn about the room. When Mr. Mayfield came for his hour, Julia would take the girls' dirty linens downstairs, where she would set them to soak until she could return and finish laundering them after the girls went to bed. As their governess, she was responsible for their clothing, just as a valet or a lady's maid was responsible for the men or women they served.

That she often lingered outside the nursery for a few minutes after leaving, and again before entering, listening to their father tease them, or sing to them, or tell them stories about their mother, was something Julia kept a secret. It was ill-mannered to eavesdrop, and yet Mr. Mayfield could be so comfortable with his daughters — playful, affectionate, and kind. Papa had been like that; he would just *be* with her.

Back then, she looked forward all day to the time she would spend with him in the evenings alongside the dogs.

There was a knock at the nursery door, and Julia turned to answer. Perhaps Colleen had come for the dishes rather than expecting Julia to return them to the kitchen.

The door opened before she reached it, and Mr. Mayfield stepped into the room.

"Mr. Mayfield," she said in surprise as she came to a stop. The girls exclaimed "Papa!" and ran for their customary hugs around his waist and knees. He bent down, smiled and complimented them, and then sent them back to finish their task of cleaning up the room. Then he turned toward Julia, and his expression changed from charming father to cautious employer. It was, unfortunately, a familiar change.

He was hosting a dinner party tonight, and the staff had been arranging dishes, polishing silver, and scurrying about for days in preparation. He was already dressed for the evening in a standard black jacket and breeches with a snowy white shirt and cravat. She'd never seen him in formal dress, and though he looked very handsome, it didn't entirely suit him and made him seem far away from the man she knew. She'd overheard a conversation about this being the first event he'd hosted since Mrs. Mayfield had died. Maybe he looked ill at ease because he hadn't worn evening dress like this for such a long time.

"I have arranged a dinner party for tonight," he said abruptly.

Julia nodded.

"I would like you to attend."

Julia felt her eyes go wide as her arms fell to her sides. "Me?" She touched her fingers to her chest.

"Yes." He looked down and straightened his already straight cuff. "Mr. and Mrs. Oswell will be there, as well as my uncle, Lord Howardsford, and . . ." He cleared his throat and looked at her with apologetic eyes. "Your mother."

"My mother!" Her own anxiety began flashing bright lights all around her head. She raised a hand to her hair out of habit, then lowered it and managed a shaky laugh. "Surely you are teasing me, Mr. Mayfield."

His expression seemed to say that he wished he *were* teasing her, which only confirmed that he wasn't. "Mrs. Oswell suggested it," he said as though trying to absolve himself of any blame. "Seeing as how your mother does not live so very far away. She felt it would be . . . helpful."

Helpful for what? Julia wondered. The

temperature of the room had risen several degrees even as her nervousness continued to build. "You invited my mother to dinner and are only telling me three hours before the meal is to begin?" She'd been careful to curtail her boldness in his presence since the day Bumbleberry had her puppies, but she couldn't manage much restraint right now.

She reached her hand up and began removing pins from her hair. Mother always told her to keep her styles soft. When the plait fell down her back, she realized she could not take down her hair in front of Mr. Mayfield.

Mr. Mayfield shifted his weight from one foot to the other. "Actually, dinner is at five. I was in Norwich all day and unable to inform you earlier. My apologies."

Unable to inform me earlier? Surely he had known her mother was coming before today. Wait, had he said *five* o'clock? She lifted the watch she kept pinned to her bodice so she could see the time. Her head snapped up. "It is already after four!"

"Colleen shall help you get ready, then tend to the children for the evening. I will have my time with them now so you might make yourself ready. I, uh, do apologize for the short notice."

He stepped forward into the room, and Julia turned sideways so he would not brush against her. Her stunned surprise quickly turned to frustration. They lived in the same house, she saw him every day, and this dinner party — and the guest list — must have been planned for some time. He could not have taken five minutes before now to inform her that he'd invited her mother? Her mother, who wanted her to live in Feltwell so she could manage Julia's life? The two letters she'd received from her mother so far had both been supportive and easy, but what her mother truly wanted had not changed.

Without another word for fear she would say something she would regret, Julia hurried to her room that adjoined the nursery. Colleen was already filling the basin with water, and the maid's warning from a few weeks earlier came to mind, that Julia should watch herself. Julia could not keep from blushing with embarrassment at the entire situation.

"I put lavender in the water," Colleen said coldly.

Julia forced a smile she did not feel. The thought of Colleen helping her into her dress and fetching her slippers was more than Julia could bear. "Thank you, Colleen.

I shall be well enough on my own, I think."

"Mr. Mayfield said I was to assist you."

"And so you have. I would not have had time to attend to the basin."

Colleen looked at her with narrowed eyes, and then left the room through the door that led to the main hall.

As soon as she was alone, Julia closed the door and began undoing the ties of her dress. The only other dress that would do for such a party was the yellow muslin she wore to church each week.

"What a man you are, Mr. Mayfield," she said scornfully as her dress fell to the floor, leaving her in her petticoat and shift. She did not bother with stays when she was not going out, which meant she would have to manage them on her own for tonight. She stepped over the puddled day dress on her way to the blocky wardrobe and began removing all the trappings she would need.

She had less than an hour to make herself presentable for a formal dinner and prepare to see her mother for the first time since fleeing Feltwell. Her position did not earn her a place at Mr. Mayfield's table for a dinner party, to say nothing of earning a place for Julia's mother — whom Mr. Mayfield did not even know. Her stomach roiled, and her head began to pound.

Chapter Twenty-Two:
Elliott

"Are you going to tell me the purpose of this dinner before the other guests arrive?" Elliott asked Peter once they were together in the parlor with glasses of sherry in hand. Elliott had been staying at Peter's for three days, and yet the two men had expertly avoided the reason Elliott had come. They'd gone riding and hunting, and Elliott had gone with Peter to Norwich that morning to deliver a foxhound to a buyer. But they had not talked about the dinner party.

Peter stared into his glass a moment, then downed the whole of it, which was not typically how one *sipped* their sherry. "It was Mrs. Oswell's idea."

"I assume *she* had a purpose for suggesting it."

Peter let out a breath of surrender before explaining that he'd asked Lydia for help while he found a new governess and she'd refused him. "She feels I will not find a better governess than Miss Julia and suggested I create an opportunity for her mother to see that my household is run without reproach." He shrugged and then added, "She did eventually agree to care for the girls if this dinner party does not go well and I still decide to turn Miss Julia out. As this evening has approached, I have questioned the entire idea; it has all the elements to make for a blasted uncomfortable evening. I appreciate *your* attendance, however. It may be the only thing that will give me any ease."

"I am happy to be here," Elliott said, sipping his drink while Peter poured himself another. Elliott had, apparently, been right about his first guess regarding this dinner — a hope that Amelia would see how well Julia fit the household here and withdraw her complaint. But Elliott's second guess was still unanswered. "And I agree with Mrs. Oswell. I cannot imagine another governess could be any better suited. I hope Amelia will see the same."

Peter stared into his empty glass. His distress was obvious.

"Are you all right, Peter?"

His nephew did not look up. "I grow both less comfortable with her presence and more determined to keep her by the day, Uncle." His tone was barely above a whis-

per. Peter poured himself another drink —
his third. The clock in the corner ticked.
The fire crackled.

Oh, dear. "Because of the notice you
confided in me before?" Elliott crossed to
the sideboard, put a hand on Peter's shoulder, and gave it a squeeze.

Peter faced him, his eyes reflecting his in-
ner torment.

Elliott put down his glass and gave his
nephew his full attention.

"She is in my employ." The pleading tone
made Elliott's heart ache. "She *lives* in my
house. Her mother is against her even being
here, and . . . I still love my wife."

Elliott swallowed against the lump in his
throat. Had he ever seen Peter so raw with
his emotions? Had Peter ever *been* so raw?

"Does Julia know you feel this way?"

Peter shook his head. "I barely speak to
her."

Odd, that, Elliott thought to himself, and
yet he believed he understood. Peter was
terrified. Of feelings he never expected to
feel again. Of what others might think of a
situation that would look too similar to the
scandal that had produced Peter. Of
Amelia's reaction, and perhaps even Julia's.

"I planned this dinner to assure her
mother that her daughter was safe and

happy here. I wanted Mrs. Hollingsworth to watch Miss Julia interact with the girls and the pack, to see that I was a man of honor, and to withdraw her complaint. Since that time, however, I have questioned the wisdom of my decision. No offense, Uncle, but perhaps Mayfield men are all broken in some way. Perhaps I *will* be her ruin."

Elliott kept his expression neutral. "I do not believe for a moment that you would ever make an untoward advance upon any woman, Peter, and you certainly would never be the cause of someone's *ruin.* You must not fear yourself, nor the feelings you have." He paused, then pushed forward, hoping that what he had to say was wisdom. It is not as though he had ever given such advice before. "You are a man, and Julia is a woman who might be exactly perfect for you."

"I cannot even think that direction," Peter said, shaking his head. "How could she be right for me? You acknowledged yourself that we are of two different worlds. Your entire marriage campaign is based upon compatibility of station."

"If this is about the campaign, I can —"

"It is not," Peter snapped. The words could not seem to get out of his mouth quickly enough. He scrubbed his forehead.

When he spoke again, his voice was calmer but still tight. "I don't need nor want your gift. You know this."

There seemed a dozen things he could say about a dozen different facets of this situation. He chose just one point of focus. "I think Julia Hollingsworth could make an excellent wife for you, Peter."

Peter closed his eyes, as though pained at Elliott having stated what he already knew. Elliott would prefer that he be relieved rather than further burdened.

The clock chimed five o'clock, which meant the other guests would arrive any minute. With only borrowed time between them, Elliott took the bolder path. "I am glad to know the whole of your feelings, Peter, and will do everything I can to support you. The first thing you need to do is impress her mother. Be kind, gracious, complimentary, and yet professional. Do all you can to assure her that Julia is safe in your home."

Peter opened his mouth, but Elliott cut him off. "She *is* safe in your home."

Peter nodded, though with reluctance.

"The second thing you must do is let down your guard with Miss Julia. You must learn if your feelings are because of her, specifically, or if they are because your heart has healed enough to entertain the idea of loving another woman — and Julia happens to be the woman you interact with most often." That such a thought came to him so quickly felt like inspiration, a confirmation that his advice was sound.

Peter nodded, thoughtful.

"*And,* if you determine that your feelings toward Julia *are* valid, then you need to move her out of your house before you propose a change of relationship between you. I don't know how to make that happen and have her stay close enough for you to interact, but surely you can find a way. This will preserve you both."

Peter looked up, surprised. "Mrs. Oswell actually offered the use of her guest room so that Miss Julia could attend to the girls during the day but otherwise live at the vicarage. I found it a very strange offer at the time."

Intriguing. "Perhaps Mrs. Oswell saw something you had not yet admitted."

Peter's cheeks pinked slightly. "She said I would know if I ever needed to take her up on the offer."

"Well, then," Elliott said with a smile. "That problem is solved."

"Should it come to that," Peter answered, avoiding certainties. "This evening feels like nothing short of madness."

A knock at the doorway caused both men's heads to turn.

"Mrs. Amelia Hollingsworth," Mr. Allen announced before bowing slightly and exiting the room.

Amelia entered the parlor wearing a rose-colored dress perfectly fitted to her frame. The fabric moved fluidly with every tentative step she took. Her hair curled around her face, her satin gloves reflected the candlelight, and her demeanor was one of elegance and grace.

Time seemed to warp around Elliott, and he was awash in memories of their time together in London all those years ago. A flush crept up his neck as a deep and abiding attraction burst forth. In an instant, he knew exactly how Peter felt: surprise at feeling what he never thought he would feel again and not knowing what on God's green earth he could — or rather, dared — do about it.

He swallowed, and Peter glanced at him with a questioning expression before putting on a smile and moving forward to welcome Amelia. Elliott remained rooted in place, overwhelmed by the awareness that Peter was not the only one confronting his feelings tonight. He somehow knew that this moment would change *everything*.

CHAPTER TWENTY-THREE:
JULIA

Julia could hear muted conversations when
she reached the drawing room door. It was
nearly a quarter after the hour, and she was
likely the last to arrive, which meant everyone would turn and look at her and she
would blush and feel ridiculous and then
wish she could run for the nursery, where
she belonged. She would not be dressed as
finely as they would be. She only had a
Sunday dress, no jewelry, and the same
shoes she wore every day. Plain. Insignifi-
cant. Out of place. And her mother was on
the other side of that door.

Why am I here? She took a deep breath,
praying it would keep her steady. *I can do
this,* she told herself as she placed her hand
on the door. *I can, I can, I can.*

She remembered to smile as she crossed
the threshold, and, as she'd feared, everyone in the room turned toward her. Her
eyes first went to Mr. Mayfield — he was

always the biggest presence in the room —
and then moved to her mother, who was
coming toward her with outstretched arms.

"Julia, dear."

It was a relief to feel genuine pleasure at
seeing her mother. Julia had been gone from
Feltwell for almost exactly a month, she realized. It felt as though so much had happened, and then nothing had happened at
all. She held the embrace, inhaling the scent
of her mother — peppermint and yeast —
and then pulled back, both of them clasping
arms just above the elbows.

"It is so good to see you, my dear,"
Mother said.

"As it is to see you," Julia answered. "How
was your travel? Were the roads good? We've
had so much rain." *Do you know why you
were invited? Why did you come?*

"Travel was quite comfortable," Mother
said. "Mr. Mayfield hired a well-sprung carriage with a skilled driver." The words were
gracious, but Julia could hear the underly-
ing coolness, and it made her already tight
stomach pull tighter.

Julia released her mother and exchanged
greetings with the other guests — Mr. and
Mrs. Oswell, as well as Lord Howardsford,
who did not look at her as intently as he
had the first time they had met. He did,

however, watch her mother a great deal. Perhaps he stared at everyone he met for the first time?

"Shall we go in for dinner?" Mr. Mayfield asked after introductions had been made and small talk had taken place. He put his arm out for her mother, who took it after a slight hesitation. Lord Howardsford then put his arm out for Julia, while Mr. and Mrs. Oswell came behind them. Julia had not attended such a formal meal since her time in London, where, gratefully, she had honed the etiquette her mother had taught her.

Relax. Do not draw attention to yourself. Enjoy a fine meal.

Lord Howardsford sat to her right and Mrs. Oswell at her left. Mother was seated across from her, between Mr. Mayfield and Mr. Oswell. Julia allowed the small talk to move around her, until, during the soup course, Lord Howardsford spoke to her directly.

"I understand that prior to coming here, you spent some years in London."

"Yes, five years. I worked for a family there." Was it all right for her to talk about her work?

"And did you enjoy your time there?"

"Very much," Julia said, carefully avoiding

negativity. "The parks are lovely."

"Ah, yes." He nodded. "I found the parks to be my favorite part of London. That and the company."

She glanced at him in time to catch him looking across the table at her mother, who looked up at the same time. Their eyes met, locked, then both of them looked away.

What was that?

Lord Howardsford continued to talk about London, asking her about Vauxhall Gardens — she'd never been — and the theater; she'd attended an opera once.

Mulling over the look she had caught between Lord Howardsford and her mother, she raised her voice and added, "My mother lived in London when she was younger. Mother, did you spend much time in Hyde Park? I understand it included more wilderness back then."

There was a beat of silence, so pronounced and obvious that Julia did not breathe for a moment. Her mother, Lord Howardsford, and Mr. Mayfield seemed caught in the silence as well, then simultaneously unfroze themselves and acted as though nothing had happened. She caught a fleeting glance between the Oswells that reflected her own confusion. The three avoided her eye, and she felt heat rise in her chest. There was a knowing here that she did not know. And no one seemed to notice that Mother did not answer her question about Hyde Park.

Mrs. Oswell was the first to speak. "Lord Howardsford," she said, talking across Julia. "Have you heard that Miss Hollingsworth is nearly as passionate for dogs as Mr. Mayfield is?"

"I *had* heard. I understand that Mr. Hollingsworth was quite invested in the field."

This time, Lord Howardsford did *not* look across the table, and neither did Mother. And Mother did not remark on a comment made about her family. Again. Instead of tracking the conversation involving her late husband, she was taking careful bites of her soup.

What was going on?

"Yes," Julia said. "My father bred Springer Spaniels all of my life."

Julia mentally began fitting together the odd pieces she'd seemingly tripped over these last few minutes. Mother had celebrated her fifty-fifth birthday just after Christmas. A quick glance to Lord Howardsford and a calculation of Peter's age, him being the first son of the second son, pointed toward the probability that Lord Howardsford was likely within a few years of Mother's age. She had debuted in London. He had lived in London as a young man. Had they known one another? Julia would have asked the question right at that moment except she knew it would disrupt the party.

"You should recount Bumbleberry's whelping," Mr. Mayfield said.

Conversation paused as the guests looked toward the head of the table. Julia felt a lurch in her stomach. Mr. Mayfield met her eye, smiled, and then looked around the table. "Miss Hollingsworth was remarkable."

"I was *present,*" Julia clarified, though she both appreciated and was embarrassed by the unexpected praise. "Mr. Mayfield was in town, and the handler was not available."

"She helped deliver the pups," Mr. Mayfield said. "And every one of them survived."

Julia's face flushed. He had never praised her so publicly nor had he mentioned her work with the dogs for weeks.

Mr. Mayfield waved toward her. "Recount the story, Miss Julia," he said with an encouraging smile. "I think they will find it of great interest."

She could tell by the slightly frantic tone in his voice and the hyper-intent look in his eyes that he was acting tonight, playing the

273

part of Lord of the Manor or some such. She didn't like it — not the clothes, not the part he was playing, not the fact that she felt like she was on the outside of something. Yet, with talk of the dogs, he was drawing her in despite herself.

Julia took a breath, and then recounted the story simply, delicately, and without drawing undo praise to her efforts. The guests were attentive despite discussing a topic that was surely not typical for such a formal dinner. Even Mother listened without interrupting, which was not what Julia would have expected since she did not like dogs and was sensitive to etiquette. She acted as interested as anyone else, though her tension was building. *Acted.* There was a great deal of acting going on tonight, only they forgot to give her a part.

"She has continued attending to Bumbleberry and the pups," Mr. Mayfield said when she finished. "And has involved the girls."

Mother put down her spoon and turned toward him. "So, Mr. Mayfield, would you say your dogs are your occupation?"

Julia sighed. A gentleman did not define himself with an occupation, which her mother very well knew.

"More of a hobby, I would say. I am lucky

to be able to pursue it."

"He sells his dogs all over Europe," Lord Howardsford said proudly. "A German count purchased — what was it — three hounds last year?"

"Four — three yearlings and a dam. He is starting his own pack and wanted clean bloodlines."

"It really is remarkable," Mrs. Oswell said. "I was already part of the household when Mr. Mayfield purchased his first two dogs. He is very efficient in his care of them."

Mr. Mayfield smiled at his former servant, and Julia felt a stab of jealousy — a completely inappropriate stab of jealousy. He and Lydia had worked together for many years, both before and after Mrs. Mayfield had died. They were family; of course, they would have an easy accord with one another.

The vicar, who had been listening more than participating, cleared his throat. "I find it very interesting that Mr. Mayfield breeds for pedigree, or, as he stated, clean bloodlines." He turned toward his host. "Will you elaborate on that, please?"

"Oh, well, I have two packs, really. One is a purebred line — the bloodlines can be traced back generations, and I have certificates to the effect. That pack consists, you could say, of perfect representations of the foxhound."

"That is the line the German nobleman purchased from?" Lord Howardsford asked.

"Yes," Peter said. "Some people prefer perfect lines."

"And the other pack?" Julia asked, noting how relaxed he became now that he was talking about his dogs.

"Are bred for attributes," Peter said. "Temperament, intelligence, or perhaps the length of the snout or tail, or overall build and bearing."

"I would expect that both would be valuable," Mr. Oswell said. "But for different reasons, correct?"

"Yes," Mr. Mayfield said. "In fact, attribute is often more valuable than pedigree for working dogs, such as hunters. There are those who want the pedigree, and will pay for that assurance, but if a man truly wants a hunting dog, he will look for attribution first. Clean bloodlines is only one aspect to consider."

"Here, here." Lord Howardsford spoke so softly that Julia thought she might be the only one to have heard it. She looked at him, who looked at her mother, who looked at her plate.

Julia then looked at Mr. Mayfield, who was watching *her.*

Chapter Twenty-Four:
Julia

The sound of the house coming awake broke Julia away from her dream, which faded as soon as she blinked at the dark ceiling of her room. Having no window meant the room was always dark, but her body had developed its own clock during her years in London. She knew it was approximately six o'clock a.m. and allowed herself ten breaths of stillness before getting out of bed and turning up the lamp. The light-blue day dress she'd dropped to the floor last night still lay in a heap, and the yellow dress was draped over the bedpost.

When she reached the servants' hall, she faced Colleen coming from the opposite direction, her arms full of clean linens. Julia smiled in greeting, but Colleen did not smile back and knocked her with her shoulder as she passed. The maid did not apologize or look back. Unfortunately, Julia had come to expect such treatment.

Julia took her blue cape from the rack near the kitchen door and let herself out into the morning chilled by night and alive with sounds and smells and colors. She pulled the sides of the cloak around her until the walking had warmed her enough that she could let the fabric billow out behind her.

The oddness of last night's party overtook her thoughts, and she reviewed and reviewed it a dozen times. The company had retired to the drawing room together rather than allowing the men their time to smoke and enjoy their port. She'd not had opportunity to ask her mother direct questions.

She'd watched Mother and Lord Howardsford circle around one another while interacting normally with the other guests, and yet she had also caught each of them watching the other without that person's notice more than once.

Mr. Mayfield had interacted with Julia differently. He was still wary but more relaxed. They had spoken of the periodical about collies she'd borrowed from his study. The more they talked about dogs, the more they both relaxed until, by the end, she'd almost forgotten he was her employer.

As the morning sun continued to rise, Julia checked the watch pinned to her bodice

— half past seven. Mother would be returning home soon. A hired carriage would come for her at noon, after an early tea, which meant Julia had limited time to get the answers she felt she deserved.

She turned back toward the house. She always attended to Bumbleberry and the puppies before she woke the girls at eight thirty, but she might need to hurry through the routine today. The girls could tend the puppies in the afternoon, which would give Julia more time this morning.

Julia let herself into the dog yard, ignoring the yipping and jumping hounds located across from Bumbleberry's pen. Most mornings, Mr. Mayfield took the foxhounds on a chase, a rabbit or pheasant tied to the back of his saddle as he galloped through the countryside. She could always tell if he'd taken the hounds out by the way they reacted when she arrived, and today it was obvious they had not yet been exercised.

She wondered if that meant she might encounter Mr. Mayfield this morning. Would he behave differently toward her now? More like he had last night, or would last night be the exception to his usual treatment? He had not treated her poorly, but he did not seem comfortable in her presence. But then she was not comfortable with him either, always watchful of her actions for fear they might be misinterpreted.

She turned the corner of the shed and nearly ran into Mr. Mayfield. She squeaked in surprise and quickly stepped back, a hand to her chest. "My apologies."

"No apology necessary." He did not step around her but neither did he let her pass. They stood facing one another for a few seconds before he spoke again. "You have already gone out for your morning walk?"

He knew she went for morning walks? She looked up from his work boots. "Yes, the rain has kept me from them the last few days."

He glanced at the sky, cloud covered but without the heavy grayness that indicated rain. "The weather has kept me from exercising the hounds as well."

She nodded, surprised that it seemed he wished to have a conversation with her. What else should they talk about? "Thank you for inviting my mother and me to dinner last night. It was lovely." And strange.

The hounds had noticed Mr. Mayfield, and the yipping and barking and jumping increased by half, at least.

"It was a very nice evening," Mr. Mayfield said loudly enough to be heard over the dogs. He tapped his riding crop on his thigh, and a breeze ruffled his hair. He made no attempt to fix it. "I have never been one for socializing, I'm afraid, so it was a relief to take off my cravat at the end of the night and not feel as though I'd wasted the evening." He shrugged self-consciously.

Julia smiled, wanting to remember the details of this exchange. "You were an exceptional host. I enjoyed myself very much, and it was wonderful to see my mother." She wished she dared ask him the circulating questions about her mother and his uncle.

"Your mother is a very gracious and kind woman. I am glad she was able to attend. Have you, uh, spoken to her today?" He looked nervous, but then again, he *was* hiding information from her. He *should* be nervous.

"Not as yet."

"Well, I hope she enjoyed the evening." It was a parting comment, but he did not move. Neither did she. He cut quite a figure in his riding breeches and boots. The riding coat he wore was not new — she could see a fraying on the cuff — but she liked the idea that he would dress for comfort more than appearance. He tapped his crop a bit faster. "I want to thank you for the generous assistance you have given me these last weeks. I realized last evening that I have been lax in showing appreciation. I do not know how I would have managed without your help, truth be told. To say nothing of your care for my daughters. You really do have a gift with both dogs and children."

Julia smiled at his reminder of their first interview in the broom closet. "Thank you, Mr. Mayfield."

"Are you happy here, Miss Julia?"

The question surprised her. Did she appear to be unhappy? "Yes, sir. I am very happy here."

"Even with my asking you to help with such unconventional tasks as caring for my dogs?"

She smiled at his worried expression. "I adore your pack — and your children, Mr. Mayfield."

He nodded thoughtfully. "And the country?" He waved his hand to the side.

"I do not think I have ever enjoyed a place as much as I have enjoyed being here." And how much more would she enjoy it if she and Mr. Mayfield could converse like this all the time. They almost felt like friends. Was it because she hadn't embarrassed him at the dinner party?

He looked past her at the surrounding country and frowned. "I do not love London. I cannot imagine living anywhere other than here."

"I can certainly understand that."

Silence descended, but it was different from the other silences that had so often permeated their interactions.

He cleared his throat. "Well, I best exercise the dogs before the early tea." He stepped around her, but she turned to match his movement.

"You are attending the tea?"

"Of course. Your mother is my guest. Unless you would prefer I not attend?"

"I did not mean that." Julia shook her head, unsure how to explain that she simply hadn't expected his attendance. At tea. In the middle of the day. With her mother.

"And, uh, what are your thoughts regarding the girls joining us for tea? Are they capable of doing so without serving as too much distraction?"

"Oh, I think they would provide plenty of distraction," she smiled. "But I think they would also behave well. We practice having tea every day."

He raised his eyebrows. "You do?"

"With lemonade and biscuits. Oh, and their dolls, of course, to make up the party. But they are learning. I think they would enjoy an actual tea with actual people."

He smiled, fine lines crinkling around his eyes, which seemed greener and brighter than usual. It made her chest warm to notice, or perhaps it was how he stood so close to her.

"Of course. Well, then, please have them attend. If they are unable to manage, Colleen can watch them until we are finished."

She nodded, though she would do everything in her power to keep from asking Colleen for help. They smiled in parting, then moved in opposite directions — Mr. Mayfield toward the hounds, and Julia toward Bumbleberry's pen.

"Miss Julia?"

She turned at the sound of his voice.

He was tapping the crop against his thigh again. "I am glad to know that you are happy here."

Julia hesitated. "Thank you, sir."

He nodded once, and let himself into the hounds' pen. She remained as she was for a moment, then turned toward Bumbleberry's pen with a smile on her face.

Chapter Twenty-Five:
Amelia

Amelia set her cup and saucer on the table, hoping she was keeping her nerves in check. She had not yet found the time to talk to Julia and was beginning to doubt the wisdom of talking to her at all. But she must. She had accepted the invitation to last night's dinner mostly so she could tell Julia about the lady's companion position with Mrs. Berkinshire. Mrs. Preston wanted Julia to come for tea with her mother as soon as possible, and if Julia would agree, all this drama and frustration regarding the Mayfields would end.

"Another scone, Mrs. Hollingsworth?"

She looked at Elliott's face as he held out the platter and shook her head. "Thank you, no, Lord Howardsford." It was odd seeing him in social settings, wondering what he thought of her, hoping they would have the chance to converse between themselves. She'd been so starry-eyed in her youth, so certain she had captured him with her grace and beauty. She stopped the direction of her thoughts, grateful for the maturity and the reason the past thirty years had taught her. She knew better than to fall victim to fantasy. Perhaps she mourned that maturity and reason a bit as well.

Amelia forced her attention away from how he seemed to want more of her company than she would offer, away from his hopeful expression. Hope for what? Likely that she would change her opinion of his nephew.

She turned to Mr. Mayfield and Julia, sitting across from one another and talking animatedly about the puppies. They had done the same thing last night, falling into conversation with just themselves. On the surface, it was rude to leave others out of a conversation, but at a deeper level, she worried about the connection.

Amelia could not hide from the fact that Julia *was* well suited for this household and that Mr. Mayfield was kind, gracious, and, from what she had seen, perfectly honorable. That her visit to his home had been so comfortable made her increasingly *un*comfortable. Julia needed to get out from beneath Mr. Mayfield's roof before the comfort she saw growing between them turned into something different.

"And how about you, young ladies?" Elliott said to Mr. Mayfield's daughters, who were sharing a piano bench and kicking their dangling feet.

Amelia couldn't help but be softened by the precious girls. They had been in the room for ten minutes and had behaved quite well for children of their age. Taking Julia from them was becoming the hardest part of her plan.

"Yes, please," Marjorie, the older one, said, as she plucked one scone from the platter without touching any of the others.

"Me too, please, sir uncle," the younger one said, then used both hands to grab two scones.

"You cannot have that many!" Marjorie wrenched one handful of now-crumbled scone from her sister and dropped it back on the tray.

Leah protested, Elliott laughed, the conversation between Mr. Mayfield and Julia stopped as Julia jumped from her seat.

"She took too many!" Marjorie exclaimed.

"He said I could have it!" Leah whined.

Julia spoke in soft tones, brushing crumbs from the girl's skirt, then wiping at the little one's eyes when she began to cry.

Amelia watched her in wonder. She was

so natural, so comfortable and calm. She had seen her with Louisa and Simon's children, of course, and Julia was lovely with them, but she took a much more maternal role with these girls. Was it because they did not have a mother, whereas Louisa and Simon's children did?

Amelia's heart tightened, and her gaze shifted to Mr. Mayfield, who was also watching the interaction. The look on his face could be interpreted in many ways — amusement, like Elliott, gratitude, or . . . desire. Her heart increased its cadence as panic began to bloom. Was she already too late?

"I shall take them to the nursery," Julia said, standing up and helping the girls off the bench. Leah's skirt caught on the edge, and she began crying again.

Mr. Mayfield rose to his feet. "Let me call Colleen.

"No," Julia said quickly. Her cheeks colored, and she spoke quickly to soften her reaction. "Only, I know Colleen is very busy. I shall settle the girls and return to say goodbye." She smiled at Amelia reassuringly, but Amelia did not feel reassured.

"I shall take them," Elliott said, surprising everyone. He set down his cup and stood, pulling down his waistcoat. In a few strides, he was around the table. "Then you might have more time with your mother."

Julia protested. Elliott insisted. He smiled and put out a hand for each of them. The girls looked at him skeptically, then at Julia, who nodded.

"I will join you as soon as I can," she said.

The girls still didn't move.

"Go with Uncle Elliott," Mr. Mayfield encouraged.

The girls reluctantly took Elliott's hands, which swallowed up their small ones. It was impossible not to find it touching to watch such a big man with two small girls. Had Elliott ever wished he'd had children of his own? Amelia could not imagine her life without her children. They gave her so much purpose — and stress and anxiety and . . .

Marjorie looked over her shoulder, and Julia waved her forward. Once they were gone, the three remaining attendees looked between one another.

The clock ticked loudly in the silence.

"I am grateful you were able to come for this visit, Mrs. Hollingsworth," Mr. Mayfield finally said. "I know it was a difficulty for you to travel so far, but I am glad to have met you."

"You were very kind to have issued the invitation." She should say more — something about how glad she was that Julia was part of such a well-run household. Or how grateful she was to see Julia so happy in her position. But she refused to say either of those things as both sentiments were connected to her growing concerns. "You have lovely daughters."

"Thank you," Mr. Mayfield said. "Miss Julia is excellent with them. She has a gift."

Amelia watched a look pass between them before Julia hid her smile by looking at her hands in her lap. The situation was dire.

"I had hoped to walk with you a bit before the carriage comes for me, Julia."

Julia looked at her mother. "I cannot be gone from the girls for long."

"Take all the time you need," Mr. Mayfield said, standing and looking relieved. "Uncle Elliott and I should be able to manage them for a time."

Julia didn't look convinced, which caused Mr. Mayfield to smile in a way that showed how disarmingly handsome he could be.

"Thank you, Mr. Mayfield," Amelia said. Yes, indeed, time was of the essence.

She and Julia left through the front door of the house.

"There is a lovely path to the east that

runs alongside a small stream. Would you like to see it?"

"Yes, thank you," Amelia said. A walk would move them away from the house and afford the privacy Amelia needed for the delicate topic she was determined to discuss.

They walked in silence around the house and through the circle yard, as Julia called it. She pointed out the dog yard to the right, but Amelia barely looked that direction. She would never understand why people would want to invest so much time and energy into smelly, rowdy animals.

"It is lovely country out here," Amelia said, trying to build some momentum of conversation.

"I adore it," Julia said. "I walk this path every morning. It is something wonderful to wake up to."

"It does not seem so different from Halling's Road."

Julia turned toward her. "Halling's Road? This is nothing like Halling's Road."

"Both run alongside a stream," Amelia offered, but she knew she'd chosen a poor example.

"Halling's Road is always full of wagons going to and from the mill," Julia said with obvious dislike. "And the cow fields do nothing to improve it."

"Better cows than dogs." The words were out before Amelia could stop them.

Julia stopped walking. She said nothing, just stared down at her mother — she was a solid four inches taller than Amelia.

"Why did you come to dinner, Mother?"

Amelia hadn't expected such a direct question — that was not typically Julia's style. "Mr. Mayfield invited me."

"I do not fully understand that either, but why did you *come*? You do not want me to work here."

"I have not said that."

Julia cocked her head to the side, staring hard at her mother. "So you support my working here, then? Working at all?"

Amelia shifted her weight from one foot to the other beneath such direct attention. "I would like you home in Feltwell. I —"

"I have not lived in Feltwell for five years, Mother. It is no longer my home."

"Do not say that."

"I do not say it to hurt you, Mother," Julia said, her tone gentler. "But it is true. Feltwell is not my home; your house is not my home."

"And this is?" She waved toward the house they could just see above the tree line.

"For now, yes. Is that why you came to

dinner, with the hope of convincing me to leave?"

This was not going the way Amelia had hoped. Where on earth had this confrontational side of Julia been hiding all these years? But Amelia had no time to waste, and she did not imagine the mood was going to improve.

"If you must know, I did come for a very particular reason." She took a breath. Said a prayer. "There is a woman in Brandon who is looking for a lady's companion. I have corresponded with the woman's daughter, Mrs. Preston, who is looking to fill the position —"

Julia's eyebrows shot up. "You have corresponded with someone on my behalf?"

She made it sound so meddling. "You would be closer to home, and —"

"Feltwell is *not* my home. And I am *not* a lady's companion, I am a governess."

"But you do not have to be," Amelia said, throwing her hands up in frustration. "You do not need to be so far away and disconnected and under some man's control."

Julia took a breath, then let it out. "We should return to the house." She began walking, and Amelia hurried to keep up with her.

"Julia, please consider this. You would

have more freedom as a lady's companion, and I want to see you, be a part of your life. I want to know you are safe."

"I *am* safe, Mother, and I enjoy my position here very much." She did not stop walking. "And I am not under Mr. Mayfield's *control.* I have my freedom here."

How could she see this as freedom? "Caring for his dogs whenever you are not caring for his daughters? You are little more than a laborer, Julia."

Julia turned to face Amelia, who also came to a stop. They were at the bend in the pathway that led back to the house. She could see the trees that rimmed the circle yard and smell the dogs. Julia's expression was tight, her eyes angry, as she stared at her mother.

"How do you know Lord Howardsford?"

Amelia startled. "Wh-what? I —"

"Is that why you came? To see him?"

Amelia flushed. "No."

"Then what is his part in this? I saw the looks between you, and I know there was something unspoken during last night's dinner."

The women looked at one another, Amelia struggling to organize her thoughts that had been scattered like so many feathers from a pillow. Julia did not look away or provide rescue. Amelia felt heat rush into her cheeks and considered a dozen different responses, ranging from telling the whole of it to pretending she did not know him. She settled for basic truth. "I knew him many years ago, in London."

"How?"

"Through our navigation of society."

Julia looked confused. "What does that have to do with me?"

Amelia looked away and folded her arms over her chest. "Nothing." The lie felt heavy, but she held to it because trying to explain everything would not only be complex, it would interfere with the point of this conversation. "But I do not have a good opinion of him or his family." That was true enough. "Their family does not have a good reputation, Julia. Do you know what has been done by those who bear the Mayfield name? Do you know the ruin they have caused to others and themselves?"

"I know Mr. Mayfield, and he is a good man," Julia said. "His family's history is none of my concern."

"It should be your concern," Amelia said bluntly. "You should know the type of family you are connecting yourself to."

"The family I am connecting myself to

includes only Mr. Mayfield and his daughters."

Amelia clenched her teeth and let out a huff. "You are being stubborn."

"And you are being judgmental and cruel. You are trying to take charge of my life. Again!"

Amelia's mouth fell open. This was her daughter? Talking to her this way?

Julia took a breath and relaxed before she met Amelia's eye again, her expression calmer. "Why is it so difficult for you to trust me to make my own choices, Mother? I do not want the life you want for me. I have no desire to hurt you, but that is the truth."

"Why don't you want that life, Julia?" Amelia had never asked the question directly, but it had haunted her for nearly a decade, and this conversation seemed to have torn down all pretenses between them. Why would Julia not find a good man and settle down? What was it about the life Amelia had lived, and Louisa and Simon, that made Julia not want it? None of *that* had anything to do with Elliott and his nephew.

Julia wrapped her arms around her stomach and looked at the ground.

Amelia waited, her nerves growing tauter

by the second.

Quietly, Julia said, "I want to make my own choices."

What? That was all? It didn't even make sense. "I don't understand."

"No," Julia said softly in a sympathetic tone that made Amelia even more defensive. "You wouldn't understand, and I'm not sure I can explain it in a way you *could* understand. A parent makes choices for their children, and a husband makes choices for his wife. I want to be in charge of my own future the way a child and a wife does not get to be."

"But being a servant does?"

Julia nodded. "Yes."

"You take care of a man's children and his dogs!" Amelia's voice was too sharp, but she could not help herself. This entire conversation was infuriating. "That is not you making your own choices."

"Yes, Mother, it is. I choose how I spend my evenings. I choose when I arise in the morning. I choose whether or not I take a morning walk, or wear the blue or green dress. I choose how I do my hair and what shoes fit me best. I choose who I like and who I don't like, and I answer to no one for those things. I also choose to take care of two beautiful girls who need me, and dogs that give me purpose. All of those things are my choice, not yours."

Amelia took a physical step backward as Julia's words moved around her, sounding like an accusation. She remembered the structured evenings she managed after Richard died and how important it was to her that the children arose at seven o'clock every morning, no matter the day of the week or month of the year. She had chosen Julia's clothes and shoes because Julia did not seem to care. She'd thought Julia had enjoyed having Amelia do her hair. But Julia had just accused her of controlling her through such things. Was that how she saw it?

Julia softened her overall tension, then stepped forward and took both of Amelia's hands in her own. "I love you, Mother. You have taken good care of me and loved me as best you could. I hold no grudges, but I want to make my own choices, and the truth is that I can only do that when I am not living beneath your roof. I am happy here, very happy, and I would like you to be happy for me too."

Amelia felt tears rising in her eyes, but she could not speak.

Julia let go of one hand, but kept hold of the other. She turned toward the house, leading Amelia along with her. She did not speak, but she did not let go of her mother's hand, either.

They came around the front of the house to find the hired carriage waiting for them. Mr. Mayfield and Elliott stood talking with the driver. They turned and smiled. Mr. Mayfield's eyes were on Julia. Elliott's eyes, however, were on her. The men strode toward them.

"Your trunk is already loaded," Mr. Mayfield said, smiling gallantly. "Thank you again for coming. It was lovely to get to know Julia's mother."

It was *Julia* now? Not *Miss Hollingsworth,* as she'd been last night?

Amelia looked at Julia, who was looking at Mr. Mayfield, and her heart sunk even more. She had failed. Julia would stay here, she would fall in love with Mr. Mayfield, and he would break her heart into a million pieces. Just as Elliott had once broken Amelia's.

The awareness was so tangible Amelia could only nod her farewell to the man who held her daughter's future in his undeserving hands. She walked past him and accepted Elliott's hand to step into the carriage. She settled on the bench and took a deep breath, trying to will away the tears.

Her stomach was twisty and hot. Was she unsettled because she had admitted to having known Elliott before? Or was she unsettled because she had lied about how well she'd known him? Her eyes closed, and tears pricked from behind.

"Are you all right, Mrs. Hollingsworth?"

She opened her eyes to see Elliott standing outside the open carriage door, watching her with concern.

She could only shake her head, overwhelmed as she was. She expected him to be a gentleman and leave her to her misery, but instead he turned toward Mr. Mayfield.

"Peter, I think I shall ride a short distance with Mrs. Hollingsworth."

Ride a short distance? Until she pushed him out on a road in the middle of nowhere?

She didn't hear Mr. Mayfield's response, but Elliott stepped inside the carriage and sat down across from her. The footman shut the door, and Amelia leaned against the cushions and looked out the window. The only other time in her life she'd felt so disregarded was when she'd held Elliott's letter in her hand, the letter telling her that he enjoyed their time together and he wished her happiness. And now they were alone in a hired carriage, and he was looking at her while she fell apart inside.

The carriage jerked forward as it began the journey to the place Julia no longer considered as *her* home. The place where Julia had apparently been so miserable that she had planned to spend the rest of her life somewhere completely different.

"Amelia?"

She did not correct him on his informal address and instead remembered a night at a ball thirty years ago. She could not remember the hosts, but she and Elliott had danced before going out on the veranda to escape the stifling room. She'd placed her hand on the rail, and he'd put his right beside hers, linking their little fingers. Amelia had worn a blue satin gown with a corseted waist and a full skirt that was the fashion of the day. She looked beautiful, she felt beautiful, and then Elliott — or Mr. Mayfield, as he had been back then — told her she *looked* beautiful.

"I was so glad to see you tonight, Miss Edwards."

She had looked at their entwined hands, then into his young, fresh, and hopeful face and thought, *I will marry this man.*

"Please call me Amelia."

His smile had widened. He lifted her hand and kissed the back of her glove before turning it over and kissing the palm. Amelia had felt fire from her head to her toes as he'd straightened and winked. "And do call me Elliott."

In the carriage, she let out a breath, trying to push the memory and regrets away. She focused on Elliott sitting across from her, but it took a few moments to remember why an older Elliott was looking at her with so much concern. Julia.

"I have found Julia a position as a lady's companion near Feltwell," she said, her voice flat. "She refused it."

Elliott was silent a moment. "Of course she refused it. Have you not seen how content she is here? This is a good place for her."

Amelia shook her head. "She is infatuated. With all of it — his children, his blasted dogs, and . . . him. Surely you see that between them."

Elliott watched her so closely it was as though he could read her thoughts. Not that he needed to since she was spewing words without any prompting from him.

"Yes, actually," he said, "I do see it, on both of their parts. I do not object, and I do not see any reason why you should object either. They are well matched, they are young, they can find happiness together."

She narrowed her eyes. Anger and hurt

and rejection and loneliness and fear and self-preservation mixed and gurgled and rose like yeast in bread dough on a hot day, bigger and headier and growing. "You are a *man,* speaking from a position of power and entitlement just as your nephew can." She waved toward the house that was no longer in view. "He will not marry her. You know as well as I do that he won't."

Elliott's eyes flashed. "You are insinuating — again — that Peter would take advantage of her, which he would not. Was your opinion not the least bit changed after sitting at his table, watching him with his children, and witnessing the respect he has for Julia?"

Amelia looked out the carriage window, which was in need of a good scrubbing.

Elliott leaned forward in his bouncing seat. "Let me tell you something, Amelia. Nearly two months ago, I presented an inducement to Peter that I hoped would encourage him to make a solid match that could repair my family's fractured past and give him additional security."

Amelia faced him while he continued explaining his plan that sounded to her like nothing short of bribery. Marriage as a commodity? Matches made for increase? She felt the rage building the longer he spoke.

"Peter did not even look at his folder," Elliott explained. "He said that he had no interest, not in my *campaign,* as he called it, or in marrying again. He loved his wife, Amelia, and was good to her. That he is beginning to see a light in his life again, that he can look at Julia the way he does, and that she can return that affection and love his children is a beautiful thing — not a manipulation or conquest. He is a good man, the best of them. His interest in your daughter is not lascivious or selfish. I understand that I hurt you all those years ago, and I am sorry for that to the depths of my soul. Perhaps if I could explain to you the circumstances —"

"I know the circumstances." She hated being placated. Hated being spoken down to, and every nerve in her body was on fire. "You inherited a title, and the daughter of a parliamentary clerk was no longer a fitting wife for you." There. She'd said the words she'd never said before. She had not been enough for him, not when his status had changed and he could have his pick of the season. Amelia had not been enough. Julia would not be enough either.

He narrowed his eyes. "That is what you believe?"

"It was quite obvious, Lord Howardford."

She could not look at him. "Never mind the promise you gave me of a future or the liberties you took with my person."

"Liberties?" he said, his eyebrows shooting up. "We kissed behind some shrubbery a handful of times. And as I remember, you were more than willing to take those liberties yourself."

Heat infused her cheeks. "How dare you —"

"I am finished with this conversation." He knocked three times on the carriage ceiling. "You have become a hard and bitter woman, Amelia, and it breaks my heart to see it. Julia is a grown woman. She can make her own decisions, and I hope that she can see the connection between herself and Peter with greater clarity than you apparently can." The carriage rumbled to a stop, and Amelia had to move her knees to the side to allow Elliott to exit. Her heart was thumping in her chest from the words he had thrown at her like arrows.

He stepped out of the carriage, but leaned his head back inside. She had no choice but to look at him, even though that was the last thing she wanted to do.

"I suggest you find a life of your own rather than trying to manage your daughter's. Good day and safe travels." He slammed the door, then hit the side of the carriage, spurring the driver to continue while he stood on the side of the road somewhere between Elsing and Dereham.

Amelia stared at the cushion across from her and locked herself up tight to keep from letting his words penetrate. He was wrong. He could never, ever, understand what his rejection had cost her or how determined she was to protect her daughter from the same. No one could.

CHAPTER TWENTY-SIX:
JULIA

Julia heard the sound of a carriage coming up behind her as she walked home from church and stepped from the road to the spongy shoulder. Last year's vegetation was matted beneath the new spring grass. While autumn would always be her favorite time of year, spring was driving a convincing campaign this year. Springtime in London, while lovely, was nothing compared to spring in the country. She was tempted to take off her shoes and run through the meadow to her left, but the sheep in said meadow kept such a frolic to fantasy. The grass was so very green for a reason, after all.

Instead of passing her by, the carriage slowed, and she looked over her shoulder to see it was Mr. Mayfield's. He had offered her a ride to services that morning, but she had graciously turned it down. Something had changed between them following the dinner party. They conversed more easily, and he spent more time with her and the girls in the nursery or when they were outside. Julia liked it — very much. Too much? Her mother's warnings still rang in her ears.

The carriage stopped, and the door swung open, revealing Mr. Mayfield. He smiled. She smiled back. "Would you like a ride back to the house, Miss Julia?"

She looked past him and tilted her head. "Where are the girls?"

"Mrs. Oswell invited them to luncheon this afternoon. I'm to return for them at four o'clock."

Julia lifted her eyebrows. "She invited the girls but not you?"

His eyebrows came together. "Odd, that, but then she and I have had some discord of late. I have known her a long time but have yet to fully understand why she does things the way she does. But, well, would you like a ride?"

"Thank you, but no. The day is lovely." Besides, it was inappropriate for her to ride with him alone in his carriage. Even if she wanted to. Which she did. Very much.

"Oh, well, yes, it is."

She hated the disappointment in his voice and yet liked it at the same time — he had wanted her to ride with him. It was not simply good manners. "Would you, instead, like to walk?"

When he paused, she nearly took back the invitation, but then he stepped out of the carriage and put his hat on. "Thank you. I shall if you are sure you don't mind."

"Not at all, Mr. Mayfield. A day like this is made for everyone to enjoy, I believe."

He closed the carriage door and walked over to explain to Stephen the change in plans. Stephen nodded, lifted one eyebrow at Julia, and then spurred the horses forward. The rumbling of the wheels lessened until the sounds of spring took center stage once again.

"It was a lovely service," Mr. Mayfield said, his hands in his coat pockets.

Julia pushed away her concern at Stephen's look. Of course the staff had noticed the change between Mr. Mayfield and herself. She should remember Colleen's words and try to prevent being alone in Mr. Mayfield's company. But she didn't. And she wouldn't.

"Mr. Oswell is easy to listen to. The vicar in my mother's parish is very young and lacks conviction, I suppose. One gets the sense that this is his occupation rather than his calling."

"And yet, it is his occupation, is it not?"

"Yes, but it should not feel that way. A good clergyman makes you forget that he would starve to death if you did not pay your tithes."

Mr. Mayfield laughed, and she decided she liked that sound very much.

When they reached a fork in the road, she stepped to the left, toward the road that provided a direct route back to the house. Mr. Mayfield, however, paused.

"There is a path, just there." He pointed to the right. "It is nearly half a mile longer, at least, but the path wanders around a lovely meadow." He met Julia's eyes and then shifted nervously from one foot to another. "But, well, it would likely be better to take —"

She hurried to speak before he talked them both out of the idea. "I have nowhere I need to be that would prevent the additional distance, Mr. Mayfield." And nowhere she would rather be right now than here, with him.

Oh, dear.

He grinned and rocked back on his heels. "Well, then — that is excellent."

They took the right-hand path, discussing the church services, the Oswells, and the dogs. It surprised her that, though she loved his dogs and loved talking about them with him, she found herself wanting to discuss other things. More personal things. This was the first time they had been alone together, after all, and . . .

Oh, dear, indeed.

"I suppose it is no surprise that you know this path," she said to change the topic. "You grew up here, did you not?"

"I did." His hands were still in his pockets, and he looked between the path before him and the view around them. "Until I was thirteen, at which time I went to Harrow."

"Did you then go on to university?"

"Yes, Cambridge. I studied for two years before coming back here. I'm afraid my interest in literature and philosophy was limited. I missed the land and the skies and the opportunities of the country."

"When you returned, you took over the management of the estate?"

Mr. Mayfield shrugged slightly. "I have essentially been managing this estate since I was ten years old, I suppose."

"Ten!" Julia looked at him to make sure he wasn't funning her. His expression was serious, though the smile on his face showed that he enjoyed surprising her.

Mr. Mayfield kicked at a rock. "My father died when I was eight. Uncle Elliott came home the following year and set things back into order as my father had been lax in his attention to most things. The estate had fallen into a great deal of disrepair and was no longer supporting itself, much less turning any kind of profit. Uncle Elliott hired a new steward — Mr. Johnstone, who is still with me — but explained to both of us that I, as the inheritor of all the holdings, needed to be involved in the management. I'm not sure how either of them took that seriously in hindsight, but it was rather brilliant because it made me feel proud of my position and eager to prove myself to them. I did very little, of course, and relied heavily on Mr. Johnstone's advice, but I learned a great deal by being involved in the necessary decisions.

"When I went to school, I corresponded with Mr. Johnstone and my uncle as best I could, and then caught up during the holidays and the summer term. It taught me the value of responsibility, and I have tried to live worthy of it — and their trust — ever since." He smiled at her rather shyly.

"I find that very impressive, Mr. Mayfield. I am sorry to hear of your father's passing when you were so young."

"Something you can relate to."

"Yes," Julia said, feeling that familiar wave

312

of sadness. Her father's death had changed everything for her. "And then you lost your mother as well?" Though Julia had told Mother she did not care about whatever scandals were in Mr. Mayfield's family line, she was curious. She had considered asking Mrs. Allen, or perhaps Mrs. Oswell, but worried it would seem like gossip to them.

"My mother was . . ." He paused, took a breath, and kicked at the ground in front of him. "She was a broken woman all of my life, more so after my father died." He glanced at her. "Surely you know the story, or rather, the scandal of it."

"I have heard some hint, but nothing specific."

He was thoughtful for several seconds, then told her the story of his parents. By the end, Julia better understood her mother's concerns yet felt even more determined that the sins of his parents had no bearing on him as a man.

"She did not leave the house after my father died, not knowing how to exist in her place without my father to draw her through a crowd, so to speak. I was sad when she passed, of course, but I was also relieved for her own sake that she did not have to suffer any longer."

"She was ill, then?"

"No." He shook his head. "I mean, yes, she was at the very end — pneumonia — but she'd suffered most of her life in one way or another. I don't believe she was ever truly happy."

"That is the very worst kind of suffering."

"Yes."

"But then *you* had a happy marriage with Mrs. Mayfield." She knew Mrs. Mayfield's name was Sybil, but it seemed presumptuous to refer to her so casually.

He startled and looked at her quickly.

She faced forward. "I am sorry. I should not have said that — any of this, really."

"No, no, it is fine." He reached up and removed his hat, letting the breeze take his hair. He swung his hat in his hand beside his leg. "I am just out of practice talking about her."

Julia smiled at him, but did not ask any questions, willing to take the conversation at his pace.

"I met Sybil when she came to Elsing to stay with her aunt for a few months. She had recently rejected an engagement and run to Elsing in order to hide — her words, not mine." He went on to explain that they'd had a good marriage, a happy one that Peter had never imagined he could have, and enjoyed their daughters. "Sybil

314

never quite recovered after Leah's birth. She could not seem to get her strength back, had no appetite, and, toward the end, was asleep more than she was awake. I finally learned that after Leah was born, she . . ." He did not continue.

Julia noted the spots of color on his cheeks. "Mr. Mayfield?"

He shook his head. "She simply did not heal well after Leah's birth."

"You mean that she continued bleeding." When he looked at the ground, Julia nudged him with her shoulder, playfully she hoped. "You forget that I am comfortable with matters of biology. She did not tell anyone? She did not see a physician?"

"I think she kept hoping her health would improve, but instead she grew weaker and weaker until winter set in. She developed a cough she did not have the strength for."

"What a horrible time that must have been." Julia put a hand on his arm, but only for a moment before realizing she should not.

He looked at the path ahead of their steps. "It was the greatest tragedy of my life."

They walked in silence for several seconds, Julia going back and forth between regretting that she'd asked and being grateful that she had. She remembered what her mother had said regarding him not being trust-worthy and scoffed in her mind. Perhaps if Mother knew how much he'd loved his wife, she would not see him so unfairly.

"There."

She looked at him, confused, then followed the direction he was pointing and gasped. A curve in the path had brought them to the meadow he had mentioned.

"You did not tell me it was a field of primroses." They had always been her favorite flower, and to have a whole meadow of them!

"Oh, well, er, I am not all that familiar with the species of flowers."

She smiled at him just enough to let him know she hadn't meant to chide him, then she turned back to the field and let the sight capture her once more. The pale-yellow tufts of primroses were bright against the intense green of the grass. Here and there was a spot of pink or a tall cluster of bluebells, but most of the blooms were the traditional butter yellow. She walked forward, turning her head slowly to see all of it and remembering her home and childhood and how Papa had once said their family was like a primrose — five petals, for five members; simple but hardy.

"Do you mind if I seek out the center?"

she asked.

He looked amused. "Not at all."

She saw a deer path, barely visible, and moved toward it, lifting her skirts as she stepped on the thin path so she would not damage the blooms as she navigated toward the center of the field. After a few steps, she turned back to Mr. Mayfield.

"Would you like to join me? The view from the edges is superb, but the view from the middle will make it seem as though the whole world is filled with flowers."

"Um, well, yes, I suppose." He followed her down the path.

When she reached what seemed like the center, she turned to watch Mr. Mayfield manage the rest of the distance, unable to hold back a laugh at the look of concentration on his face. He looked up when he heard her laughing, and smiled before returning to his careful steps.

"Can I show you a trick my brother, sister, and I would do when we were young?"

He closed one eye slightly and gave her a suspicious look. "Does it result in me having petals, grass, or dirt in my mouth? If so, I know that trick."

Julia laughed so loud that she put a hand to her mouth in surprise. Which made him laugh. She dropped her hand. "It is not that kind of trick."

He nodded, and so she turned him around so they were back to back. She had to step on a few flowers to manage it, but felt justified that the overall effect would be worthwhile.

"We have to link elbows," she said, twisting and taking hold of his arms in order to help them get into position.

"I don't understand what we are doing."

"You will see. Now, link elbows with me — yes, like that."

They were back to back now, elbows locked. Julia stepped to the side, forcing Mr. Mayfield to do the same. He caught on quickly, and they began to pivot in a slow circle, turning the field into something magnificent, a view of flowers that never stopped. They made a full circle before Julia broke the silence with an explanation.

"Papa called this a panorama — each of us seeing the same thing on our own time but without missing a single detail."

"It is remarkable."

She let the compliment, so sincere and simple, fill her up as they continued to turn, slow and steady. Julia imagined them as the center of the world with everything else moving around them. She closed her eyes in order to focus her senses on the smells of growing things, the sounds of birds and rustling leaves, a river in the distance, and the feel of the sun and the breeze on her face. Mr. Mayfield's warm back against her own . . . which had not seemed the least bit sensual until she really considered it. Since she had not intended such a sensation, she decided she could not be faulted for enjoying it a bit longer. It was almost as though they were dancing, back to back.

After they'd made another revolution, she opened her eyes, and with all of her senses keen, took in the whole once again. "Have you ever brought Marjorie and Leah here?" she asked.

"I have not."

"You should."

After another three rotations, they came to a stop and stood for several seconds until he somehow managed to untangle himself from her elbows with far more ease than she'd gotten them into the position. They both turned to face one another and, though they were no longer spinning, she had the same sense of being the center of something. He stared at her as though he could see her every thought. What if this moment could exist separately from the world they lived in?

After several seconds, he smiled and bent

down, straightening a moment later with a single bloom between his fingers. He brushed her hair from her face, and her entire body shivered as he tucked the flower behind her ear, beneath her bonnet. How his touch could be light as a butterfly's wing and yet burn like coal was a mystery. He lowered his hand and cocked his head to the side, frowning slightly. "It is nearly the same color as your hair. I'm afraid I can hardly see where the petals end and you begin."

She bent down herself, plucked another bloom, straightened, and tucked the flower into the pocket of his overcoat. "Well, the color is stark against your coat. I supposed that means you are the better canvas."

"Certainly not."

She looked from the flower to his face. Did she imagine that he leaned in, just so? She leaned forward as well, just in case, and felt an even stronger pull between them. She could see the pulse in the base of his throat and imagined that hers had sped up to match his. She was captured by his eyes and felt an unfurling inside herself. It didn't matter what he was to her or what she was to him. She leaned in another inch, and she heard him inhale deeply, then he lifted his hand to run the backs of his fingers along the curve of her chin. She closed her eyes and savored the delicate fire of his touch.

"Julia?"

She opened her eyes and saw that his expression had changed. The soft desire she'd seen a few moments ago had turned to anxiety. He stepped away, and heat flushed through her chest and neck before taking over her face. She looked around at the flowers again while she mustered a polite smile. "Well, um, thank you for bringing me here, Mr. Mayfield." *My boss. My employer. The man my mother fears is a cad.* "It is magical — the kind of place one can get lost in."

She did not meet his eye or wait for him to respond but instead lifted her skirts and followed the deer path through the meadow to the other side, where it joined the wider footpath. Her heart was pounding, her face still hot, but she was aware of Mr. Mayfield following a few steps behind her.

They reached the main path and walked for a few minutes in complete silence. Julia tried to determine how she felt. Embarrassed, but then . . . not. She could not remember who had taken the first liberty and realized she did not care. There was something beautiful and innocent about the moment, and she refused to let regret overtake it, though she was unsure how to accomplish that.

"The eastern edge of the estate is not far from here," he said eventually.

"Oh. Very good."

They walked in silence.

"I do think the girls would like this place very much," she said when the silence again became unbearable.

"I believe you are right. Perhaps you should bring them here."

You, not us. *Of course not us!* More silence. And with the silence came memories of that moment — a moment she wished she could cut from the fabric of time and preserve forever. But she was twenty-seven years old and still a silly girl. She wanted to keep him talking. If they could talk, the words could be like steps taking them farther from this place. Maybe with enough words, they would nearly forget it. Nearly.

"A new week is ahead of us," she said, changing topic.

"Yes." He'd quickened his pace, and she glanced at him from the corner of her eye. Was he embarrassed? Angry? He continued to look straight ahead. "Queenie has me worried. She should deliver Tuesday or Wednesday but isn't eating much."

Dogs. Good. They could talk about dogs

for hours without inviting any of the intimacy that had been building between them so strongly a few minutes ago. They could rediscover the proper place for themselves. She caught sight of the yellow flower in his coat pocket and wondered if the one he'd tucked behind her ear was still there. She didn't dare check.

"Really? Is that normal for her?"

He shook his head. "No, she lost a pup with her last whelping, but kept her strength and appetite throughout the pregnancy . . ."

CHAPTER TWENTY-SEVEN: JULIA

A knock on her door caused Julia to sit straight up in bed, then wonder if she'd actually heard it. When the banging sounded again, she fumbled out of bed and made her way to the door that led to the hallway. En route, she hit her knee on the washstand, and then stubbed her toe on the footboard, causing her to wince but also wake up more fully. She pulled open the door and blinked against the light of a candle held by the new dog handler, Henry. Mr. Allen stood behind the man, a jacket thrown over his night-clothes. It must be very late Wednesday night or very early Thursday morning.

"Mr. Mayfield needs you to come," Henry said, chest heaving and eyes scared. "Queenie be having a rough go with the whelping. He said you would come."

After her conversation with Mr. Mayfield about Queenie a few days earlier, after that moment in the meadow, Julia had taken to checking on the dam every morning before looking in on Bumbleberry, who was no longer in the shed. The door that led from Queenie's pen to the whelping shed had been open for almost a week, but she had shown little interest in it, despite her litter being nearly due. The only thing Julia had managed to get Queenie to eat was some bits of chicken she got from Cook.

"I just need a moment." She turned back to get her shoes, leaving the door open so she could see, at least somewhat. When she appeared in the hallway less than a minute later with the laces of her boots tucked into the tops and cinching the sash of her dressing gown around her waist, both Henry and Mr. Allen looked at her with surprise.

"Perhaps you ought to dress yourself properly," Mr. Allen said, followed by a discreet cough.

"If Mr. Mayfield has requested my help now, he surely needs me now." She walked between the two men and heard Henry follow behind her as she hurried down the servants' stairs and through the hallway and kitchen. She pushed through the door and was immediately hit in the face with a hard rain. She gasped and pulled back inside. But Henry was right behind her, so she stumbled backwards into him. She had not realized before now that he was soaking wet.

"The storm is somethin' fierce, it is," Henry said, staring past her into the dark.

She set her jaw and hurried into the night and the rain — there was nothing else to do.

By the time she reached the whelping shed, the bottom six inches of her dressing gown were coated in mud, as were her boots, the laces of which had fallen out. She let herself into the shed, Henry right behind her, and he pushed the door closed against the wind and rain. She wiped at her face in hopes of clearing her vision. Once she could see, she took in the room. Two lanterns hung from the walls, the whelping box was in the center of the floor, as it had been for Bumbleberry, and Queenie lay on her side, panting heavily with her eyes closed. Nothing seemed especially wrong until Julia looked at Mr. Mayfield. He held a towel in his lap, rubbing something inside it.

"A pup? Already?" Julia asked.

"Henry found it in the yard around midnight," Mr. Mayfield answered.

"Don't know how long it been there," Henry said. "I been checking on Queenie every few hours the last few nights. This time I found a pup. Still warm."

"The sack was broken, but Queenie had

left it and gone back to her shelter." Mr. Mayfield continued to rub the pup, but looked at the dam. "Henry carried her in here, and she's straining some, but . . . she doesn't seem to care what's happening. She seems asleep most of the time." He looked at Julia with heavy, frightened eyes, and she read what he didn't say aloud: *I wasn't sure what to do.*

Julia moved around to the side of the box closest to Queenie's head. She pulled off her muddy shoes and dressing gown, all of which were only a burden. She pushed her hair from her face and caressed the dam's head.

"Queenie," Julia whispered, stroking the dog with slow, even movements. "What is wrong, my girl?"

The dog did not respond, but her chest heaved with panting breaths.

"I think she is unconscious," Julia said softly. "When was she last responsive?"

"Perhaps ten minutes," Mr. Mayfield said. "Have you seen something like this before?"

"Not like this, no," Julia said, still stroking the dog as she thought over her experiences. What would her father do? With one hand, Julia pulled back the side of the dog's mouth to inspect her teeth, then assessed her belly. She'd always felt Queenie was

327

older than Mr. Mayfield knew but hadn't taken the time to determine it for herself. "Queenie is not your pureblood dam, is that right?"

"No, that is Sheila, and I've only bred her once. Queenie is bred for size, agility, and speed."

"And the breeder you bought her from said she was two years old?"

"Yes, and had birthed one successful litter. I've bred her twice since."

"I am sorry to say this, Mr. Mayfield, but I would guess Queenie is nearly eight years old. If you bought her as a breeding dam, she likely had ten or more litters before coming to you."

"The seller said she'd only had the one," Mr. Mayfield repeated, confused.

Julia smiled kindly. "He lied."

Mr. Mayfield's expression fell.

"Tell me about her last litter." She lifted one of Queenie's paws and separated each toe, watching to see if the dog responded to what should be uncomfortable.

"There were ten puppies — a large litter. Nine survived."

"What about the one that didn't survive? What went wrong?"

"The whelping took several hours, and she was exhausted by the effort of it. The last puppy was stillborn, but with a litter that size, I didn't find that too unexpected. I waited two cycles to allow her to regain her strength before I decided to breed her again."

Mr. Mayfield was passionate, but not yet an expert. Julia moved to another paw, spreading the toes again. On the second one, Queenie tensed. Julia paused, then did the next toe. Queenie tensed again.

Julia looked at Mr. Mayfield, who was still rubbing the puppy they both knew was already lost. "I believe I know what to do, Mr. Mayfield, but I will need you to do everything I ask of you."

He nodded vigorously. Julia looked at Henry. "Take the pup from Mr. Mayfield into the house. See if you can warm it by the fire. Blow into its face and try to clear its nostrils." The effort was likely futile, but it would give Henry something to do and allow Mr. Mayfield to help her directly.

The pup was passed over, Henry left, then Mr. Mayfield rolled up his shirtsleeves and knelt on the floor of the shed. Their gazes met across the box.

"Thank you," he said softly.

Julia shook her head. "Don't thank me yet. This will likely be a long night for all of us."

She turned her attention to Queenie. She rolled the dam onto her other side, eliciting a whimper in the process. That was good, even though the sound hitched Julia's heart. She guessed that Queenie'd had a stroke.

Hours later, as the birds began to chirp, Julia found herself alone with Queenie in the shed. Mr. Mayfield had taken the four surviving pups — one had been stillborn — into the house nearly half an hour ago. She'd told him they needed the warmth of the fire, which they did, but she was also trying to spare him these final administrations. Queenie lay on a blanket on the floor in front of Julia, the stillborn pup between her front paws.

"You did a wonderful job, Queenie," she said, stroking the dog's side as the breaths came slower, with longer pauses between. Julia had ceased the regular, and painful, methods of reviving the dam, finally letting her rest. The dam had fully roused only once during the whelping, and then fallen immediately back into unconsciousness. Julia and Mr. Mayfield had delivered the puppies without her help, and now, the task done, her body was failing completely. "Four puppies, Queenie. Four beautiful, healthy pups."

Another breath. Another pause. Bit by bit,

Queenie's body relaxed, her mouth hung open, and her tongue lolled to the side.

"Bumbleberry will be a good mother to them," Julia continued, her throat thick.

Another breath. Another pause.

"Mr. Mayfield will care for them as best he can. He didn't know you were so used up. If he had, he'd have never asked so much of you."

Another breath. Another pause. Then nothing.

Julia pursed her lips together to keep from crying. She waited another minute, and then pulled the corner of Queenie's blanket over her and the tiny pup that had never taken a breath. Julia sat back against the wall of the shed and let the exhaustion and emotion envelop her. She was sobbing with her head on her knees when she heard the door of the shed creak open.

Thankfully, it was Henry and not Mr. Mayfield. He looked from her to the blanket and back to her. "She dinna make it?"

"No," Julia said in a tremulous voice, wiping at her eyes. "I don't want Mr. Mayfield to trouble himself." She'd watched him wrestling with his emotions as the whelping had progressed. He'd never been involved in a situation like this.

"I understand." Henry stepped inside and

lifted the blanket-encased body from the floor.

Julia came to her feet and tucked the corners of the blanket in around Queenie. "I don't know what to do with her," she said, resting her hand on the dog's head.

"I do," Henry said. "Donnah you worry."

She wiped at her eyes again. "Where is Mr. Mayfield?"

"In the kitchens." Henry nodded toward the house. "Did ya hear that first puppy revived?"

She looked at him in shock. "It did?"

Henry grinned widely, showing his missing eyetooth. "Almost an hour after I done took it in. Jacob had taken over, and he must have the right touch."

"I thought there was no chance," Julia said, her chin trembling as more tears threatened. She was completely wrung out and unable to school her thoughts or demeanor the least bit.

"Well, there was. I'll take care of our Queenie."

Julia nodded, wiped at her eyes again, and then rested her forehead on the wall of the shed for another minute or two until she felt as though she had control of herself.

The worst was over, but there were still issues to address regardless of how tired she felt. She put on her boots, encrusted with mud, and threw the still-wet dressing gown around her shoulders. The rain was less intense than it had been, but she was muddy and wet again by the time she let herself into the kitchen. She stood on the mat, dripping and shivering.

Several heads turned to look at her, but she only saw Mr. Mayfield sitting in a chair by the fire, a blanket on his lap. She took off her boots and walked barefoot across the cold flagstones to him. When she arrived, he looked up with a question in his eyes. She smiled sadly but said nothing. She reached out and turned back the corner of the blanket. Five tiny white-and-brown pups barely moved within the nest he'd made for them.

Julia felt tears threatening but resisted. "They are beautiful."

"They are," Mr. Mayfield said.

Julia rested her hand on his shoulder as though it were the most natural thing for her to do, and he placed one of his hands over hers just as easily.

"We should introduce them to Bumbleberry as soon as possible," Julia said.

Mr. Mayfield held her gaze, then he pulled the corners of the blanket over the pups and stood. When Julia turned toward the door, five different staff members tried to hide the fact that they had been watching the interaction. Julia was too tired to care what they thought.

She went to the back door and sat heavily on the bench. She dreaded having to put her wet and muddy boots back on.

Mr. Mayfield watched her for a moment before turning toward the housekeeper. "Mrs. Allen, have we any work boots Miss Julia could wear?"

"Certainly, sir." She nodded and left down the servants' hallway.

Mr. Mayfield nodded toward her boots. "Those should be put in the fire, Julia. They are unsalvageable."

"They are not," Julia said, pushing them beneath the bench and feeling her heart flutter at him having called her Julia. Not Miss Hollingsworth or even Miss Julia. "I can save them with a brush and some water. But I would appreciate another pair on loan until I have the chance." Mud had gotten inside the boots, which was quite uncomfortable.

Mr. Mayfield looked around the other staff members until his eyes landed on Mr. Allen. "Will you please send a note to the vicarage requesting that Mrs. Oswell come and care for the children today? Tell her that

Miss Julia and myself were up all night with a new litter. Have Jacob deliver the note immediately."

Julia tried to amend the request. "That is not —"

She stopped when he turned to her with a look that said quite clearly that he would not be swayed. The argument disappeared in her throat; in truth, she wanted nothing more than to sleep.

"Yes, sir." Mr. Allen left the common area for the office he shared with his wife.

Mr. Mayfield turned to Cook and Colleen, the only two staff remaining in the kitchen. "Miss Julia and I will need breakfast when we return, something hot and filling." He turned to Colleen. "Prepare Miss Julia a bath in the copper tub in the upstairs washroom. Make sure the water is hot so that she can bathe when we are finished with breakfast."

"Yes, sir," both women said, but Julia cringed, knowing that her relationship with Colleen was only going to get worse after this. But a hot bath and a hot meal sounded too divine for her to argue against.

Mrs. Allen returned with a serviceable pair of boots, only slightly too big, and an overcoat with patched sleeves and missing buttons. She would look like a scarecrow, but she would be warm and dry. "Thank you, Mrs. Allen." Julia pushed her arms into the sleeves, pulled the collar around her neck, and smiled at the housekeeper. "Wonderful."

Mrs. Allen held out an umbrella, nodding toward Mr. Mayfield. "To cover the pups."

Julia thanked her again, and then she and Mr. Mayfield made the journey to the dog yard, Julia holding the umbrella over the precious cargo he carried.

"It's too cold for the pups to be outside," Mr. Mayfield said as they approached the pen.

Julia agreed. "The shed, then," she said and opened the door for him. It was warm, though a bit more coal would warm it up even more. She closed the door to Queenie's pen and opened the door leading to Bumbleberry. Half an hour ago, Queenie had taken her last breath in this shed. Poor Queenie.

"You have used a dam for another's litter?" Mr. Mayfield asked.

Julia nodded but kept her uncertainty to herself. Father had had a network of farmers to call upon when such a thing was needed, farmers with dams used to taking in other pups than their own. But she had heard stories of litters being killed by dogs other than their own mother. Bumbleberry was a first-time mother with eight four-week-old pups.

"Let us see how she reacts. If she doesn't take to them, perhaps Henry can go into town and ask after another dam to try."

Mr. Mayfield nodded, and Julia felt the weight of his trust. He placed the blanket gently into the whelping box, then stepped back. "I shall fetch Bumbleberry, but maybe it would be best if I stayed outside for the first bit."

Bumbleberry responded to Mr. Mayfield better these days, but seeing as how there were new puppies involved, perhaps him keeping his distance was wise. Julia nodded, then stroked and cooed at the puppies, who were crying with hunger, while she waited. The first thing she saw was Bumbleberry's nose sniffling around the door leading to the shed, then her face poked through.

"You thought you were almost done, didn't you?" Julia said.

Bumbleberry came directly to Julia, seeming to ignore the new puppies completely. She licked Julia's face, and Julia scratched her ears and nuzzled her neck. Then she pulled back and took Bumbleberry's head in her hands like she would do with one of the girls when telling them something that required their attention.

"I have a very important thing to ask of you, Bumbleberry. You have proven yourself an excellent mother, and I have five puppies in desperate need of one." She turned Bumbleberry's head toward the mewling puppies. After a few seconds, she let go of Bumbleberry's head and held her breath as the dog leaned forward to sniff the puppies. She looked at Julia as though asking her what she was supposed to do with these annoying creatures.

"Please, Bumbleberry," Julia encouraged, turning her head toward the pups again.

Bumbleberry walked to the other side of the box and leaned in, sniffing again. Once she'd investigated the puppies fully with her nose, she began to lick them, eliciting protest from the newborns. With a huff, Bumbleberry stepped into the box, nudged the puppies out of the way, and then settled down on her side as though accepting her fate. She licked and nudged the pups into position with far more instinct than she had showed toward her own litter.

"Good girl," Julia cooed while helping to position the puppies. The first puppy latched on, then the second, third, and fourth. After several poor attempts, the fifth did as well. Julia stroked Bumbleberry's head while praising her excellent mothering skills. After a few minutes, the shed door opened, and Mr. Mayfield came in.

Bumbleberry tensed and lifted her head, growling low in her throat.

Julia could not help but laugh at the fallen expression on Mr. Mayfield's face, though she put a hand over her mouth to hide it.

"I had hoped she and I were past this." He sighed with exaggeration, and then smiled. "She is lucky to have you here, Miss Julia. As we all are."

Warmth bubbled up in Julia's chest and went straight to her cheeks. "I have only done what anyone else would have."

"No," Mr. Mayfield said, looking at her with soft eyes. "*Anyone else* would not — nor could not — do what you have done. You truly do have a gift."

Bumbleberry growled again, and Mr. Mayfield put up his hands in surrender. "All right, Miss Bumbleberry, I know when I am not welcome." He put his hands down and turned to Julia. "Shall I await you in the breakfast room?"

Breakfast with him? Was that what he'd meant earlier when he'd said they would need a hot meal?

If she weren't already blushing, she would be now as she imagined herself sitting at his fine mahogany table set with china dishes and crystal goblets. The fantasy made her painfully aware of her current state. She lifted a hand to her hair for the first time in who knew how many hours. She'd plaited it before bed, but a fair amount of curls were now tangled around her face. She could feel bits of mud dried in clumps and could only imagine how she looked.

"I am humbled and grateful for the invitation, Mr. Mayfield, but I dare not accept. I am an absolute wreck."

"As am I." He spread his hands to present his muddied breaches, unshaven face, and tousled hair. But if anything, he looked more handsome in this state. She was still in her nightdress, for heaven's sake, with boots that were too big and a coat with patched elbows. But that was not the real reason she could not eat with him. She'd thought back to the meadow of primroses a hundred times in the days since it had happened. The memory was delicious, but it could not happen again. *You best watch yourself,* Colleen had said. Julia needed to follow that advice.

"A bowl of porridge after the bath will be sufficient." But how she wanted to sit at his table and share a meal with him.

"Julia, after this night —"

"Anything more than that would be inappropriate, Mr. Mayfield. But I thank you for the offer." Her insides clenched. Offending him was the last thing she wanted to do — well, other than overstep her position. She remembered her hand on his shoulder and his hand on hers. That could be justified by the intense emotions of the circumstances, but nothing could justify more than that.

He crossed his arms over his chest, setting off his shoulders, which she'd noticed before, and looking as though he were formulating further argument, which she both adored and dreaded.

She looked back to Bumbleberry, who was still watching him — a perfect excuse for a change of topic. "Though I'm disappointed that she's reverted to her old opinions of you, Mr. Mayfield, I think it is a good sign that she's as protective of these pups as she was of her own."

"Yes, I suppose it is." He did not sound happy. She told herself it was because of Bumbleberry's rejection, not hers.

"Someone will need to stay with Bumbleberry every hour for the next day or so," she said. "To make sure she doesn't reject the litter. And we might need to wean her own litter sooner than we planned. It will depend on how her milk production is affected by these extra mouths to feed. Some dams will produce enough for both litters; others are unable to. Thirteen puppies is a lot to ask of a new mother."

"I shall have Henry stay with them this morning, and then Cook can prepare the beef gruel I use to wean pups from the dams. We can supplement as best we can."

Julia nodded. "I will stay until Henry can relieve me. Thank you for . . ." She wanted to say his acceptance, his kindness, but she could not decide what was appropriate, so she said nothing.

"I shall send him in straight away." They locked eyes another moment before Mr. Mayfield turned and left the shed.

Bumbleberry rested her head once more and fell asleep without understanding that she had saved five little lives today.

Chapter Twenty-Eight: Peter

It was four o'clock in the afternoon when Peter awoke, disoriented and sluggish. Mrs. Oswell had taken the girls to the vicarage, and they would return in time for bed. He checked on the puppies — Bumbleberry's and Queenie's. Henry was keeping the litters separated, and he'd wrapped a bundle of blankets in an old sheepskin that Queenie's puppies were snuggled with when they were not eating — Miss Julia's idea, he said. Peter asked the groom to spell Henry for the night with the promise of making better arrangements come morning.

Peter did not ask after Julia, though he was sorely tempted. She had been remarkable last night, and when she'd put her hand on his shoulder, he'd realized how much he wanted her beside him . . . all the time. Every thought of last night brought him back to her and the knowledge that things had changed for them. Equaled them somehow. And he needed to make some decisions.

He dressed slowly and ordered tea to be brought to his study, where a stack of correspondence was waiting for him, as well as two days' worth of newspapers and a new periodical he'd ordered from London. He put the papers aside and skimmed the periodical instead — there was an excellent article on dog racing — while he ate; Cook had included a generous ham-and-cheese plate with an assortment of tarts and scones.

He turned to his correspondence. There were two invitations he would send polite excuses for, a notice of a new constable appointment in Elsing, and then a packet that at first confused him until he saw the return. Mr. Hastings of Hastings Staffing Services. He unfolded the packet to find four individual letters and a short note from Mr. Hastings.

Dear Mr. Mayfield,

My apologies for the delay in sending these letters of application for the position of governess. I know that time is of the essence in regard to your situation and hope that it hasn't been too uncomfortable keeping Miss Hollingsworth on longer than you would have liked. However, I hope that the wait will be proven worthwhile as you peruse these applicants — all of whom have a great deal of experience, as you requested. Two of them, especially, seem to be very well suited for your situation.

I look forward to your response and instruction on how you would like to proceed. I am at your service, as always.

Sincerely,

M. L. Hastings

Peter dropped the letter on the desk, the four applications spread out beside it. The decision he needed to make had become urgent. What was he prepared to do?

Both Lydia and Uncle Elliott had said Julia was perfect for his household, and he could finally admit to himself that they had not meant only as a governess. His stomach flipped at the thought, and he wondered how things could have changed so quickly.

But perhaps it hadn't been so quickly. Maybe he had simply been too scared to admit what could now be apparent from their first meeting in the broom closet. Julia was everything he did not know he wanted, and now that he'd accepted that knowledge, he was eager to move forward. However, the situation was delicate, and he needed to proceed with practical logic.

He folded Mr. Hastings's letter around the four applications and put them aside in order to open his appointment book. He scanned the next few days in order to refresh his memory. There was a livestock show in King's Lyn day after tomorrow, and then a buyer was coming to look at the hounds on Saturday. Monday, however, was open. He penciled in "Mrs. H in Feltwell," felt another flutter of anticipation in his belly, and closed the book. First things first.

CHAPTER TWENTY-NINE:
AMELIA

Amelia found plenty to keep her hands occupied, if not her mind, upon returning to Feltwell. She helped bake for the weekly dance at the assembly hall. She dusted and gardened and made bread and tried to forget her visit to Mr. Mayfield's house. And the confrontation with Julia. And Elliott's parting words. She felt more and more brittle with every passing day.

On Monday, she'd gone to Louisa's house to help little Sophie learn her letters. How on earth would that family squeeze another baby into that tiny cottage? She had been dreading a lonely evening at home when she turned up the walk of her house and saw a man standing there. It took a blink and another moment before she recognized Mr. Mayfield.

"My apologies for startling you, Mrs. Hollingsworth." He held the brim of his beaver hat in his hands, turning it nervously. "I had hoped you would be returning soon and decided to wait."

She was not prepared to see him or speak to him. Goodness, she could barely let herself think of him and her daughter living in that house and what could be happening between them. Each time she did, such fear and regret rose up in her throat that she felt she were choking.

"What are you doing here?" she asked, not even trying to keep the tightness from her voice.

"I wanted to speak with you."

What on earth would he want to speak with her about? And then she knew. He was going to try to convince her to withdraw her objection. Or, she considered hopefully, perhaps he had determined to turn Julia out and wanted Amelia's help with the transition. He had told Elliott from the start that he didn't want the slightest hint of scandal; perhaps his honor had won out.

"We can speak in the parlor," Amelia said, looking around as she made her way to the front door in hopes that none of her neighbors were watching. She'd had half a dozen people ask her after Elliott's visits about the fine gentleman who had called on her, and she did not like being the center of gossip. How long had he been waiting for her in full view?

He stepped aside so she could open the door, then followed her into the parlor.

"Let me prepare some tea," Amelia said without sitting.

"Please do not do so on my account. I am well enough without it."

"I just finished helping my daughter with her children." She didn't know why she told him as much, but she was nervous and wanted him to know how devoted she was to her family.

He sat only when she did, putting his hat on his knee. She really should take his hat, but she didn't want him to feel too welcome.

"Well, then," she said, keeping her chin up. "What was it you wanted to discuss with me?"

Mr. Mayfield stared at his hat a moment. He opened his mouth, then closed it. Took a breath. Opened his mouth again and then finally spoke. "I would like to ask your impressions of my household."

Amelia furrowed her brow. "I am not sure what you mean."

"I am aware of your concerns with having Julia in my home. I would like to know if your opinion has changed since your visit. I hope that you saw how well she cares for my daughters and how honorable my intentions are toward her."

"Intentions?" she repeated, raising her eyebrows and solidifying her position. A shimmer of power swept through her chest, fortifying her resolve. "I do not see how an employer should have any *intentions* toward his hired help."

He closed his eyes for a long moment, then fixed her with a level gaze. "I can assure you that nothing inappropriate has ever passed between Julia and myself. I have been a gentleman in every respect and have done nothing to break your trust."

"I have no trust to break, Mr. Mayfield. I have been uncomfortable with the situation from the moment I heard of it."

"Yes, but I had hoped that perhaps the dinner party changed your mind."

"It was a lovely evening, but it did nothing to change my mind. My daughter is not safe in your household."

He paled slightly, and she felt a pang of conscience. He hadn't personally done anything to earn her determination against him. But she wanted nothing to do with the Mayfields. She held his eyes until he looked away.

"You are still set against me, then."

"Yes, sir, I am. A mother wants what is best for all her children."

350

"As does a father," he added, his voice becoming sharper, which only set Amelia's back up that much more. "Julia loves my daughters as her own, and she is one of the kindest and most capable women I have ever known. I came today to ask for your blessing in formally courting her."

Amelia stared at him in shock. *He wants to court my daughter.*

She remembered being in Vauxhall Gardens with Elliott. Him leading her to a secluded corner, and her being the one to step forward, showing her willingness and wantonness. He'd run his thumb along her cheek and told her how beautiful she was and that he felt more alive when he was with her.

Lies.

At Almack's a few days later, she had learned that his father had died and he'd returned to East Ashlam. He hadn't written her before he left town, but she could forgive him as he must have been overwhelmed by the turn of events. Then she'd realized that he would inherit, which meant he would have more reason to marry. And soon! She would become Lady Howardsford and live in a grand house and save her father and love Elliott with her whole heart. It had been wicked to think that way in the

351

light of the tragedy of Elliott's father's passing, but with her father pressuring her to make a moneyed match and the invigoration she felt being with Elliott, how could she not have seen everything as a positive turn of events?

A week had passed. Then two. She wrote him twice, and when he did not reply, she comforted herself with the reminder that he was in mourning and certainly had a great deal of work to do with the transfer of the title. And then she did receive a letter, the words of which seared into her as hot as a branding iron. He had enjoyed their time together and wished her the best, but family matters were such that he would not be returning to London, perhaps for some time.

He'd broken her heart into a dozen pieces with that letter. Rejected. Abandoned. Not enough. The parting with Julia earlier this week came back to her as well. Rejected. Abandoned. Not enough.

"Mrs. Oswell has offered to house Julia," Mr. Mayfield continued, interrupting her painful reminiscence. "Julia can still care for the children, but she will not be living at my home. I will do everything that is honorable and right by her, Mrs. Hollingsworth."

"You have already discussed this with Julia? You have made this plan without having spoken to me, even though you know my concerns of this very thing?"

"I have *not* spoken to her of this," he responded. "I have come to you out of respect for you as her mother and because I am aware of your concerns and hoped to resolve them. But I am . . ." He took a breath. "I care a great deal about your daughter, Mrs. Hollingsworth, and would like the chance to see if we are as well suited as I believe we are, but that cannot happen without a formal and respectable courtship. I ask this of you with the hope of making her my wife and ensuring her comfort and happiness for the rest of her life. I can assure you that I will be a devoted husband to her in every way, should we suit as well as I hope."

Lies! Just like Elliott's endearments all those years ago. Amelia could not separate the two circumstances. "Of course you have fallen in love with her — that is what you Mayfields do. But she is not of your world, Mr. Mayfield. She has not been raised to be the mistress of an estate, the hostess of fine parties with people to wait on her and coddle her. She is your *servant,* and it would disgrace to both of you should you pretend she is anything different."

His jaw went taut. "I care nothing for dinner parties and society, nor have I any intention of changing her. I love her as she is — *because* of who she is. Does that mean nothing to you?"

"Pish," Amelia said, waving away his proclamations. "Love grows *through* marriage. It does not spring up like lust and infatuation does. I also know about your uncle's bribery — the financial gift he plans to bestow upon your marriage, which gift can only give you further motivation to take advantage where you can." She narrowed her eyes and dug to the very depth of her cruelty. "I would think you would know better than anyone the difficulty of an uneven match."

Heat rushed up her neck as her words rang in her ears. Had she truly flung his parents' scandal in his face? And not because she believed their sins made him a sinner but because she knew it would hurt him.

His neck reddened. His fingers clutching the brim of his hat were nearly white. "You will not give me your blessing, then."

"No, I will not, though I expect that you will no doubt move forward without it."

He stared at her, she stared back, but her heart was thumping. She reviewed everything that had been said. *I am right about this.* But it might not matter. Julia was of age. Mr. Mayfield was of the type who was used to getting his way, and he held all the power.

"I will not go against your wishes, Mrs. Hollingsworth. I decided from the moment I heard of your concerns about your daughter working in my household that I would do nothing to interfere with the relationship between mother and daughter."

He stood and seemed to catch sight of Richard's portrait for the first time. He stared at it for several seconds; she kept her eyes on him. He looked back at her, nodded, and headed toward the doorway, but he had only taken a few steps before he turned back to face her.

"Since you and I shall likely not cross paths again, I feel I must say that your holding so much against my uncle when he sacrificed his own happiness for the good of the rest of us is equally unfair. He has spent his life caring for us and doing what he could to restore our family name. I have done my best to prove that his sacrifice was not in vain, and I wish very much that you could see it. But, then, bitterness can become a comfort for some." He was unable to hide his disappointment. "Forgive me for speaking so plainly and wasting your time. I will set about replacing Julia as you have wanted from the start. I can only hope she can find as much happiness in her life as she could have had with me and my daughters. Good day."

Amelia stayed seated as he stalked from the room and let himself out. She expected him to slam the door, but he closed it softly. His parting words reverberated throughout the room. She pushed away the unwelcome and unreasonable regret rising up inside her. Mr. Mayfield didn't mean it when he'd said he would not go against her wishes. He would get what he wanted because he wanted it.

Amelia stood to leave, overcome with the need to do something, spare herself from replaying this moment in her mind. She remembered Mr. Mayfield looking at Richard's portrait and found her eyes drawn to him again.

How different things would have been if he had not left her alone. She'd never been as good without him as they had been together. What would he think of what Amelia had just done? She had wanted Julia to make a match and have a family — she'd never understood why Julia would want anything different — yet she had just sent that opportunity away. Because of her own pride? Because of her own fear? Her anger and hurt gave way to sorrow and regret, tears stinging her eyes before they fell.

What is wrong with me?

Richard would not have done what she just did. Not in a hundred lifetimes.

CHAPTER THIRTY:
JULIA

Leah hit the ball with the croquet mallet, and it went through the hoop — finally.

"Well done," Julia said as though this was Leah's first attempt, not her seventh.

"Is it my turn yet?" Marjorie asked.

"Almost." Julia positioned her mallet, but then hit the ball from the side so she did not overtake Marjorie, who was in the lead. "Gracious," she said, shaking her head and leaning on the mallet. "I was sure I had that lined up right."

Marjorie's eyes lit up with excitement as she hurried to take her own shot. The tip of her tongue showed between her lips as she focused. She pulled back her mallet, and then hit the ball as hard as she could. The ball went through both hoops and hit the post at the end.

"I did it!" She dropped her mallet and jumped up and down.

Julia should correct such unladylike behavior, but, then, these girls would only be little for a short time longer. They had plenty of time to learn the appropriate way of celebrating victory. Or, rather, not celebrating. But that lesson was for another day, not when one was eight years old and mastering the fine art of yard croquet.

Julia applauded. "Well done, Marjorie."

Leah threw down her mallet and stalked away from the circle yard.

Julia hurried after her. She might choose not to teach appropriate celebration behavior, but children were never too young to be taught sportsmanship. It took some doing to convince Leah to finish her game, but neither girl noticed that Julia's ball seemed to disappear into the rose bushes, leaving all the focus on Leah as she hit the ball over and over and over again. Eventually it made its terribly inefficient way through the last two hoops. Fortunately, Marjorie cheered for her sister. Leah beamed with pride.

Mr. Mayfield was gone today, though Julia did not know where, of course. They had developed a habit of being in the dog yard at the same time every morning this last week. She attended to the new puppies and to Bumbleberry, who was a fabulous adoptive mother, while Mr. Mayfield worked on weaning the older litter of pups onto the beefy gruel Cook made every night. They would talk — about the girls, about the dogs, about the weather, about livestock prices and crop expectations. Everything he said was interesting, and he listened to everything she said even if it wasn't.

He had told her that morning that he had an errand and would not be back until late but would check on the girls when he arrived. It was hard to remember how avoidant he had seemed in the past or how uncomfortable she had been in his presence. As to what it all meant . . . She avoided forcing an answer. It meant she was happy here. It meant he was too. For now, that was enough.

After luncheon was letters and numbers. Then supper. Then reading. Then bedtime. Julia tucked in the girls, explaining that their papa would come kiss them good night when he returned home. She took the supper tray to the kitchen. A plate of chicken and potatoes had been left for her, and she thanked Cook for supper before taking a candle with her to the third level.

Mr. Mayfield had told her she could avail herself of his books in the study anytime she liked, and she'd acted on the offer several times before. She told herself that was why she'd come tonight, to get a book, not in hopes that Mr. Mayfield had returned and she might "accidentally" encounter him.

Focus, she told herself. *You came for a book.*

That evening, she had told the girls the story of Moses being sent down the Nile in a basket and found herself wondering if there was more to the story. Did historians know which pharaoh it was that Moses' mother was trying to protect him from? Mr. Mayfield had a collection on Biblical teaching and interpretation, and she hoped to find something that would expand her understanding.

He was not in his study, though the candles had been lit in anticipation of his return. She put down her own candle and ventured into the room that smelled like him. She ran her fingers across the lacquered top of his desk, imagining him sitting behind it, studying the facts and figures that made up the running of his estate. The cover of a periodical discussing the treatment of racing dogs caught her eye, and she reached for it, but paused. He wasn't finished with it; he'd said so that morning when they had discussed it in general. It wouldn't be well-mannered of her to read it before he'd had the chance. Her eyes stayed on the cover as she moved toward the bookshelves, however.

She perused the shelves until she found an interpretive guide to the Old Testament. On her way back to the door, she fantasized about lighting a fire in the grate and putting her feet up on his stool. The thought made her smile, and then her eyes were drawn back to the periodical on the desk.

It was late, and Mr. Mayfield likely wouldn't be home in time to read it tonight, considering he wasn't back already. She could return it tomorrow on her way out of the house for her morning walk. He wouldn't know it was gone, but then he wouldn't mind if she borrowed it anyway. They could discuss the article tomorrow morning. She reached for the periodical for the second time, and her hand paused again, but not because of second thoughts.

Instead, her eyes settled on something else on the desk. A letter with familiar script and a familiar return — Hastings Staffing Services. She picked it up, and four letters fell out. Letters from Miss Gertrude Robinstone, Miss E. L. Housend, Miss Elizabeth Champion, and Mrs. Samantha Evenbrite.

She hadn't realized the household needed a new female staff member, but then she turned her attention to the letter that had been wrapped around the others and was now in her hand. The word *governess* jumped off the page. She paused barely a moment and then read every word of a letter not meant for her, though it was very much *about* her.

Julia swallowed once she finished, blinked back the tears rising behind her eyes, and read Mr. Hastings's letter one more time: *". . . I hope that it hasn't been too uncomfortable keeping Miss Hollingsworth on longer than you would have liked."*

Chapter Thirty-One: Peter

It was after ten o'clock Monday night when Peter returned from Feltwell. His mood had not been improved by the drizzly return trip, which became so intense at one point that he'd had to duck into an inn and wait out the worst of the storm. It was hard to believe his meeting with Mrs. Hollingsworth could have gone so badly. He remembered seeing the primrose border that led to the front door of her home and how he'd thought it a good omen to see some portion of that primrose meadow reflected there.

Fool.

Now he was left having to determine what he could do about it. He'd told Mrs. Hollingsworth he would replace Julia rather than pursue a courtship without Mrs. Hollingsworth's blessing, but with every mile, he had regretted such a promise. He had hoped his assurance would help Julia's mother realize how sincere he was in protecting their relationship, or maybe he was just playing the role of martyr, but the honor had further complicated the situation.

He wanted Julia in his life so badly his chest ached to consider the alternative, but to have her now meant going against her mother, in addition to the already-existing complications. If he broke his promise, he would prove himself the exact kind of man Mrs. Hollingsworth believed him to be. He had put himself in an impossible situation.

The girls did not rouse when he kissed them, and he pulled the covers to their chins, leaving as quietly as he had entered. He could see a light beneath Julia's door and considered knocking. She would come to the door, perhaps with her hair loose over her shoulders and wearing her nightdress. He could ask her about the girls and what she had done with them today. She might lean against the doorframe. They might laugh together at some silly thing Leah said or wonder where Marjorie came up with the questions she asked.

What would Julia do if he took her face in his hands and kissed her breathless?

He forced his feet down the hallway and away from her door.

Peter did not sleep. Instead he tossed and

turned and paced and raged until he determined his course — he would tell Julia everything. About her mother and Elliott. About his early determination to replace her but how that had become impossible for him to consider now. He would confess having promised her mother that he would not move forward without her blessing. It would be betraying her mother, but he could not hold this for a moment longer.

Perhaps Julia would be aghast at his assumption of her feelings and not even want to stay. The possibility terrified him, but every course he chose now presented a risk of one kind or another, and one truth had risen to the top: Julia was the center of fears and prejudices she knew nothing about. Her ability to make any choice was impossible when she did not know what it was she was choosing for or against. How he wished he'd confided in her before now instead of trying to be so blasted honorable!

It was still difficult to sleep, but easy to get out of bed when dawn lightened the room. Mornings had become something he looked forward to now that he and Julia had time together without anyone else looking on. They cared for the dogs together, talked, and got to know one another. Those minutes together when the day was brand-new were when he believed he had truly fallen in love with her.

Julia wasn't in the yard when he arrived, so he fed the hounds and checked on Sebastian and Viola. He had started running the greys with the other hounds, only they were faster than his horse and would be on either side of Peter from the start. After twenty minutes, they would lag, and once back in their pens, they would sleep most of the day, completely spent.

When he finished his tasks in the yard, he looked into the shed, expecting to find Julia there. Instead, Bumbleberry raised her head from the whelping box and growled. Queenie's five puppies were tucked in about her, sleeping. Her own puppies had overnighted in the yard alone for the first time last night, using the sheepskin dam for comfort and warmth. Peter backed out of the shed but did not look away immediately, struck by the realization of how well Bumbleberry had taken to raising Queenie's pups.

A cobwebbed fear he had not pulled from the corner for some time — that no one could love his daughters the way Sybil had — came forward. Maybe that was true, though he would never know because Sybil was not here to show the contrast. But his daughters had been loved since Sybil's death. Deeply. By Lydia, and now by Julia. The invigoration of the realization quickened his blood and increased his eagerness to talk to Julia as soon as possible. He had to know her heart. Then he — or they — could know how to move forward.

Bumbleberry growled again.

"I am not coming in." Peter began to close the door, then noticed that the food and water dishes were full and the dog had already been brushed. Julia had come already? Before seven o'clock?

He left the dog yard for the second floor of the house. The girls were still asleep, and there was no answer when he tapped on Julia's door. Short of asking after her with the other staff, he was unsure where else to look. Then he remembered her morning walks. He followed the path he'd seen her take, but she was not there, either. Some part of him knew he ought to be worried about her, but she hadn't gone missing, she'd just changed up her usual routine.

Peter's anxiety grew. He wanted to go inside and double-check each place where she could be, but he did not. Instead, he tied one of the rabbits Henry had hung in the stable to the back of his saddle and ran the foxhounds for an hour, then changed to a fresh horse and ran the greys at a full gallop until they began to lag behind.

It was nearly eleven before Peter returned to the house, changed into his everyday clothes, and settled himself in the study. He paced for a time, trying to find a solution or the appropriate approach, but his mind was choked with anxiety. He looked longingly at the doorway, mapping in his mind how this hallway led to that one, which led to the other that would take him to the nursery. Was it better to wait until the children's hour? Perhaps he should invite her to join him for dinner — but she'd refused his invitation to breakfast last week. He finally settled himself behind his desk, took a breath, and turned to the tasks waiting for him. He would be patient and keep to as normal a routine as possible.

When he entered the nursery for children's hour that evening, he tried to catch Julia's gaze, though she did not meet his eye. She draped the girls' dirty linens over her arm and then slipped through the door while the girls were wrapped around Peter's knees and he could not go after her. During playtime with his girls, he tried to keep his mind off their governess, but it became harder by the minute.

When Julia tapped on the door to signal

her return, he quickly kissed his daughters and hurried to intercept her, meeting her at the threshold and blocking her entrance. She stepped to the side as though allowing him to pass. He, instead, stepped forward, forcing her to step back into the hallway.

He closed the door behind him. "Could we talk, Julia?"

"I need to ready the girls for bed, Mr. Mayfield." She still would not meet his eyes.

"Is something wrong?"

She shook her head but continued to look at the floor.

He put a finger beneath her chin and tipped her face toward his. Her eyes were sad, her demeanor cautious.

"Something is the matter," he said.

The door behind him suddenly opened. He stepped away from Julia and dropped his hand as the door swung wide and Marjorie shot into the hall.

"Miss Julia! I get to choose the first story tonight."

Leah ducked under her sister's arm. "No, me. Miss Julia said I could choose."

"That was last night. Tonight is my turn."

Julia took advantage of the interruption and moved around him. "I do believe Marjorie is right, Leah. But we must have our nightgowns on before we read."

Peter watched Julia enter the nursery and close the door softly. She didn't meet his eyes.

It was almost an hour later when she let herself out of the nursery, and she startled when he pushed himself away from the wall where he'd been leaning, listening to her put the girls to bed.

"Mr. Mayfield!" she exclaimed. She looked at the door and listened for a reaction from within. When a few seconds passed without the girls seeming to have noticed, she turned back to him but only met his eyes a moment before she looked at the floor.

He kept his arms crossed over his chest. "What is the matter?"

She fiddled with the watch pinned to her bodice. "Nothing is the matter, Mr. Mayfield."

He put his finger beneath her chin and raised her eyes to meet his as he had before, praying they would not be interrupted this time. "Something is wrong."

Tears filled her eyes, but instead of wilting, she hit his hand away and stepped back. They stared at one another. He found himself at a complete loss for words. He'd seen her sad and uncomfortable and shy, but he'd never seen her angry.

"When were you going to tell me?" she snapped.

Peter let out a breath. She knew he'd gone to see her mother without telling her and, as much as he hated that she was hurt by it — or angered, apparently — it was somewhat of a relief since he would not have to confess himself. "I am sorry. I had not expected it would be necessary for me to tell you beforehand. I had hoped —"

"Not necessary?" She looked even more offended, and her hands went to her hips in the universal display of angry women. "I may be your servant, Mr. Mayfield, but I am also a person and a woman who has to find her own way in the world. Were you just going to bring her in one day and turn me out? Did you not think for one moment how I might be affected by your decision?"

"Bring her here?" Peter said, trying to keep pace with the conversation. "I wanted her blessing."

Julia's eyebrows came together as she stared at him. "Her blessing?"

He took a breath, any hopes of having a well-crafted conversation about this topic lost. "She would not give it. What's more, I promised her that I would not move forward without it."

Julia's looked completely confused.

372

"Promised who?"

"Your mother."

Julia's hands fell to her sides. "My *mother*?"

The confusion was catching. "What exactly are we talking about?"

"The governess you are hiring to replace me."

Peter opened his mouth to explain he wasn't hiring a new governess, but he realized that should things go well with Miss Julia, he *would* be hiring a new governess. How would he explain this? "I think we are both a bit confused right now."

Julia did not seem ready to admit as much and took a breath. "I know about the letter."

Peter proceeded with caution. "What letter would that be?"

"The one I read was from Mr. Hastings, but it was apparently in response to a letter *you* sent in hopes of replacing me. Why? Because I have done a poor job? Because of my mother and her interfering ways?"

"No," Peter said quickly, putting out his hands in surrender. "Well, perhaps in part because of your mother, but . . . ."

She opened her mouth to speak, and he hurried to cut in before things became even more muddied. "I did write to Mr. Hastings after I learned of your mother's concerns, but by the time he sent the response, I had changed my mind, quite a lot."

She crossed her arms over her stomach, still confused but not so angry.

He stepped closer, and though she watched him skeptically, she did not move away. He reached for one hand, then the other, before pulling her closer, knowing as he did so that he was making all of this more complex. She did not resist, but neither did she drop her suspicions. Her hand felt so right in his. "I should have told you all of this before I spoke to your mother."

Her expression changed yet again. "You spoke to my mother?"

"I wanted her blessing."

He could nearly see her repeating the words in her mind. She blinked, and for an instant, he thought she might turn and run. He tightened his hold on her hands, just in case. They could not afford another conversation like this one, and he was prepared to explain everything. At the same time, the things he had thought reflected feelings on her part suddenly seemed ridiculous and overly optimistic. But to retreat now would be the end of his opportunities — he could feel it.

"I went to Feltwell yesterday to ask your

mother's blessing so that I might court you. I had assumed I would return with success and things would change between you and I in all the ways I have hoped they would and feared they couldn't."

She blinked at him. "What?"

He said it all again, slower and without missing a detail.

"You wanted to court me?"

Was she disgusted? He could not tell and simply nodded.

"Sh-she refused?"

He swallowed and nodded again. He saw her jaw tighten slightly. Dare he hope that was a good sign?

When she spoke, her voice did not have the shock and surprise of her other responses but was a bit harder. "Did she say why she refused?"

"To sum up her feelings, I suppose she distrusts my family and therefore myself. It seemed I could say nothing to convince her I am an honorable man." He paused and shook his head. "Perhaps she is right."

Julia turned her head slightly, watching him.

"As I left, I gave her my word that I would not pursue you without her blessing, but I fear that may be the first promise of my life I am unable to keep."

"I need to make sure I have this right," Julia said slowly. Her hand seemed to relax within Peter's grip. "You were aware of my mother's objections to my being here some time ago. When?"

"Within two weeks of your arrival here," Peter said, swallowing his regret. "I was not yet convinced of how much we — myself as well as the girls — needed you, and my reaction was to protect us all from scandal, which is why I wrote to Mr. Hastings."

"Why did you not tell me of my mother's complaint?"

"I did not tell you because it was not my story to tell. I believed that replacing you quickly was the best course, though I see how unfair it would have been. You know of your mother's connection to my uncle, then?"

She nodded, though slowly. "They knew each other in London and did not get on." She withdrew her hands from his and took a small step back.

Peter hesitated, but could not help but attempt to further defend himself, and his uncle. "They were all but engaged when my grandfather died, and I am afraid my uncle fairly broke your mother's heart. My uncle blames his poor explanation to your mother as the root cause for her objection to your being here. You did not know?"

"No," she said with a degree of tightness. "I did not know the whole of that story."

"It was easy, I am sure, for her to compound her bad opinion with the scandalous behavior of my parents and my aunts. I could not necessarily argue against her concerns, and I did not feel it was my place to tell you. This was early in your time here, before I had come to . . . to love you. Now I find it impossible to imagine my family or my home without you."

She smiled, but then returned to a neutral expression and shook her head as though not yet ready to believe it.

Peter had never felt so vulnerable in his entire life and wondered how such careful living could have put him in the middle of so much complication. "I wrote to Mr. Hastings in an attempt to protect us all — you, your mother, and myself. His response a few days ago forced me to admit that the extent of my feelings had changed."

Her expression remained cautious. "And rather than giving me any hint of such feelings, you went to my mother?"

She made it sound foolish. "It was the honorable course," he reminded her. "A gentleman procures the blessing of a parent or elder brother before he moves forward with a courtship. You must know how hard I have attempted to live an honorable life, Julia. It has been the goal of every step I have ever taken."

She nodded slowly, thoughtfully, then met his eye and cocked her head to the side. "And my mother refused to give her blessing." She spoke evenly, not letting a hint of her feelings show.

"She did."

"Does that change your feelings?"

"Not at all." If his heart weren't already beating like a woodpecker against his ribs he'd have surely noticed it speed up. He had said so much out loud already and felt completely naked while poised on the edge of a cliff, waiting for her to react to his confessions.

Julia closed her eyes briefly and clenched her jaw before looking at him again. "You must know, Mr. Mayfield, that —"

He reached for her hand without thought and squeezed it. "For the love of heaven, you must call me Peter." He could not be Mr. Mayfield, her employer and the father of her charges, right now.

Instead of pulling away, she took a step toward him, and a warm shiver calmed him. Somewhat. "You must know, Peter" — she gave the slightest smile before continuing; a

378

smile that lit the sun — "I am a grown woman and do not need her blessing."

He swallowed. "I gave my word." He would give anything to go back and undo that promise. Put his heart before honor, once and for all.

She didn't reply, but took another small step closer to him. Her eyes were bright and a little bit nervous, but excited, too. She reached out her free hand and touched his forearm as though asking his permission to be this close. "Does her opinion mean more than mine?"

Words failed him. He slipped his hand around her waist and pulled her closer still, watching her face as she followed the silent instructions. She was only a few inches shorter than he was, which made it so easy to duck his chin and brush his lips across her own. Light and fiery. She startled — or at least he thought she did. Maybe it was him. He began to pull back so they could consider, reassess, decide together what to do from here, but she took sudden hold of his arm and, as easy as it was for him to duck his chin, it was just as easy for her to lift hers and kiss him back.

More fire than light this time, and completely maddening.

His hand at her waist slid around her

back; her hand on his arm moved to his neck. Touch and sound and warmth and silence. Vertigo. A crashing wave. He thought he ought not deepen the kiss, suspecting she had never been kissed before, but he'd no sooner thought it than he was pulling her closer still, drawing her in, pressing for more until everything disappeared except for the two of them and the cracking passion.

When he finally pulled back, her eyes fluttered open, and she stared at him, then smiled — thankfully. He smiled back without releasing her.

"I promised myself I wouldn't do that," he whispered, watching her mouth and barely holding himself back from doing it again.

"Then I have never been so pleased to have a promise broken."

He kissed her again, but when the aching turn frenzied, he released her.

She leaned forward, not letting him go, and it was like starting and stopping the most beautiful piece of music ever played, until finally, he took a step away.

"If we do not stop, I fear we never will."

"I do not think I would mind." She smiled, and he began to drown again.

He laughed and lifted one of her hands to

his lips — perhaps to remind them both that he was still a gentleman and she was still a young woman who deserved his restraint. He held her eyes. "I do not want to be the reason for a breach of your relationship with your mother."

Julia's expression hardened, which made it a bit easier not to kiss her. Reality was returning for both of them. "You will not be the reason . . . Peter. She is the one who created this situation. I will talk to her," Julia said.

Peter shook his head. "I can't let —"

She raised her eyebrows, which was all the reprimand he needed. Was he going to give more credit to her mother's wishes than their own? After that kiss? After her confession of feeling that fit his own so thrillingly?

He reached a hand to her face, unable to stop touching her smooth skin. He trailed a thumb to her lips, still warm from his earlier attention. *Gracious.* "You will need to move to the vicarage."

She furrowed her brow.

"So that I might formally court you."

She smiled and cut the distance between them again with a single word spoken from breathless lips. "When?"

CHAPTER THIRTY-TWO: ELLIOTT

"Mrs. Hollingsworth to see you, my lord."

Elliott looked up from where he was playing chess against himself. Life as a gentleman bachelor could be very boring. "Mrs. Hollingsworth?" He scrambled to his feet, and the hot-water bottle he'd been resting on his knee fell to the floor.

Brookie nodded. "I put her in the blue room. Tea is already being prepared."

"Perfect, excellent. Thank you." Elliott pushed back from the desk and headed for the door before remembering he'd taken off his shoes — his feet got so blasted hot sometimes. He went back to his chair and slipped back into his shoes, then remembered that he'd untied his cravat.

"Brookie," he called out, reaching the doorway in time to see the servant turn back. "Please send Heathrow to my chamber to help make me presentable."

"Yes, my lord."

Elliott hurried to his bedchamber, changed his coat to the blue one, and then to the charcoal instead. Amelia had once told him in London that gray made his eyes look bluer. Once he had the new coat on, he realized his red-and-green-striped waistcoat did not match. By the time Heathrow arrived, the room was strewn with discarded articles, but Elliott had settled on the right combination — a blue-and-gray waistcoat with the charcoal coat and black breeches. Heathrow kept his fashion judgments to himself and crossed to tie Elliott's cravat while Elliott stared at the ceiling and wondered why Amelia had come.

Finally, he was ready. He turned side to side in the mirror to make certain, then nodded to Heathrow and left him to clean up the mess while he hurried down the stairs. Outside of the blue room, he paused to take a breath before entering.

Amelia was standing, looking out the window. He hoped she was impressed by what she saw, even though that made him feel childish. She was wearing a lavender gown with a white shawl over her shoulders.

"Good afternoon, Mrs. Hollingsworth." He bowed slightly when she turned to face him. It was a relief to see she was not angry, but he could not read much else into her expression. She looked tired, mostly, but then she'd traveled some fifty miles, which meant that her errand was important. "I apologize for making you wait. Had I known you were coming, I'd have been at the ready."

"I thought not informing one another of visits prior was our arrangement." She smiled, which allowed him to smile too. She was making jokes — that was a good sign. Still, her overall demeanor remained subdued.

"Would you like to sit down?" He waved toward one side of the large room where two semicircular, blue-velvet settees ringed a small table. Elliott had called them "moon chairs" when he had been a child.

"Thank you." She moved from the window and sat. Brookie had made the right choice in putting her in the blue room as opposed to the west parlor or the front parlor, which was filled with a nauseating array of floral patterns. His mother had decorated it years ago, and Elliott hadn't the heart to change it after she passed, but he found the room too busy to be comfortable.

In the blue room, however, with its big windows and muted tones, Amelia was presented at her very best — bright and . . .

well, not quite cheery.

Elliott sat across from her. "To what do I owe the pleasure of your visit?" Their last interaction had been in the carriage leaving Peter's house. He'd rewritten the conversation a dozen times since then and wished that reliving time could be so easy. Even in his editions of what he wished had transpired, however, he'd known he could not change *her* feelings or reactions. Today, her posture included an air of humility he had not felt from her before.

She took a breath and then let it out, her back perfectly straight. "I want to know what happened when your father died."

Elliott blinked. "Oh. Well . . ."

"Is it difficult for you to talk about?"

"Not necessarily," Elliott replied. "Just unexpected."

A sound in the doorway drew their attention, and they both looked to see the first footman coming in with the tea tray. Brookie hovered behind him as though supervising his charge. The footman set the tray on the small table, then the two servants departed.

"May I pour?" Amelia asked when they were alone.

"Certainly," Elliott said.

He watched the graceful and confident movements of Amelia's hands as she prepared their cups — his with only cream, just as he liked it. Her age showed on her hands, the map of her life etched upon them. They were not the hands of a lady — flawless and smooth and meant for nothing more taxing than pushing a needle through fabric. These were the hands of a woman, a mother, a wife — someone who had worked hard and given much.

Yet she had the manners of a lady: moving with a whisper, setting cups upon saucers without the barest sound, stirring without scraping the spoon on the bottom of the cup, and then tapping the spoon twice on the rim before setting it aside. She chose one of each of the items from the kitchen — a pecan scone, a lemon biscuit, and a cheese tart — then put his plate in front of him. When she looked up, she blushed to find him watching her.

Why was it that no matter how often he saw the worst in her, he never forgot that *this* was under the surface? What he wouldn't give to help her step out of the hurt and fear she surrounded herself with so tightly and see this version of Amelia each time he encountered her.

"Thank you, Amelia."

She inclined her head, then prepared her cup. She took one sip before returning it —

noiselessly — to the saucer. She looked at her knees a moment, then lifted her head. "I remembered this morning on the drive here that, shortly before you left London, you had wanted a horse for your birthday. It was a black stallion you'd seen at Tattersalls, and you asked your father to purchase it, but he responded that you were too old for birthday gifts. You were quite frustrated, do you remember?"

"Not really," he said, shaking his head. "Much of what happened then mashes together in my memory. My father died a few weeks after I turned twenty-four." Other memories did stand out, however. Did he dare admit them to her? She made him feel both vulnerable and cautious, and yet he longed to . . . what? Be at peace with her? Feel as connected to her as he once had? Be understood instead of accused?

"Do you truly want to know the whole of what happened, Amelia? I have no wish to burden you, so if what you want is for us to be friends again, then we are friends. I have no quarrel with you, I never have, and I have already determined that I will have no additional interference with Peter's household. You and I need not cross one another's paths ever again if that will bring you peace."

"You are far more kind than I have been, and I acknowledge that. You have tried to tell me, at least twice before, the circumstances concerning breaking off our courtship, and I have not wanted to hear it. I would like to hear it now, however, if you do not mind telling me."

It was on the tip of his tongue to ask her why she wanted to know *now,* but he did not want to risk getting off track. He had wanted to tell her the truth, for both their sakes and for Peter and Julia's too. Now she was asking. He prayed that neither of them would regret it.

And so he told her. About his father and his family. About his responsibilities. And she listened. Without interruption, without defense. What was more, he could tell that she understood. He finished, and the air seemed to buzz with the words already said. She looked at her lap and fiddled with the strings of her shawl. "I wish I had known all of this back then."

"Why?"

He expected her to be defensive, but she was thoughtful and quiet.

"I don't know why, Elliott, truth be told. I was hurt and embarrassed and certain that my life was over, but . . ."

Elliott shifted. Was the bridge they had

built these last minutes strong enough for him to ask questions too? He decided to chance it. "When I returned to London after those first two years, I learned you had married shortly after I'd left. You already had a son. I can appreciate how painful my leaving must have been at the time, but your heartbreak was only temporary." His tone changed dramatically as he'd said these last words. "Your banker filled your heart pretty well after I left, I believe."

She lifted her head, humility checked. "*My* banker?" she repeated.

"You'd told me of him once," Elliott reminded her, sitting back slightly and lacing his fingers in front of him. "You had met him when visiting your aunt in Feltwell. I remembered because the village was not so far from Howardhouse and my father had used *his* father in some matter of business or another. He wrote to you when you were in London. You found his attention flattering but silly as he was lower class than your family."

Her face flushed, but she did not lose her temper as Elliott half expected.

She took a breath and spoke in an even voice. "My father was eager for me to marry when he sent me to London. He had debts he hoped to pay off if I made a good match.

I am the youngest of four daughters, and none of my sisters had married all that well. I told him about you, of our mutual interest and the conversations we'd had about a future together. I admit I exaggerated somewhat in hopes of impressing him, and it worked. He was less critical — after all you were the heir to a viscountcy — and then you left. Without even seeing me. I was humiliated. My father was angry and refused to support my stay in London any longer. I went to stay with my aunt, and there was *my banker.* No one else wanted me — not my father, not you. Richard was kind and hardworking, and he adored me. I realized I could make a good life with him."

"Did you love him?" Elliott asked, his chest feeling strangely empty, as though his heart were echoing through a cavern. So many secrets. How many more secrets and broken promises did society hide from each other?

"I loved him enough — in the beginning. But in time, that love grew into something beyond my expectations." Amelia paused, and an air of reverence settled about the room. "He was a good husband to me, Elliott. He was kind, attentive, and steady, especially when I wasn't. He was an excellent father, and he took good care of us.

When he died" — she blinked quickly, perhaps holding back tears he could not see — "I learned that *actual* heartbreak was not the unfulfilled fantasy of a young girl. *That* pain was nothing compared to losing the man I loved so completely, my partner in life and the father of my children."

Elliott had felt envy when he'd seen Richard Hollingsworth's portrait above the fireplace in her modest home. He had felt envy when he'd met Julia and seen in her the traits of both her parents, evidence of a life he could have had. But he realized now that he could not have had *that* life with her.

Had he married Amelia, things would not have been the same. She would not have had the lifestyle they had both expected she would have with him because Elliott would not have been able to apply himself to his family's rescue. He may not have experienced the cultures outside of England that helped him develop his theory of how important strong family ties could be. Julia would not be his child; there would be no Julia at all.

"I am happy to know you had a good life, Amelia. It is what I had always wanted for you. But I am sorry you have been alone for such a long time and that you still feel the weight of those past hurts. I had hoped that leaving as I did would spare you pain, and I am very sorry that it did not."

Amelia began blinking rapidly, and she put a hand over her mouth and closed her eyes.

Elliott leaned forward. Was she crying? "Amelia? Are you all right?"

She nodded, then paused, then shook her head.

Elliott pulled his handkerchief from his pocket and held it out to her across their now-cold tea. She took the cloth from him and dabbed at her eyes. He looked around, feeling lost. What else was a man supposed to do in a situation like this?

She took a deep breath and then spread the handkerchief out on her lap, smoothing all the corners and looking at it rather than Elliott. "Peter came to see me yesterday."

She spoke so quietly that Elliott almost didn't hear her. "He did?"

She looked up. "You didn't know?"

"That he was going to visit you? No. I have not spoken to him since the day after the dinner party. What was the purpose of the visit, if I might ask?"

Her chin trembled. "He wanted my blessing to court Julia. He said she would move in with the vicar, that he would be a perfect gentleman, and that he loved her and wanted to marry her."

"You don't say," Elliott said, leaning back in his chair and feeling his chest swell with pride to know that Peter had taken such initiative. Good for him.

"I told him no."

Elliott froze. "What?"

She looked at him, her eyes pleading. "I told him that I would never be comfortable with Julia in his house, that she was too far below him to be happy in such a match, and that he was selfish and spoiled and undeserving of my blessing."

Elliott braced his elbows on his knees and dropped his head into his hands. He could picture Amelia saying those words — the woman had a razor tongue — and how such words would have cut Peter. His heart ached. "Oh, Amelia," he said under his breath.

She continued. "He told me the grudge I held against you was unfair, that you had sacrificed your happiness for everyone else. I did not know what he was talking about."

Elliott remained where he was, head in his hands and heart in his throat. After nearly a minute of silence, Elliott straightened. "Julia is of age, Amelia. His asking for your blessing was a courtesy, not a requirement."

"I know." She dabbed at her eyes again. "I told him I was sure he would go forward anyway, but he said he wouldn't. He said he hadn't confessed his feelings to Julia before he'd come to me."

"No, he would not put you and Julia at odds with each other by talking to her first. He will, instead, bury his feelings and convince himself that he isn't worthy of your trust or Julia's love. He's lived beneath the shame of his birth all his life and has never felt as though he deserves the good he's had. He'll replace Julia with a new governess so as to spare them both, and then you will have exactly what you wanted."

Amelia closed her eyes, and a tear dripped into her lap.

Some part of him wanted to offer her comfort while the rest of him was revolted by what she'd done. How could a good woman — and he knew she *was* a good woman — be so cruel? Not only to Peter but to her own daughter.

Her shoulders shook, and she dropped her chin to her chest.

Elliott remained in his chair, trying to think of possible solutions to this muddle. Could it be as easy as Amelia apologizing and giving her blessing? *Should* it be that easy?

Taking a chance, he stood and crossed to her settee. He sat beside her and put his arm around her shoulders. She turned her face into his shoulder and sobbed.

"Amelia," he said softly after she'd regained some of her composure a few minutes later.

She lifted her head to look at him, torment showing clearly in her red-rimmed eyes and fallen countenance. He was prepared for her to pull away, but instead she relaxed against him, her head on his shoulder and her hand against his chest. The sensations of holding her close, of being needed, were invigorating.

They sat in silence for several seconds until Elliott finally spoke. "Peter confessed to you his love for Julia. Do you know how she feels about him?"

She shook her head. She did not pull away.

"Did you ever think to ask?"

CHAPTER THIRTY-THREE:
AMELIA

Elliott invited Amelia to stay at Howard-house Tuesday night, and she accepted. Elliott explained to her that he had hired an Indian cook because of his love for the region's food, and they ate what he called Tandoori chicken. It was a spicy chicken served over long-grain rice with flatbread and chutney on the side. While the chicken was *quite* spicy, she liked the flavors, and the flatbread was delicious. They talked about India, and Amelia's children, and parliament, and Elliott's bad knee. It was comfortable and nice.

Amelia slept in a guest room in the south wing. Elliott had been a perfect gentleman, not even kissing her hand when they parted for the night, though she would not have minded if he had.

They enjoyed breakfast together, and then he walked her to the front drive where, instead of the hired carriage she'd asked for, his own barouche waited.

"Elliott," she said with mild reprimand.

"Don't argue with me, woman." He strode ahead of her to open the door. She hesitated, but then allowed the kindness to break through her pride and accepted his hand to help her step inside. She enjoyed the feel of her hand in his and wished she had the courage to tell him that. Last night, with its ease and honesty, had been healing.

"You are on to Feltwell, then?" he asked once she had settled onto the bench.

They had talked about many things, but not what she would do next — not since she'd melted into him and he'd let her cry out all her regrets. She should be embarrassed, any other woman of breeding would be, but all she could feel was grateful. And strengthened. "Elsing, I think."

"You think?" he asked with raised eyebrows and a teasing grin. "It might be best if you make the decision at the beginning of your journey rather than the end."

She shook her head; what a tease he was. "Elsing, then." She needed to talk with Julia, with perhaps more humility than she had allowed herself to express, or even feel. For so long she had needed to be so certain. Of everything. To admit that she had gone too far and embraced her fears at the expense of her daughter's best interest was overwhelming. She did not know how to fix it, but she feared, if she did nothing, the rift between her and Julia would never heal.

Beyond that, what if Peter Mayfield was the man to give Julia the life Amelia had always wanted for her? The irony she could see now that her vision had cleared made her sad. All she had wanted was for Julia to settle down and be a wife and mother. Yet that was exactly what she had fought against.

Elliott had not closed the door yet. "Would you like me to come with you?"

"Yes," she said automatically, then shook her head. "But no. I think Julia and I need to have this conversation between ourselves." How her stomach rolled at the difficulty of what lay ahead. Yet, in the space of one hour, she and Elliott had resolved thirty years of hurt and ignorance. She was learning that the truth held great healing power.

"Very well," Elliott said. "I wish you the best, and thank you for staying the night. It was the nicest evening I have had in a very, *very* long time."

"For me as well." And she meant it, which was remarkable. She had been so angry with him for so long, even when she thought she wasn't. And now the anger was receding, and while regret lingered in its place, she felt calm and relieved of the burden. She stretched out her hand. He took hold of it and squeezed her fingers. "Thank you, Elliott." She didn't specify what she was thanking him for.

"You are very welcome, Amelia." He brought her gloved hand to his lips and kissed the fingers while holding her eyes. A sense of energy rushed throughout her body. It was something she had not felt for so long, and though she was tempted to stay and explore that sensation, she felt it wiser not to. Her relationship with Julia was paramount. Whatever might follow between her and Elliott would come later, but she hoped they had found a new starting point.

Chapter Thirty-Four:
Peter

Peter stood beside his desk with his hands behind his back as Mrs. Allen led Colleen into the study. He invited them to sit, which they did. Mrs. Allen's expression was perfectly neutral. Colleen was barely hiding her fear.

"Thank you for meeting with me, Colleen," Peter said. He did not want to increase her anxiety, but neither did he want to make this too easy. "I have spent this morning puzzling through a situation, and I think I have found the root of it. I am hoping you can help me."

"I-I will try, Mr. Mayfield. If I can." She swallowed.

"I spoke with Mrs. Allen this morning about an upcoming change in my household and was reminded that you have helped with the girls for some years as needed, correct?"

Colleen glanced at Mrs. Allen, then back

to Peter, still confused. "Yes, sir."

"And you once harbored a hope of being their governess."

"Yes, sir," Colleen whispered.

"Mrs. Allen and I did not entertain that request. Do you know why?"

Colleen shook her head.

Peter glanced at Mrs. Allen and gave her a nod.

"Miss McCormick, or rather Mrs. Oswell, was a nursemaid," Mrs. Allen explained. "She taught the girls basic letters, but she did not have the formal training Miss Marjorie needs, especially now that she is older. She was not musical, for instance, or schooled in literature or mathematics. Mr. Mayfield's advertisement for the governess position specifically requested someone with teaching experience so that he would be able to have the girls educated at home."

"We had no qualms with the way you interacted with the girls," Peter said, drawing Colleen's attention away from the housekeeper. "And if I had only been looking to replace Lydia, you would have been the first choice since the girls are so familiar with you, but I was looking for a teacher. Do you understand?"

She nodded slowly.

"I have heard that you have not been

particularly welcoming to Miss Hollingsworth. Is this why, Colleen? Have you been upset that she took the position you felt should have come to you?"

She began to cry, her round face crumpling as her shoulders pulled forward. "Are you turning me out?"

Peter handed her a handkerchief. "I am not sure."

That Julia was willing to entertain the idea of Colleen taking on some of the responsibility for the girls was yet one more affirmation of Julia's good-hearted nature.

"Miss Hollingsworth has been an exceptional governess, Colleen, and, as I'm sure you have heard whispered about, will very likely become the girls' mother in a few months' time. I trust in my staff to be able to make this transition and afford *everyone* the respect he or she deserves. Based upon your history with Miss Hollingsworth, do you feel that you can do that?"

Colleen nodded. "I *am* sorry, Mr. Mayfield. Please do not turn me out."

Good. Peter and Mrs. Allen shared an encouraged look. "I do not want to turn you out, Colleen. You have served this household for a long time, and this is the only complaint against you. Even with the struggles you have felt toward Miss Hollingsworth, she says you are remarkably helpful with the girls, and Mrs. Allen vouches for your good character and work ethic."

Were it up to him, Peter would likely have simply let Colleen go rather than risk additional difficulties between her and Julia. But it was not up to him. A rush of pleasure and excitement coursed through him at the thought that soon he would have Julia beside him to help make these types of decisions all the time. To make them a family again.

"I love those girls, Mr. Mayfield." She began to cry again. "They are my very heart. I have . . . I have been so envious, and it was very wrong of me."

"Well, then, I have a proposal."

She blinked quickly at him and held her breath.

"Miss Hollingsworth will be a hands-on mother. She will manage their education and a good deal of their care — it is her nature. I will not be hiring another governess, but I will need someone to act as a caretaker for the girls. This person would need to work directly with Miss Hollingsworth, which would require some humility and cooperation. Would you be interested in such a position?"

"Do you mean it?" she breathed.

He smiled for the first time. "I do, if you think you can manage."

"Yes!" She nodded vigorously. "I can manage, and I will make up for all my poor treatment of Miss Hollingsworth. You must know I am not a cruel person."

"If you were, Colleen, we would not be having this conversation."

CHAPTER THIRTY-FIVE: JULIA

Julia arranged the letter tiles into a word for Marjorie to transcribe onto her slate, then turned to Leah sitting on the other side of her and went through a list of words that started with the short *e* sound, which was where she was in today's lesson.

"Eh-lephant," Julia said. "Eh-verything. Eh-legant."

Leah dutifully repeated each word.

The door to the nursery opened, and Julia glanced up, hoping it was Peter, even though he was at the vicarage making arrangements for her to move there this weekend. Yesterday evening had changed her entire world. They had seen one another that morning in the dog yard. It had taken them twice as long as usual to do the morning chores, but the privacy was priceless, and the ease in which they had transitioned from employer and governess to something else was surprising and very welcome.

405

It was not Peter at the door; it was Mr. Allen. He gave her a slight frown she could not immediately interpret, and then stepped aside to reveal her caller.

Julia felt a jolt of surprise at seeing her mother tentatively step into the room.

"Thank you, Mr. Allen," Julia said after the initial shock had passed, glad no one could tell how her chest thrummed with the increased speed of her heart. Her plan to go to Feltwell next week and *announce* to her mother what direction her life was taking crumbled in an instant. The confrontation would take place now, and Julia was not very good at confrontation.

The butler nodded and backed out of the room, leaving Mother standing just over the threshold.

Julia whispered to the girls to continue with their lessons, then stood in a measured way, determined to present herself in a calm and mature manner.

Mother looked ill at ease standing in this room that had become so comfortable to Julia.

"Good afternoon, Mother," Julia said, more polite than cool, she hoped. She kept her voice low to keep the girls from over-hearing. "I was not expecting you."

"No, I am sure you were not." She cleared

406

her throat, looked past Julia to the girls, who were not disguising their interest very well, and then back to Julia. "Could we perhaps speak in private?"

Julia opened her mouth to agree, then closed it. She did not have to agree to her mother's wishes and put everything and everyone else aside to comply. She steeled herself and then spoke. "We have another half an hour of lessons, then the girls will take their quiet hour. We could speak at that time, quietly."

Mother looked about the room as though evaluating whether or not it was a fitting place for whatever it was she'd come to discuss. "We cannot, perhaps, take a walk in the gardens during quiet hour?"

It was hard not to give in, but Julia was determined to stand her ground. She could not very well prove herself a grown woman capable of making her own decisions if she allowed herself to be bullied in something as small as this. "You may converse with me here in half an hour, or you can wait until five o'clock when I leave the nursery so the girls might have time with Mr. Mayfield. I'm sure Mr. Allen can set you up in the drawing room with some tea in the meantime. There is a good collection of books in that room."

Her mind filled with the idea that she was giving direction above her place in this home, and yet when she and Mr. Mayfield married, this would be her home as well. She would be mistress of it. A shot of anxiety passed through her chest. How would she manage that?

Mother considered Julia's suggestion without irritation, which Julia found surprising. "I should prefer to converse with you during quiet hour, then."

"Very well." Julia waved toward the writing desk and chair near the window. "You are welcome to rest while we finish."

Julia knew she was being unreasonably determined. There was no reason why she could not have quiet hour now and resume lessons later — she'd done it often enough when one thing or another interfered with their daily routine — but she was feeling stubborn. Mother "forbidding" Julia's relationship with Peter was reason enough to make her wait.

"Might I help with the lessons?" Mother asked. She remained standing, fidgeting with the side of her skirt and looking uncertain — something Julia had rarely seen. Her mother was the type to command a room or organize a committee, and yet right now Julia was the one in charge. Interesting.

"That would be appreciated, Mother. Thank you."

Mother joined them at the teaching table, a circular table with two curved benches. Mother sat beside Leah, and Julia quickly explained what they had been working on so that she could take up reciting words with the soft *e* sound, allowing Julia to focus solely on Marjorie's penmanship.

They worked separate from one another, though Julia kept an ear tuned to her mother's interactions with Leah. Despite herself, she felt her heart softening with memories of when she had been the pupil.

Mother would sit with her for hours, teaching letters and numbers, then words and equations. Simon had gone to a boarding school when he turned ten years old, despite it being a dear expense and unusual for their class. Louisa and Julia had attended a local parish school. Most girls only attended to the age of fourteen, though Louisa and Julia had stayed until they were seventeen, and Julia had stayed on two more years as an assistant teacher.

It was only later in her life that Julia realized the sacrifice her parents had made to educate them so far above the expectations of their class and sex. Her parents had wanted their children to have choices and opportunity. How ironic that Mother had then disagreed with nearly every choice and opportunity Julia had followed since then.

Leah had worked through the list of soft *e* words, and so they moved on to the *f* sound.

"Oh, this is an easy one," Mother said, looking at the primer in her hand. Julia prickled slightly. If it turned out that it was not easy for Leah, then what?

"*F*— first. Sometimes in a game you go first."

"Sometimes Marjorie goes first," Leah said in a complaining tone. "She says she should *always* go first because she is the oldest."

Marjorie leaned past Julia and Mother to scowl at her sister. "I do not always say that."

"We are focused on *your* work, Marjorie." Julia redirected her attention.

"*F*— finger," Mother said. "How many do you have?"

"Ten!" They counted Leah's fingers.

"Did any of those numbers start with an *f*?"

Leah paused, then exclaimed, "Five!"

"Yes," Mother praised. "Excellent. There's one more number that started with *f*."

Leah was quiet for a few moments. Mother was changing up the exercise, but not in a bad way. Just not Julia's way.

"Four!"

"Yes. Oh, that is very good. What are some other words that begin with *f*?"

"Fuh-fuh-fuh — furry. The puppies are very furry."

Julia had an idea and arranged the letter tiles into the word *furry* for Marjorie to write.

"Excellent. And I bet they are also fuh-friendly."

"Yes, they are *so* friendly, Mrs. Mother," Leah said. Julia pursed her lips together to keep from laughing.

"You may call me Mrs. Hollingsworth."

"Mrs. Holl— eng— uh . . ."

"How about 'Mrs. Amelia,' " Julia offered. She caught her mother's eye, and they both smiled slightly. They were building something here.

They went back to their work, Mother helping Leah identify words and Julia arranging the tiles for Marjorie to write those words on her slate. It became a challenge for Marjorie to transcribe the word before Mother and Leah moved on to the next one. As it turned out, there were a great deal of attributes that started with *f* to describe the puppies — furry, friendly, frolicking, fat, funny.

"Here's one that isn't about the puppies," Mother said. "*F*— forgiveness."

Julia tensed but arranged the tiles.

Mother did not turn her attention from Leah. "Do you know what that means, Leah?"

"It means you feel bad."

"Well, somewhat. When you have done something you should not have done, you can apologize, and the person you hurt then has the chance to forgive you."

"The Bible says to forgive," Marjorie chimed in as she finished writing the word. "It says we have to."

Everyone was quiet for the space of a tick of the clock. "That has been a hard one for me," Mother said. "I am not very good at forgiveness."

Julia furrowed her brow. She'd thought Mother was asking for *her* forgiveness, but this was something different.

"I am very good at forgivingness," Leah said.

"Then you are *f*-fortunate," Mother said. "Were you not so good at it, you would find that not forgiving can make you very un-happy. It can make you bitter and hard-hearted and . . . blind."

Leah looked at Mother in horror. "It can make you blind?"

Mother gave the girl's shoulder a squeeze. "Not the blind that makes your eyes not see — more of a blind heart, where you cannot feel the way you should."

"That is confusing."

Mother chuckled. "Yes, I suppose it is. How about the word *feel* — that starts with an *f*."

Julia spelled it out in tiles for Marjorie.

"How about fear?" Mother suggested. "Fear can make it hard to forgive, and to trust other people."

"And it makes you afraid!" Leah added helpfully.

"Yes, it does," Mother said. "Do you know what an opposite is?"

"The different thing," Leah said. "Marjorie is the opposite of me because she likes asp-ruh-gus and I hate it."

"That's not an opposite," Marjorie interjected. "An opposite is like black and white or night and day or hot and cold." She sat back, smug in her wisdom.

"Yes," Mother said. "And the opposite of fear is another word that starts with *f*— *faith.*"

Julia arranged the tiles for Marjorie, who was getting faster at writing.

"Faith is saying your prayers," Leah informed Mother.

"That is part, but I think faith is mostly about believing you don't know all the answers but that, even when it seems impossible, things usually turn out all right in the end if you treat people fairly."

"*Fair* starts with *f*!"

"Very good," Mother said. "You are a very smart little girl."

"That's because I am six."

They spent a few more minutes on the lesson before Julia announced it was time for quiet hour. Though the girls had protested — vehemently — when Julia had first introduced this part of the day early in her employ, they had come to accept it as routine. Marjorie selected a book from the shelf on her way to the area that Julia had set with thick quilts and pillows, a spot that was in full sun on the days when the sun was out. Leah grabbed her doll and the tin of soldiers, but Julia knew she would fall asleep before she fully executed whatever game she had in mind with them. That girl could sleep!

Julia gathered up the letter tiles, taking more time than necessary to arrange them inside the small wooden box.

"I am sorry, Julia."

414

Julia let those words seep deep into her heart so that she might see them clearly enough and determine if they were sincere. Her heart did not spit them out. She put the lid on top of the letter box. Part of her wanted to soften, forgive everything and put it in the past, but it was time for Mother to know that Julia would manage her own life, and that meant confronting this. All of it.

"What, exactly, are you sorry for, Mother?"

"Many things," Mother said softly. "I'm sorry for selling the dogs when your father died."

Julia startled, then tensed, waiting for the justification that would surely follow. It didn't.

"And I'm sorry I was not more affectionate and concerned about the pain my children felt then. I was far too caught up in my own hurt. And I'm sorry for trying to force you into marrying when you did not feel ready." Her eyes got glassy, and her voice cracked as she continued. "I am sorry that I chose your clothes and criticized your hair and felt so sure that I knew the way you should do every little thing in your life. I'm sorry that I was not soft and open to you as a mother should be, and I'm sorry I did not support your first position in London. I am ashamed of myself for never once coming to see you there."

Julia pulled her eyebrows together. She had not expected any of this and struggled to take it all in and formulate a response. "I never expected you to come to London, Mother."

"I thought of coming a hundred times." Mother shook her head as though disappointed in herself. "My youngest child had traveled further than any of my children had. And I know London. I lived there for a substantial part of my life. I could have shown you the parks and helped you understand the workings of society. But I felt that if I came, I would be showing support for a choice I did not agree with, and so I did not come. Not one time in five years."

Julia said nothing. Would she have wanted her mother to come? She couldn't decide because it had never crossed her mind that she would, for the very reasons Mother had admitted.

"I suppose, overall, I am sorry that I have been so set on what I wanted you to be that I have not realized what an exceptional woman you truly are."

Julia blinked. "I had thought you were going to say you were sorry for withholding your blessing from Peter."

"Oh, that, too." She smiled a vulnerable yet hopeful smile.

Julia did not know what to say. Manners dictated that she should also apologize for something, but she could not think what to apologize for that would not somehow unravel the power of these last few minutes. Her mother was so real right now, so open and fair-minded. "Thank you, Mother."

"You're welcome." She paused for a breath and then looked up from her hands in her lap. "I assume that you and Peter have reached an understanding."

Julia could not help but smile. Peter was the best thing that had ever happened to her. "I'm half in love with him, Mother. If things continue as they have the last twenty-four hours, I expect to be full in love with him by sunset."

Mother took a breath, nodded, and let it out.

"You should also know that I will not listen to additional objections. You had *no right.*" Her voice dwindled to a hiss, and she paused before she continued, her voice stronger. "You had no right to speak with him the way you did or presume to manage the course of my life."

"You're right," Mother said with a surprising lack of defensiveness. "It was wrong of

417

me, and I am very sorry."

They looked at one another, and Julia thought back to Marjorie writing the word *forgiveness* on her slate.

"I also owe you an apology for not telling you the truth about my connection to Lord Howardsford." She looked at Julia as though gauging how much she knew. Julia did not tell her, forcing her mother to explain it herself.

"Did you love him?" Julia asked, feeling an ache in her chest, mostly for her father. He had adored Mother, and it made Julia sad to think that her mother's heart had been divided.

"I am not entirely sure," Mother said with a shrug. "I thought I did, at the time, but then the way I felt toward your father was so different, so much . . . more." She held Julia's eyes. "I did not pine after Elliott, Julia, not after those first months. I was hurt, and when I thought of him it was painful, but not because he was the love of my life."

"But you've reacted so strongly to him now."

Her mother pulled her eyebrows together as though trying to puzzle that out. "Yes, I have, but that does not mean I have regrets for how things happened for me."

"What if Papa were alive now?" Julia

asked. "And I'd taken a job in this house?"

"Well, I'd have had him talk to you about it, to be sure." She smiled at the almost-joke, and Julia could not help but smile back, though a bit sadly.

She could see how things would have happened if Papa were here, but then, would she have become a governess if Papa were here? Would she have been a teacher? There was no way to unravel who she would be if he had not died.

Julia glanced across the room to where Marjorie was lying on her stomach reading a book and Leah was enacting what looked like a battle between her doll and the soldiers. And if Sybil had not died? What then?

She looked back to see Mother watching her. "I think we could drive ourselves mad trying to make sense of what could have been. I've learned that lesson all over again these last weeks. I think that the best any of us can do is to hold on to joy when it comes and enjoy it fully while it lasts so that we might draw every lesson from it and be better for the hurt we suffer."

A bubble of warm confirmation deemed those words both true and wise. Julia nodded. They sat in silence a few moments, then Julia brought the conversation back

419

around to the reason her mother had come. "So, we have your blessing now?"

"Yes. I do, however, have some concerns."

Of course you do, Julia thought, then wondered why she was keeping such a thought to herself. "Of course, you do," she said aloud, readying her arguments.

"My concerns do not undo my apologies, Julia, and I am trusting you to at least try to believe that. I have been wrong about you, about Elliott, about Mr. Mayfield — about so many people and things. However, I am still your mother, and I would like your permission to share my concerns, not to talk you out of your course, but to give you the chance to consider these things."

The beautiful apologies Mother had offered hung in the air, waiting for Julia to decide if she could believe them after all. It was also her right to tell Mother to keep her concerns to herself, but her own curiosity was growing. Things had changed quickly between her and Peter, and she was mature enough to know that what lay ahead would not be easy. She nodded her permission.

Mother let out a relieved breath. "If you are to enter into a formal courtship with Mr. Mayfield — well, any courtship with Mr. Mayfield — it is inappropriate for you to remain in his employ."

420

"No, it isn't."

Mother opened her mouth, but Julia cut her off. "It is inappropriate for me to live under his roof, but not to remain in his employ."

Mother paused, then nodded. "I suppose that is what I meant."

"Arrangements are even now being made for me to stay at the vicarage. We shall court, formally, as you said, for a while before we have the banns read. We are determined to make this work only if it is a solid match."

"Oh, well, that is very comforting for me to hear."

"And your other concerns?"

"I mean nothing personal against Mr. Mayfield, but the family as a whole has not earned itself a favorable reputation. If you marry Mr. Mayfield, you will be entering into a world of noblemen and society where such things matter a great deal. I only caution you to be mindful."

"I shall consider that."

Peter had told Julia the litany of scandals his family had been involved in, including his sister, who was in exile for her adultery and his cousin who was a rather flagrant rake in London. Julia had been shocked, but mostly because Peter was so very un-

421

scandalous. And, ultimately, Peter's character was the only one that mattered to her.

Mother seemed surprised that Julia did not ask for details but after a few seconds continued. "Lastly, I raised my children as best I could and as close to the expectations of the upper class as I could manage, but you were not raised to be the mistress of a house like this." She waved her hand to encompass the estate at large. "Nor have you had the necessary training in regard to being a hostess, socializing, or preparing Mr. Mayfield's daughters for their place in a world you have only been in as a servant. Mr. Mayfield will be the sixth Viscount of Howardsford, and his daughters will be presented at court one day. There are so many things about this world that are completely unknown to you, and I fear for your happiness if you find yourself at a disadvantage."

This was, perhaps, the most important concern, and one Julia had only thought of in the abstract. Anxiety built in her stomach as she considered it fully. She would have to rise up to a place she had never seen executed — even the Cranstons were not noble class, though she had at least seen some of the workings of the polite world by being in their home. She would be a countess! The solution to Mother's fear, however, presented itself immediately.

"You are right. I do not know the details regarding such a position, and I have a great deal to learn. Will you help me?

Mother visibly started, her eyes wide and her eyebrows jumping up her forehead. "Me?"

"You were a gentleman's daughter," Julia reminded her. "You have told me of helping your mother host events, being presented at court, and dancing until wee hours at balls in London. Who better to help me find my way in a world I do not know than someone who does know it and will not think ill of me when I ask for guidance?"

Tears filled her Mother's eyes and overflowed her cheeks. Julia reached her hand out, and Mother took it, holding it tightly. "I would do my very best to help you in that way, Julia."

"Thank you." She paused, felt braver, and continued. "Things have not always been right between us, Mother, but I never doubted you loved me and wanted my happiness." *You simply could not believe that my course could be different from the one you had already chosen for me.*

There was a knock at the door, and Julia rose to answer it just as it opened slowly.

423

Peter stepped through, and Julia felt her entire being lift at seeing him. He was smiling, but she could sense his wariness as he stepped into the room and looked from Julia to her mother.

"Mrs. Hollingsworth," he said, inclining his head. "I had not expected —"

His words were cut off as Leah barreled into his legs, wrapping her arms around them so tightly that his attempts to catch himself failed and he tumbled to the floor completely. Marjorie began yelling at her sister, Leah laughed, and Julia hurried over to untangle Leah and help Peter right himself.

That led to him assuring his daughters he was all right, straightening his coat, and then reaching for Julia's hand. They turned toward her mother together, and Julia watched Mother's eyes go from their joined hands to her face and then his.

"Apologies for my uncoordinated entrance, Mrs. Hollingsworth." He looked down at Leah, who had sat upon his feet with her arms wrapped around his knees.

Julia really did need to work on this girl's behavior. Even if she found it adorable.

"I assure you," Mother said in a soft and kind voice. "I am not the least bit put off by seeing up close how much these girls love

424

their father." She looked at Julia, her eyes glassy with tears. "I knew a girl who was very much the same, and I should never have wanted anything less for her than a man so much like the one she loved best."

CHAPTER THIRTY-SIX:
PETER

Peter stood at the base of the stairs across from Mr. Oswell, who was dressed in his full vicar regalia. Two dozen people stood behind them, awaiting the bride and her bridesmaids to join them, just as he was. He and Julia had chosen a short ceremony to cover the practical and legal necessities, then a wedding luncheon to share with their few but cherished guests.

Mrs. Hollingsworth had been living at Mayfield House these last three months, who was staying at the vicarage, to help Julia learn the ways of navigating society and managing a household. Colleen had taken over roughly half of the care for the girls, allowing Julia to learn the additional tasks of her position as mistress of the house. It had not been easy or entirely smooth, and there would still be patches of difficulty, but, then, life could often be messy. Fortunately, most messes could be cleaned up with enough

426

time, attention, and elbow grease.

A hush fell over the quiet conversations taking place between the guests, and Peter looked expectantly to the top of the stairs. Julia was dressed in a champagne-colored gown, a bouquet of pale yellow flowers he could now identify as primroses in her hands. Marjorie and Leah walked behind her in white dresses and wearing laurel wreaths upon their heads.

The image from my dream, Peter thought as he watched the procession move down the stairs toward him. He'd all but forgotten it, and yet here it was, revealed as unexpected prophecy.

Julia looked nervous, her eyes wide and her expression saying loudly how uncomfortable she was to be the center of attention.

He smiled at her encouragingly, not moving his eyes from her face until Leah whispered, "Hello, Papa."

The guests giggled, and Marjorie scowled at her younger sister. Peter put a finger to his lips and winked at his daughters.

The procession reached the base of the stairs, and Lydia stepped forward to take Julia's bouquet and then lead the girls to stand with the other guests.

Peter took both of Julia's hands in his and

427

hoped that the onlookers were disappearing to her just as they were disappearing to him. He gave her hands a squeeze, she squeezed his back, and the vicar began.

CHAPTER THIRTY-SEVEN: AMELIA

The wedding carriage left the Mayfield house at a quarter past one o'clock. Some of the guests left for their respective homes since the weather was fine — including both of Amelia's other children and their families — but half a dozen guests stayed, which kept Mr. and Mrs. Allen and their staff busy throughout the day.

Amelia helped to manage a cold supper and the preparing of rooms for the night, performing the tasks that Julia would be doing in the future. Julia would do well here, and Amelia felt like the mother she always wanted to be, helping her daughter prepare for her new place.

After supper, those remaining at the house conversed in the drawing room. Amelia quite liked Peter's younger brother, Timothy, and had enjoyed meeting a few of the other prospects for Elliott's marriage campaign. One by one, the guests retired until only Amelia, Timothy, and Elliott remained.

Amelia was reading Peter's copy of *Paradise Lost* while listening with half an ear to their discussion of mining rights currently being debated in parliament. When the topic was exhausted, Timothy stood. "I must be off to bed, Uncle, Mrs. Hollingsworth. I leave for London first thing and may not be able to make my farewells."

Goodbyes were shared, and then Timothy left, leaving Amelia and Elliott in silence. She tried to continue reading the book but could not concentrate. Elliott had visited several times over the last months, and they had been able to conclude that they had both done a good job with their past circumstances. It was a relief to say as much and believe it of Elliott, too. Amelia looked up from the book to find him watching her.

"It was a very nice day," he said.

Amelia smiled, thinking of how happy Julia had been and the expression on Peter's face each time he looked at her. What a heavy weight she'd have had to carry if she'd managed to prevent today from happening. "It *was* very nice," she confirmed, closing the book. "How long will you stay?"

Elliott looked at his shoes. "I am as yet undecided." He met her eyes again. "I thought perhaps you might need help with the girls."

Amelia nodded with feigned gravity. "I am sure I will. They are complete terrors and far more than Colleen and I could possibly manage on our own."

"Oh, yes, they are quite possibly the worst children I have ever encountered." He grinned, paused, and then spoke, but without the jovial tone. "You would not mind if I hung about?"

Amelia shook her head and enjoyed the fluttering sensation in her chest. He was flirting with her after all these years. And she was flirting back.

Though they had enjoyed one another's company these last months, they had avoided any talk of their future. Perhaps because they had to make sure they liked these older and wiser versions of each other. Perhaps also in order to not detract from this marriage between two people they so dearly loved. But the wedding was over. Peter and Julia's futures had begun, and Amelia had already decided not to stay much longer once Julia returned. The new Mr. and Mrs. Mayfield would need to define their new family, and though her intentions would always be good, Amelia would not be able to help inserting herself. Too much, as was her tendency.

"I would not mind you're staying at all, Elliott." She set the book aside completely. "The moon is bright tonight, and the evening is mild. I wonder if you might be willing to escort me on a walk, to settle the nerves of the day and —"

"I would consider it an honor." He nearly jumped to his feet, then cringed and bent over to rub his knee.

By the time she'd crossed to him, he had his arm out for her to take, and she did so, stepping closer to him than she needed to because she felt he would not mind. They left through the front door and followed the path that went around the east side of the house. They remarked on the wedding again, the meal, the weather, and then the people who had attended.

"Your niece and nephews are quite engaging," Amelia commented.

"Yes, they are," Elliott says. "I have seven nieces and nephews, you know, and am doing my utmost to see them all settled and happy with good families of their own. Peter and Julia are my first success."

"I know this already."

"Yes, but I wanted to make sure you did not forget. You have now met three of my next projects. It is important that you know I intend to follow through with my plan.

Timothy shall be doing the pretty rather soon, I think."

She looked at him, his profile lit by the silver moon, the light reflecting off the gray strands in his hair. "I am still not convinced that your campaign is the right way to go."

"I assumed as much, but seeing as how it is *my* campaign, and it has been wildly successful thus far, I am not convinced that your opinion matters." He winked at her. She chose not to continue the argument and faced forward once more.

"And is Peter still ignorant of his wedding gift?"

Elliott nodded. "The portfolio remains in my study at Howardhouse. I meant to bring it but forgot, seeing as how he gives it no attention whatsoever. Each time I suggest it, he tells me to keep it in the drawer."

"Will you tell me what it is?"

He gave her a sideways look. "I am not sure. Can you carry the burden of knowing such a thing?"

"I assure you I am perfectly capable — cross my heart." She made an X over her chest.

They had reached the circle yard, and Elliott led her to one of the four stone benches that skirted the round of grass. He brushed off the surface and then indicated for her to sit. Once she was seated, he joined her, then laid his hand on the bench between them. She looked at it a moment and then placed hers beside his, their little fingers entwining as they once had.

"Peter's was the hardest endowment to decide upon," Elliott began. "He inherited from his father — though it was as much a burden as a bounty at the time — and then he is my heir as well, so he does not want for many things. He also lives below his means — very ungentlemanly of him."

Amelia laughed and Elliott continued.

"However, I made a determination I think he will like, even more so now that Julia is a part of his life. There truly could not be a woman better suited for him."

Amelia nodded in agreement. "What did you decide upon?"

"There is a man in Germany by the name of Arthur Steveltsorg. He is well-known for his canine husbandry, specifically with greyhounds. Should you ever want to know everything about this man, you only need ask Peter. He can talk about the man and his advances in breeding practices for hours. It is he who inspired Peter to procure his first pair."

"I am glad for the warning that Peter is passionate of this topic so I know never to ask." She liked Peter a great deal, but the man could talk when the topic suited him, and they had spent many evenings just the two of them after Julia had returned to the vicarage. Amelia had heard more than her fair share of dogs and husbandry and puppy birthing. Julia was just as bad. The two certainly were a perfect match on that topic.

Elliott continued. "Peter's endowment is a trip to Germany, with his new wife and the girls, where he will stay with Mr. Steveltsorg and learn from the master for a month. They shall then get a pup from the newest litter after they return. I communicated with the man's steward — which was not easy, let me assure you, as I do not speak a bit of German — and he agreed to the idea, for a price, of course."

"Of course."

"I shall present Peter and Julia with the portfolio when they return. All I shall then need to do is pull the strings I have put in place to have it come together."

"They will be overjoyed, I think," Amelia said. "The opportunity of a lifetime."

"You approve, then?"

"I don't care much for dogs myself, but I believe Peter and Julia will be beside themselves. Only promise me I will not have to go with them."

Elliott laughed. "I am sure Colleen could go as nurse so that you might avoid the unpleasantness."

Elliott looked twenty years younger in light of her praise. The breeze ruffled his hair and caught the hem of her dress. She bent forward to smooth her skirts, then righted again. The garden was lovely, with rows of primroses making up the boundary of the circle — that had been Amelia's idea. She had missed her own gardens and felt no landscape was complete without the prim and perfect flower. When given as a gift it meant "I can't live without you." She'd given them to Julia, and Julia had then used them in her wedding bouquet.

"You do not feel I am manipulating my niece and nephews by creating these endowments?"

"Oh, I think you are *absolutely* manipulating them, but that does not mean it is a bad idea or that it is not incredibly generous." She cocked her head. "You have truly given them everything, haven't you?"

Elliott lifted their clasped hands and kissed the back of her fingers. "They have given me purpose and joy. A man could not ask for much more than that."

"Much more?"

He held her eyes. "There is only one

regret I have regarding my actions these last thirty years, one choice I made that I have relived a dozen times in my mind."

"We have spoken of this many times, Elliott. Let us leave it where it belongs."

"In the past?"

She nodded.

"Because everything worked out just the way it should?"

She laughed. "Yes. Everything has worked out just the way it should, perhaps even you and me sitting on a bench in the moonlight with life yet ahead of us." She could hardly believe such words had come out of her mouth, and yet she felt them to the tips of her toes. She did not look away from him even though she was embarrassed by her boldness.

He grinned slowly, took both her hands in his, and pulled her closer to him on the bench. "Mrs. Amelia Edwards Hollingsworth, will you forgive me my trespasses against you and allow me to spend the rest of my days making it up to you?"

"Only if you can forgive me for nearly ruining Peter's chance at happiness."

"Already forgiven."

She leaned forward before he could and pressed her lips to his, past and present and future mingling together in a kiss that was both new and familiar. Desire rose up within her to be with this man, to share his future, his life, and even his marriage campaign, which, so far, was off to a strong start.

His hand moved to the back of her head as he returned the kiss with all the ardor of their youth.

When she pulled back, she rested her forehead against his. "Before we allow things to progress too far, I do have some stipulations."

"Why does this not surprise me?"

She laughed, then went serious. "I like to bake my own bread in the mornings. Peter has allowed me to do so here, though his cook dislikes my being in her space. We have found our rhythm though, but I should not want to give that up."

"My cook cannot manage English cooking all that well anyway, so I do not think he will mind your baking bread. Anything else?"

"My children must be welcome, and I must be free to be invested in their lives as much as they will allow me to. The wife of a nobleman such as yourself shall have expectations placed upon her, all of which I shall rise to my utmost abilities, but do not ask me to change who I have become. At my age, I do not think I could do it, even if I tried."

"Oh, my dear Amelia," he said, running his thumb across her cheek. "It is who you have become that I have fallen in love with all over again."

She sat back so she could look him in the eyes. "Then I accept your proposal, Lord Howardsford. There is nothing that would please me more than becoming your wife."

"And joining me in my marriage campaign? I fear Peter may be the easiest to see settled."

"I am happy to be a lieutenant in the fight to save your family from themselves."

He said nothing, but kissed her again instead. She had never been so glad to be proven so very wrong. About Elliott, about Peter . . . about herself.

ACKNOWLEDGMENTS

A very big thank-you to my agent, Lane Heymont, of the Tobias Agency for inspiring this series idea and helping me develop the stories that would fit within it. Thank you to my critique group for helping me plot out the series: Ronda Hinrichsen (*Unforgettable,* Covenant, 2018); Becki Clayson; Jody Durfee (*Hadley, Hadley Bensen,* Covenant, 2013); and Nancy Campbell Allen (*Kiss of the Spindle,* Shadow Mountain, 2018); my beta reader Jennifer Moore (*Miss Leslie's Secret,* Covenant 2017); and Whitney Schofield, my sister-in-law and resident canine expert.

Thank you to Shadow Mountain for embracing the story and then helping it be better, specifically Heidi Taylor Gordon, production manager for the Proper Romance line; Lisa Mangum, editor extraordinaire; Heather Ward and Richard Erickson, both amazing designers; and Malina Grigg, skilled typographer. I am continually re-minded that writing the story is only one part of the creative effort that goes into making it a book, and I appreciate everyone who makes that possible. Big thanks to my readers — without you I would have no reason to do what I love. I am a very lucky girl.

Thank you to my kids for giving me a full and happy life, and my sweetheart, Lee, for the battles he fights for me, and for us, and for our family. Lee and I will celebrate twenty-five years of marriage this year, and I can't imagine my life without him. For all of the above, and so much more, I thank my Father in Heaven, who has given me so much perspective, purpose, and patience.

ABOUT THE AUTHOR

Josi S. Kilpack is the author of twenty-five novels and one cookbook and a participant in several coauthored projects and anthologies. She is a four-time Whitney Award winner — *Sheep's Clothing* (2007), *Wedding Cake* (2014), and *Lord Fenton's Folly* (2015) for Best Romance and Best Novel of the Year — and the Utah Best in State winner for fiction in 2012. She and her husband, Lee, are the parents of four children.

You can find more information about Josi and her writing at josiskilpack.com.

The employees of Thorndike Press hope you have enjoyed this Large Print book. All our Thorndike, Wheeler, and Kennebec Large Print titles are designed for easy reading, and all our books are made to last. Other Thorndike Press Large Print books are available at your library, through selected bookstores, or directly from us.

For information about titles, please call:
(800) 223-1244

or visit our website at:
gale.com/thorndike

To share your comments, please write:

Publisher
Thorndike Press
10 Water St., Suite 310
Waterville, ME 04901

445